*brickhouse*

## By Rita Ewing

HOMECOURT ADVANTAGE
(*with Crystal McCrary Anthony*)

# brickhouse

## rita ewing

An Imprint of HarperCollins*Publishers*

HarperCollins books may be purchased for educational, business, or sales promotional use. For information please write: Special Markets Department, HarperCollins Publishers Inc., 10 East 53rd Street, New York, NY 10022.

FIRST EDITION

*Interior text designed by Elizabeth M. Glover*

Library of Congress Cataloging-in-Publication Data

Ewing, Rita.
  Brickhouse / by Rita Ewing.—1st ed.
    p. cm.
  ISBN 0-06-057055-5
  1. African American women—Fiction. 2. African American businesspeople—Fiction. 3. Physical fitness centers—Fiction. 4. Harlem (New York, N.Y.)—Fiction. 5. Political corruption—Fiction. 6. Female friendship—Fiction. 7. Businesswomen—Fiction. I. Title.

PS3555.W54B75 2005
813'.54—dc22                                                2004020995

05 06 07 08 09 JTC/RRD 10 9 8 7 6 5 4 3 2 1

*Brickhouse is lovingly dedicated to my shining stars,
Randi, Corey, and Kyla
and my Forever Angel, Karin.*

The following acknowledgments are an absolute must, for without these individuals, *Brickhouse* would just be another old-school classic soul favorite: Denise Stinson, you knew this would work! Thank you! Carrie Feron, you are one incredible editor, a fun friend, and loyal blessing . . . thank you so very much for your continued belief in me and *Brickhouse*. Victoria Christopher Murray, you are an amazing talent! I cannot thank you enough for your assistance with *Brickhouse* . . . may God continue to bless you! Last, but certainly not least, my own personal trainers, Jeanne Marcus and Nancy Fuentes, for introducing me to the world of fitness and making it fun!

# *one*

The airplane continued its descent, and Nona leaned back in the seat, gripping the leather armrest. As the L-1011 slowed, she opened her eyes and sighed, taking in what were the still regal edges of the New York skyline. The Empire State Building, the Chrysler Building, and even the gaping hole where the twin towers of the World Trade Center had once stood welcomed her into the city. Despite the deep pang that jolted through her as she fought back the memory of September 11, Nona found herself saluting Lady Liberty as she caught a perfect aerial view of the famous monument.

Home sweet home. Those were the first words she thought every time her returning plane's tires touched the tarmac. Today, though, she felt those words deeply. Fifteen days was the most time she had ever spent away from home while on business. She couldn't wait to lie on the smoothness of her own silk sheets and sink her head into the softness of her own feather pillows.

Her heartbeat matched the slowing of the plane's speed until it no longer raced. She spent what seemed like forever in airplanes; still she didn't like the takeoffs and landings. As the plane taxied toward the gate, Nona began returning the papers on her lap to the leather folder she'd placed on the empty seat beside her. She glanced through the appointments marked on her upcoming week's schedule, which her assistant had faxed to her. She shook her head. The 168 hours in each week were not enough to accomplish all that was expected of her. But that didn't matter—her to-do-list would have to wait. She planned to put aside as much as she could for a few days to make room for her most important priority—her daughter.

The thought of Kelly made Nona smile. Still, her heart ached with thoughts of her eleven-year-old and how she hadn't seen her in over two weeks.

The jetliner jerked as the plane came to a complete stop and before the "Fasten Seat Belt" sign clicked off, Nona was standing with her backpack slung across her shoulder.

"Ms. Simms, here's your jacket," the flight attendant said, handing Nona her ankle-length cashmere duster.

"Thank you." She beamed her practiced smile with her picture-perfect teeth and stood at the door as the jetway moved toward the plane. She impatiently tapped the tips of her Gucci pumps, waiting for the airplane's door to open.

Nona wouldn't fly unless she could have seat 1B in first class. That way, she never spent a moment longer than she had to in the confined space. When the door opened, Nona hurried through, and was greeted by Marco, who had a special pass to meet her in the terminal.

"Hey, Nona." Marco smiled as he reached for her carry-on.

"It's so good to see you," she replied. "Now, show me just how good you are and get me home to my baby."

Marco laughed. He'd been her bodyguard for the last fifteen months—ever since the mass marketing of her last video made it impossible for her to go out without being mobbed. "The car is circling," Marco said. "By the time we get to baggage claim, you'll be able to go right to it."

Nona nodded her thanks, put on her sunglasses, and lowered her head. They walked quickly, past the shops in the Delta Air Lines terminal. At five-feet-eleven, Nona strutted like a model, and her arms swayed with the elegance of a ballet dancer. With her short black hair slicked back, her chiseled facial features were even more prominent. Many had wondered why Nona Simms wasn't gracing the runway for a top European designer. But even with her looks, modeling had never entered her mind. Nona was all about business.

She had scheduled her arrival for the middle of the afternoon; still the terminal was filled with people, and in moments, Nona began to feel the stares. Then, a few minutes more and the stares turned to shouts.

"There's Nona Simms."

"Hey, Nona. I love your books. Especially the last one."

"What's up, Nona? I have every one of your workout tapes."

She kept her head down, but could still see the glare from a flashing bulb. She hoped it was one of her fans rather than the paparazzi. She'd had enough of made-up tabloid stories.

Her bodyguard kept Nona at arm's length from her admirers, but Marco couldn't stop the swell of the crowd that followed her. As they trotted down the escalator, the screaming requests continued.

"Can I get a picture, Nona?"

"I just want your autograph."

"I just want to touch her," Nona heard someone say. "Maybe some of her looks will rub off on me."

The people around her laughed, but Nona's eyes remained lowered. She didn't want to be rude, but she couldn't stop—not today. She'd given herself to her supporters for fifteen days. It was time to go home.

By the time they reached baggage claim, they were almost running. "I'll go back for your bags."

"Let's just get you into the car, where it's safe," Marco yelled above the crowd's cheers.

Nona took a deep breath as they swept through the automatic doors into the chilled New York air. Just as they stepped outside, her black Cadillac Escalade with the license plate "BRCKHSE" veered to the curb. Marco opened the rear door for her, and the automatic running board hummed as it dropped.

"Excuse me, Ms. Simms. May I have your autograph?"

It was the gentle voice that made Nona turn. While the rest of the crowd had remained inside, two young girls had followed her. They couldn't have been more than twelve or thirteen. The one who spoke was tall, almost five-seven, with her head covered in hundreds of microbraids.

The other girl stood behind her and was at least four inches shorter. But what she lost in height, she made up in weight, and the shorter girl lowered her eyes when Nona looked their way.

"We just bought your new exercise video." The taller girl took another step closer while the other stayed in place. "We're your biggest fans. Could we have your autograph?" she repeated.

Nona stared at them for a moment. Times had certainly changed. Today girls who had barely reached puberty were working out and starving themselves, trying to conform to some made-up American standard.

Nona's objective had always been to encourage people to

develop a healthy body through a healthy lifestyle. But some-how that had become twisted. Now, girls who should have nothing more on their minds than school and friends and music and movies were thinking about dieting and trying to exercise until they looked like Halle Berry—or even worse, until they looked like her. That thought made Nona shiver as her own daughter's words flashed through her mind.

*Mom, I just wanna look like you.*

Nona stared at the girls for a moment longer, and this time when she smiled, it wasn't rehearsed. She took the torn loose-leaf pages from the girl's hand.

"What're your names?" she asked softly.

"I'm Leslie," the tall one said. "And this is my friend Kelly."

Nona stared blankly when she heard her daughter's name, but then regained her composure. She signed the pa-pers and handed them to the girls.

"Thank you," they said in unison.

Leslie added, "I can't wait for your next video. When I grow up, I want to look like you."

Nona almost shook her head. Was this the new teenage mantra? She wanted to tell the girl the same words that she voiced to her own daughter over and over. But instead she waved good-bye, and then slipped into the car.

"I need to do something about that," Nona muttered.

"Did you say something, Ms. Simms?" Ray, her driver asked.

"No." But she made a mental note. She would produce a video or write a book geared toward teen girls. If they were watching her videos, she needed to make sure they were getting the correct message.

She leaned back against the soft leather of the seat. This was the first time in days she'd sat still, without a pen and paper in her hand, or a cell phone pressed to her ear. Feeling as if she hadn't slept in days, she closed her eyes. But a moment later, she opened them when she heard a tap on the front window.

"This is for immediate loading only," the airport security guard snarled when Ray rolled down the window. "You're going to have to move, buddy."

As Ray eased the chrome-trimmed vehicle from the curb, Nona sighed. This would slow down her trip home. Kennedy Airport had been a circle of mass confusion for as long as she could remember. New construction was constant, and with the traffic, it would take them at least fifteen minutes to get back to Marco and her luggage.

She leaned back again, closed her eyes, and focused on the breathing techniques she taught her clients. She inhaled and began counting, "One, two, three . . ."

*And this is my friend Kelly.*

Her eyes snapped open when she heard the girl's voice in her head. But it was her daughter's face that her mind's eye saw. Recently, almost any thought, word, or sound made Kelly come to mind. It was as if guilt had its hands gripped around her throat. She was constantly being reminded of how her frenzied schedule kept her from giving the most important gift to her daughter—her time.

What made it worse was that Kelly never complained. Her eleven-year-old suffered through her mother's absences and workaholic pace like a martyr. She was an expert at the role, having been forced to play the part since she was two.

Nona hadn't designed it this way. When she started Brickhouse, it was going to be a neighborhood health club—something she would do part-time in the evenings and on weekends.

It seemed like such a good idea at the start—a perfect marriage of her several years of experience as marketing director for the New York Fitness Club and her love for a community that every major health club facility ignored. Her idea came only after the New York Fitness Club denied all her requests to open a facility in Harlem—even though she was responsible for selecting new locations, and during her tenure she'd never been wrong; every one of her recommendations turned into a hot new club.

It didn't make sense to her. The New York Fitness Club reveled in being first and best in the industry. So, when they turned down her Harlem recommendation for the third time, Nona approached her boss.

"Marilyn, we're passing up a great opportunity," Nona said one day while they were at lunch in the Jamaican restaurant One Love. "Maybe you should come up to Harlem with me so I can show you the location I'm recommending."

Nona had almost laughed at the horror that flashed in Marilyn's blue eyes. She could imagine her boss's thoughts: *Me, in Harlem? Isn't it enough that I'm eating peas and rice with you?*

Nona was sure that Marilyn's only exposure to black people were the few she worked with and her weekly visits to One Love.

It took Marilyn a few moments to swallow the lump that had formed in her throat and gather what she thought were the politically correct words, "Nona, I appreciate your enthusiasm, but let's be real. Harlem doesn't fit the demographics . . . no matter how you fudge the numbers."

"I didn't fudge anything, Marilyn. The numbers prove that Harlem is as promising as any of the other locations. With all the new construction and conversion of apartments to condos, Harlem is not the community you saw on *Eye-witness News* twenty years ago." Nona reached for her folder. "Maybe you should look at the numbers again."

Marilyn held up her hand. "There's no need to discuss this. Case closed."

But it wasn't closed for Nona. She was tired of fighting "the man's" stereotypes of her people. According to them, black folks didn't exercise, read, or appreciate the finer things in life. Right then, she decided to stop her battle with Marilyn and turn her energy elsewhere.

As Nona worked, she made mental notes, determined to learn every aspect of club management. A few months later when she read an article stating that diabetes affected ten percent of African Americans, compared with only five percent of the general population, she knew what she had to do. It was then that she decided it was time to bring an exercise facility to Harlem. She would help her people get on the healthy path to living, just like the rest of America. She'd be damned if African Americans weren't given the same opportunities for a healthy lifestyle that the major chain gyms afforded millions in the general population.

It took one week to work out a deal with Reverend Zolle of Mount Sinai Baptist to use the church's basement. Then she spent the next two weeks developing a schedule and printing flyers, which she mailed to area churches and other organizations and distributed through two teenagers she hired to be her street team. She called her program in the holy facility the African American Wellness Center since she wanted it to be more than a gym. It was going to be a complete information center.

On the first day, only six people came to the aerobics class, each paying ten dollars for four sessions. Another three joined them for the free lecture on diabetes that she held after class. The attendance was a disappointment, but Nona worked as if fifty people had attended.

Within two weeks, fifty people did show up. It was as if a hot new jazz club had opened uptown. The word spread faster than gossip did over the old Harlem party lines.

Every Monday, Wednesday, and Friday she held two exercise classes—one for seniors over the age of fifty-five and the other for everyone else. On Saturdays she brought in guest speakers who were experts in their fields. Lectures were held on everything from AIDS to lupus.

It was an exhausting schedule, but an exhilarating one. With her fine arts degree in dance, her master's in business, and her experience with the New York Fitness Club, she began to think of this small community health club as something more than a part-time gig.

Within a year, the classes swelled to fire-hazard levels, and Nona had to rent three rooms in a four-story walk-up next to the Apollo Theatre. Now she had classes every evening and twice a week during the day. Allen Wade, one of the trainers from the New York Fitness Club, believed in her mission so much, he joined her, covering her during the day while she continued to work. She never worried about staying with the New York Fitness Club, as she built her own facility, and her contract did not prevent her from freelancing. She knew none of the big boys like Bally's, Gold's, Equinox, or even her current employer were willing to touch Harlem—not even with a ten-foot pole. She was no competition for them, or so they thought.

A few months later, Nona developed a special workout that combined muscle-sculpting aerobics, kickboxing, calisthenics, and yoga. A regimen that had Nona looking finer than ever. With her tall, lean frame and shapely, toned assets, Nona quietly accepted the Brickhouse nickname her brethren folk bestowed upon her as she walked the streets of Harlem. What quickly became known as the Brickhouse Technique brought more people to Nona's place in Harlem. When the time came for Nona to name her place of business, there was no doubt in her mind that Brickhouse was the perfect fit and her only option.

Although the hours were long, it was a welcome indulgence—her job and her small business were distractions from her faltering marriage.

In the end, her marriage hadn't survived, but her business had thrived. While she was proud of what she'd accomplished, it was hard to reconcile it with what she believed she missed at home.

"Ms. Simms," Ray called, bringing her thoughts back to the present. "Marco's outside now. We'll be out of the airport in a few minutes."

Ray slowed the SUV, and Marco tossed her bags into the trunk. Then he slid into the car.

"Ms. Simms, is there anywhere you want to stop first?"

Nona glanced at her watch. She wanted to be home when Kelly arrived from school. But today she'd have an extra hour since Kelly had her acting lessons—or was it dance class today? "Take me to the office, Ray." She could spend a little time with her other baby—Brickhouse. Only forty-five minutes, and then she'd go home for sure. She wouldn't allow herself to slip back into her old bad work habits. She smiled; with a bit of planning she could have it all.

Ray snaked the Escalade through the heavy Friday airport traffic, and Nona settled back again. It was difficult to remember a time when she wasn't being whisked through cities in limousines or jetting across the country for special appearances. As she let the past years fly through her mind, she found it hard to believe how far she'd come. But what was even more fascinating was what lay ahead: more books, more videos, more appearances, and the opening of her new restaurant in the new mall in Harlem. Sarah, her assistant, told her there was even a movie script sitting on her desk for her review.

But nothing excited Nona more than her upcoming Central Park production. It was going to be a video—taped live from New York's urban oasis—that combined exercise with a discussion on how to live a healthy life. She had just inked a record-breaking deal with HBO to provide international coverage and sponsorship.

As Nona's thoughts drifted, various hues of gray whizzed by the tinted car windows in the form of nondescript factory buildings, box-style two-level homes, and leafless trees that lined Grand Central Parkway. By the time the truck passed through the E-Z Pass lane and crawled over the Triborough Bridge, all that was on Nona's mind was what she had to get done when she reached the office.

But once they exited on 125th Street, she pushed thoughts of work aside, relishing the fact that she was now truly home. They moved slowly in the heavy traffic, but Nona didn't mind. There were faster routes, but Ray knew Nona loved this street. The slower they moved, the better for her. It gave her a chance to really welcome herself home as she soaked up the atmosphere of the place she loved so much.

An eclectic mix of the past and present, 125th Street was lined with buildings that had been standing since the turn of the century—five-story walk-ups that housed families who had lived in the neighborhood for as many generations.

But the old Harlem was being infiltrated by the new. The Apollo Theatre stood in all its glory, the sound of decades of music almost audible even through the closed windows of her truck. Yet not far away, a crowd gathered under the green and cream striped awning of Starbucks, where young black professionals sipped three-dollar cups of coffee and waited for an occasional glimpse of former President Clinton arriving at or leaving from his Harlem office.

They turned onto Lenox Avenue and headed south, toward 116th Street. Seventy-five minutes after she got off the airplane, they entered the parking lot of Brickhouse. Ray slowed the car as they passed parked Mercedes, Lexuses, and Jaguars with license plates covering the tri-state area.

Nona peeked through the window at the massive three-level redbrick structure—her second home. It was an old factory that had been renovated to become what *Muscle and Fitness* magazine called "the sleekest gym in America."

The SUV barely came to a stop before Nona opened the door. She smiled as Allen Wade trotted down the brick stairs toward her. Even after all their years working together, she still marveled at Allen's Hollywood good looks. She almost laughed now as she remembered their first meeting and how she'd mistaken him for Rick Fox. Nona probably would have been offended that Allen had never tried to ask her out back in the day, but she had been so fixated on her plans for her gym, the thought of dating her business partner never crossed her mind.

"Hey, you," she exclaimed.

Allen grinned and pulled her into his massive arms. "How's my girl?" He squeezed her tightly.

She rested for a moment against his large, muscular frame. "Tired and glad to be home." She turned back to the car. "Ray, can you and Marco take my bags over to my place? Odessa's there."

Ray nodded. "Will you need anything else this evening, Ms. Simms?"

Nona shook her head and wished again that Ray would call her by her first name. But after almost two years as her driver, he said he felt more comfortable with "Ms. Simms." "I'll drive my car home tonight," she said as she took Allen's hand and climbed the steps into the building. "It's still here, isn't it?" she asked Allen teasingly.

He nodded and laughed.

"So, how are things?"

"No questions until we're in your office and you tell me how much you missed me." He smiled. Allen had a natural flirtatiousness about him, but when it came to Nona, he remained the consummate professional.

Nona laughed, but gave Allen a long glance. There was humor in his words, but not in his tone. And the glow in his light brown eyes had dimmed.

They walked through the wide reception area, filled with the early after-work crowd.

"Hey, Nona."

"Good to see you, Ms. Simms."

"Oh, no. You're back. I'm still hurting from your last class."

Nona chuckled and waved to the clients, feeling as if she were walking through the airport once again. They moved through the long narrow hall, past the administrative offices, to her office suite in the back of the building.

"It's good to have you back." Sarah grinned from her desk outside Nona's office. "The drums are beating overtime. Everyone knows that you're returning today, and the phones haven't stopped ringing. Should I put your calls through now?"

Nona shook her head. "Pretend I'm not back . . . yet." She grinned and pulled Allen into her office.

It was a private haven. Soft earth tones covered the plush furniture, and the massive white oak desk was different from the streamlined chrome, glass, and steel designs throughout the rest of Brickhouse.

When Nona closed her office door, she lost her smile. "So tell me, what's going on?"

The ends of Allen's lips turned down a bit. His eyes darkened, becoming almost as black as his jet hair. "You know me, don't you?"

"Being best friends has to count for something more than free workouts. Now stop stalling. Tell me."

Allen sighed, walked across her wide office, and reached for an envelope on top of the pile of mail stacked high on her desk. He handed it to her.

Nona scanned the manila envelope with the green card attached that signified the letter had been sent certified.

"It's not good news," Allen whispered. "It's from Reverend Watkins and the Harlem Empowerment Office—specifically, the rezoning committee."

Nona frowned. "Is this about the new mall off Harlem River Drive? What's it being called again?"

Allen lowered himself into one of the massive cream chairs in front of the desk. "Harlem East. They announced the name at a groundbreaking ceremony three days ago. It seems they've devised a strategy to force businesses into the new retail complex. They're rezoning, turning this entire area into a residential-only zone." He allowed his last words to settle before he continued, "From the look of things, Reverend Watkins and his cronies have the support they need to do it."

"What?" she gasped.

Allen knew he didn't have to explain further. But he continued. "That would mean Brickhouse wouldn't be able to stay in Harlem."

Nona sank into the plush chair behind her desk. "Why would—"

"So that every major retail business has to operate from Harlem East. This is all being done with the mayor's, City Council's, and New York City Zoning Commission's blessing."

Nona stared at Allen for a long moment, then she stood. She paced behind her desk. "Are these people crazy?" she asked, stopping in front of Allen. "So you're telling me they're going to close every business in Harlem that is not part of the new mall?"

Allen nodded. "All retailers east of Frederick Douglass Boulevard that are over a certain size. Only the smallest of the mom-and-pop shops and street vendors will be safe."

"That's ludicrous. Besides it being crazy to try and force everyone in Harlem to shop in one place, don't these people understand that they're going to be destroying businesses?"

"The plan offers compensation—if you close down or move your business into the new mall. In your letter it says that the mortgage on this building will be completely paid. Guess whoever sent out this form letter doesn't know that you paid off your mortgage a long time ago."

"They can't really expect me to leave this building that I own and then *rent* forty thousand square feet in the mall."

Allen nodded.

"That's insane. Those developers are charging a premium— midtown leasing rates for that space. Not to mention that moving this gym out of this residential area would be operational suicide. People go to malls to shop and to eat. Not to work out."

"I think they realize Brickhouse will be out of business," Allen whispered, as if he didn't want to speak the words too loud. "It just doesn't matter to them."

"But what about all the taxes we pay, all the people we employ?"

Allen shrugged. "From what I've been able to find out, we're nothing compared to the plans Reverend Watkins has for Harlem East."

"So he's just going to push me out? Make me walk away from my business?" Nona's voice rose a decibel with each syllable. "We built Brickhouse from the ground up. I own this building, and no one is going to take this away just because some insane, Bible-thumping, Al Sharpton-wannabe has decided that Harlem needs a mall. Has everything become so political?"

Allen stood and raised his hands in the air. "Calm down, Nona. Remember, you thought the mall was a good idea."

"I thought it was a good idea before this." She picked up the envelope, then slammed it on her desk. "I agreed to put my restaurant in the stupid mall . . ."

"I know."

"Reverend Watkins gets my commitment and my money for the restaurant and then he does this?" she screamed.

"I know you're upset, Nona, but—"

"Upset?" She squeezed her hands into fists. "No one has seen upset yet." She turned toward the glass wall behind her desk. Cars and buses fought for their space along Lenox Avenue. Pedestrians rushed from the subway to catch buses, or strolled on the street, stopping in the market, or cleaners, or liquor store on the corner. She could see the new yogurt shop that had opened across the street. Many of her clients purchased protein smoothies after their workout from there instead of from Brickhouse's restaurant. But Nona didn't mind. There was enough business for all of them. It was about everyone doing well. At least, that's what she thought.

She turned and pointed her finger at Allen. "I think Reverend Watkins had this plan all along. You know he's known for underhanded schemes. He always planned to rezone and push me out. But he figured I was in too deep. That I'd already committed to my restaurant in Harlem East, and that would be enough for me. I'd let Brickhouse go, but I'd still do the restaurant with him because I'd never say no to Harlem . . ."

"And he's right," Allen whispered. "You could have chosen any city in the world for your next venture, and you insisted that the restaurant be here. Reverend Watkins had nothing to do with that."

Nona crossed her arms and tried to breathe deeply. But all she could feel was the pounding in her chest.

"Nona, maybe you could meet with Reverend Watkins—"

She held up a hand, stopping her friend. There was no way she'd meet with that son of a—"I should just pull the plug on everything. Take my business and my money and walk away."

But even as she spoke, she knew she wouldn't do it. And she didn't have to look at Allen to know that he knew this was only her anger speaking.

Harlem was more than her home; it was her mission. She had built her business as much for herself as for the community where she'd been born and raised. Harlem flowed through her blood in a way that few could understand. She remembered how her fellow students at Barnard College had looked at her when she told them she was from Harlem. Their eyes said what their lips were too polite to speak—*Harlem, oh, my goodness.* She didn't have the heart to tell them that at least while they were in school, they were residents of Harlem too.

Although the students at Barnard never uttered their disdain, others were not so kind. She couldn't count the number of well-meaning fans who suffered from foot-in-mouth disease.

"You're from Harlem and you still live there? Why? Aren't you making money?"

"Don't you have a child? How can you raise her in Harlem?"

"Aren't you afraid to go out at night?"

With as wide a smile as she could muster, she addressed their comments, chalking up the stupid statements to the fact that these people didn't know what she knew. That Harlem was a true community, where she knew everyone who lived in the building she'd grown up in across the street from Marcus Garvey Park. That she was blessed to live in a multicultural city where she learned Spanish from the girls in her Girl Scout troop who lived in Spanish Harlem, and French from the Haitian women who sold their native wares on the street. That her neighbors were in her life as much as her own parents.

Harlem was her home, her love, her past and future. No matter what kind of hardball the reverend and the Harlem Empowerment Office were playing, she would stand firm at home plate.

Nona turned back to Allen and blinked to keep the tears from her light brown eyes.

Allen moved to her and pulled her into his arms. "We'll get through this. I believe you'll be able to keep Brickhouse exactly where it is and open your restaurant in the mall."

She leaned back. "Sounds like you've got a plan."

He nodded, directed her back to her seat, and then perched himself on the edge of the desk. "It's going to be a battle, but it's a war we can win. The only thing is that you're going to have to fight this from the front line."

She squinted and motioned for him to continue.

"The community will rally behind you, Nona," he said. "The people know you and what you've done. We're a faithful group of people." He paused. "Remember O.J.? And you have a much better reputation," he joked, trying to lighten the moment.

She almost smiled as she nodded at his words. Yes, she had built quite a name. When God granted the miracle allowing her to buy this building, it had been as much of a blessing for Harlem as it had been for her. She'd become a major employer—with almost one hundred employees. And she poured her dollars back into the community. She advertised in the local newspapers, used local suppliers, and contributed to any Harlem-based fund-raiser—from supporting the new day care center to speaking at the annual Harlem Hospital Kids' Day program. She was so recognizable that many times people cheered when she walked down the street.

"But . . ." Allen's voice forced her away from her thoughts. "There's a catch to all of this."

She remained silent.

"You're going to have to be here to make sure this happens." Allen leaned toward her. "You're going to have to change your focus. The book tour, the appearances, all of the traveling is going to have to stop . . . for now. You have to spend time reestablishing your old ties . . . going to the other neighborhood businesses, speaking at churches . . . depending how things go, even leading a neighborhood rally. You'll have to become the politician, building your own support base so that it's more than just you saying no to Reverend Watkins."

Nona nodded.

"I think you should start by contacting other businesses,

but you'll have to do it rather quickly. The first hearing is in two weeks."

Nona stayed quiet, staring at Allen, absorbing his words. Finally she said, "I can do it. I'd already decided to slow down a bit and stay closer to home," she said. She needed to cut back, not just for this rezoning issue, but there was something far more important than all of this—she had to make time for Kelly. "Let's do it." She felt suddenly rejuvenated by Allen's talk.

The door to her office burst open, and Toni Lee glided in as if she were floating on a magic carpet. She was dressed in a winter-white pants suit, with a matching ankle-length cape draped over her shoulders. Her blond hair hung straight, blending in with her outfit. Her green eyes sparkled as she smiled wide.

"You are here," Toni exclaimed as if she were surprised. "Sarah wasn't at her desk."

Nona wanted to be annoyed. Her friend had, after all, blown into her office while she was in the middle of this important issue. But Toni's glow only made Nona smile.

"It's so good to see you." Toni's words slipped through her lips in her affected actor's tone. With one hand, she flung her cape over a chair, and with the other, she tossed a gold envelope onto Nona's desk. "You're both coming, right?" Toni asked, placing one hand on her hip.

Nona matched Toni's stance. "What ever happened to 'Hello, Nona. How was your trip, Nona? How are you, Nona?' " She rolled her eyes, feigning frustration. "This ain't no scene in one of your movies, girlfriend. If you keep this act up, you can just turn around and waltz your li'l butt right out of here."

Allen laughed as he watched the two friends, knowing their usual tag-team banter was about to begin.

Toni fluttered her French-manicured fingernails in the air as if the motion would cast Nona's words aside. "Just look at you. Obviously, everything went well." Toni fell into the chair. "So, are you coming," she asked, glancing at the envelope on the desk.

Nona sighed and picked up the packet. "What is this?"

"You're kidding, right?" Toni paused. "I know you didn't forget the premiere. *Love's Desires* is opening, and I must have the two of you there." Her eyes moved between Nona and Allen. "It's going to be more fabulous than my last picture."

"Really? I didn't think anything could surpass *Scandalous*."

Toni didn't seem to notice Nona's sarcasm. She moved to the edge of her seat. "You know who's going to be there?"

Nona sat behind her desk. Toni had been her friend for more than five years, but she still amazed her. Nona would have loved to talk to her friend about her issues—the rezoning challenges, Kelly, everything. But that would never happen. At least not yet. Not until they exhausted every issue in Toni's life.

Nona sighed. The self-centered, egotistical, top-billed actress also had a golden heart. Toni had come to Nona's rescue on countless occasions—the most important time being when she helped Nona get the financing for Brickhouse.

When Nona was finally ready to move to a much larger facility, she had taken her expertly honed business proposal to every major lending institution in Manhattan. Not one loan officer had been willing to risk such a large investment on this black woman, even though Nona was no novice. She came to the table with credentials, experience, a sizable amount of her own money, and an already profitable operation. If the money brokers weren't willing to give her a loan, she couldn't imagine whom they would finance.

Then Toni stepped in. She introduced Nona to one of her past suitors, John Bradford—a very young, very handsome, very savvy manager of a private asset management group. It was a wealthy group of private investors who afforded Nona the opportunity to break ground for Brickhouse.

It had turned out to be a win-win situation for everyone. Nona had her business and had paid back her investors in record time at a handsome interest rate. Today she owned Brickhouse free and clear, with no regrets, and only Toni to thank.

"So, who's going to be there?" Nona finally asked, knowing that Toni would not leave until she had poured out all her news.

"Der . . . rick." Toni dragged out the name as if it had seven syllables.

Nona shook her head. This news did not make her day any better. "Don't tell me that he had something to do with whatever's in this fancy li'l envelope?" Nona said, flicking at the sealed gold package as if it were a bug crawling across her desk. "I tell you, no matter what I do, I can't seem to get away from that man."

"And why would you want to?" Toni grinned. "I can't get enough of him."

"I don't understand you at all, Toni. After what he did to you. He's nothing but an overbearing, pompous jerk."

"Derrick's company was involved with this?" Allen asked, holding up the invitation. "Damn."

Toni laughed, and Nona rolled her eyes.

"Don't be impressed," Nona smirked.

Toni turned to Allen. "Don't listen to her. Be very impressed."

"I am. Man, he got to work with Dreamworks on this project? Derrick must be at the top of his game."

Nona sighed at Allen's tone, but Toni ignored her friend and continued addressing Allen.

"Derrick produced the soundtrack for the movie, and of course he's directing all of the videos." Toni leaned across the desk. "Do you know how many nights I pretended I wanted to help with the editing just so I could be in that man's presence? He is so fine." She waved her hand at her face as if she were trying to lower her body temperature.

Nona looked at her friend as if she were crazy. "I don't care how fine he is. He's nothing more than a fine asshole. He's a bear to work with, and I don't see how you can even look at him. You act as if nothing ever went down between the two of you."

Toni slumped back in her chair and pouted.

"That's my cue," Allen said. "Toni, I'll be at the premiere. Also, do you still want to do two sessions a day next week?"

She sighed, but nodded. "Of course. How else will I fit into the fabulous Vera Wang dress that the studio sent over for the premiere?" Toni waited until the door was closed before she said, "I wish you wouldn't do that. Especially not in front of other people."

Nona wanted to gag, but instead she softened. "I'm sorry, Toni, but you've got to accept that there are very few people on earth who are as bad as Derrick Carter."

"When are you going to get over it?" Toni asked. "I have."

"And I don't know how. The man left you pregnant—"

Toni held up her hand and stood. "I don't want to go over this again, Nona. I've moved on, and I thought you had too when you hired him again for your Central Park production."

Nona shook her head. "He wasn't my choice," she

snapped, remembering how she'd fought with the marketing director against having Derrick Carter. But even though she hated the air that he breathed, Nona had to admit that his work surpassed excellent. He was the reason she'd sold fifteen million copies of the first mass-production video. It looked more like a Hollywood creation than an exercise tape. After thirteen months on the market, sales were still strong.

Toni grabbed her cape. "Well, I'm going to get out of here." She walked to the other side of the desk and rubbed Nona's back. "Hey, you just got home. Don't be mad at me."

Nona shook her head. "I'm not. I just want you to know what I know. You have too much going for you to be running after Mr. Carter like he's the only man you could ever be interested in."

"Honey, you know me. Don't worry. There are too many men for me to just think about one." She slapped Nona's arm playfully. "I'm not serious about Derrick. I just don't have the same problems with him that you do. I don't mind working with egotistical, overbearing, controlling, anal perfectionists. Just as long as I look damn good on the silver screen when it's all said and done."

Nona twisted her lips in doubt.

Toni leaned forward and added, "And anyway, I just want to know if he still tastes as good as he looks." She chuckled.

Nona raised her hands in exasperation. "What do you see in that man?"

"Girl, everything. Have you ever really looked at him?"

"No, he's a repellent to me."

Toni laughed. "Well, my hope is to add a little cream to his coffee again one day."

Nona hesitated, then said, "You know what? Go for it, Toni. Make him feel like a king for a day. Maybe he's changed. And if he's good for you, maybe I'll be able to handle him too."

"That's the attitude." Toni draped her cape over her shoulders, and her smile disappeared. "Remember one thing, Nona. People are not as bad as the worst thing they've ever done. Derrick is a good man. He just has some commitment issues."

Nona wanted to scream as she watched Toni walk to the door, but she knew it wouldn't do any good.

Suddenly Toni turned and rushed back to Nona's desk. She leaned over and hugged her friend. "It's good to have you home, honey. I've missed you. Maybe later we'll get to talk about you. See you in class tomorrow." With a smile and a flutter of her hand, she whisked out of the office in the same manner that she had entered.

Nona sighed. Her business issues were piled high on her shoulders, and now she had a feeling that Toni would be added to her list of concerns—if she was going to get involved with Derrick Carter again.

She shook those thoughts from her head and began to sift through the mail stacked on her desk. She opened the first envelope and scanned the letter. Another request to make Brickhouse a franchise. These solicitations constantly bombarded her—from hotels to airports, the requests poured in, asking permission to open Brickhouse gyms around the world.

She had declined all offers. Instead she had patented and trademarked the Brickhouse exercise technique. Nona's personal program was being taught at top gyms around the country. The latest addition was Adonis Gym, which found it was losing members because it was a year behind the other national facilities like Fitness Forever and Physique International, which had long ago jumped on the Brickhouse train.

That was as far as Nona had gone. She was determined not to add anything else to her plate until her life was in order.

She laid the letter on the desk, leaned forward, and held her head in her hands. Sometimes it seemed this life was too much. But how could she complain when she was living her dream? How many people would give all they had to be all that she was? She would just manage her issues the way she did everything in her life—like a professional.

She looked at her Cartier watch and jumped up. How had the time slipped away? It was well after five. Kelly was sure to be home by now.

She stuffed the stack of mail into her bag. It was time for her to take on the most important role in her life—time for her to be a mother.

"Good evening, Ms. Simms," the parking garage attendant said as he opened the door to her Mercedes. She stepped out. "Welcome home."

"Thank you, Lewis. Believe me, it's good to be back." She handed him her keys, then walked up the slight incline that led to 138th Street. Autumn's nighttime darkness had descended on the city, but Nona welcomed it. She feared nothing. These were her streets. People could think what they wanted about New York City and Harlem specifically, but she knew she was safe.

Nona crossed the street and trotted up the steps of her brownstone—one of the distinguished row houses that lined the street known as Striver's Row since the late 1800s.

She balanced her briefcase and backpack in one hand

while she put her key in the door. She entered the small anteroom, then walked into the main living quarters.

"Hello," she yelled.

"Ms. Nona." It was Odessa's excited voice that she heard first. "Welcome home." The petite housekeeper put her slender arms around Nona's neck.

Nona hugged her back, but her eyes focused over Odessa's shoulder, peering at the top of the ornately carved, curved staircase that led to the bedrooms. The huge brownstone was more than seventy-five hundred square feet, but Nona was sure that Kelly heard her come in.

She leaned away and smiled at her housekeeper. "How's everything?" Nona dropped her bags by the door.

"Just fine." Odessa picked up the bags, then followed her into the living room. "I didn't know what time to expect you. Marco brought your bags over earlier. I assumed you were at Brickhouse?"

Nona nodded, her eyes still looking past Odessa.

Odessa leaned toward Nona and lowered her voice. "Kelly's in her room," the housekeeper said, as if reading Nona's thoughts.

"Is she doing her homework?"

Odessa shook her head. "I checked on her a while ago when I heard her stereo. She finished her homework." Odessa patted Nona's arm. "I'm sure she's anxious to see you."

Nona knew that Odessa didn't really believe what she said. "Thank you, Odessa."

As Nona walked upstairs toward Kelly's bedroom, Odessa called out. "I'll fix you something to eat."

Nona held up her hand. "I'm not hungry . . ." She paused. "Has Kelly eaten yet?"

"No. I have a salad for her, though. She said that's all she wants."

Nona shook her head. "She has to have more than that. Why don't you broil some chicken, and I'll eat with her."

Odessa nodded. When she disappeared into the kitchen, Nona took a deep breath and continued up the stairs. At the top, she knocked on Kelly's door. When there was no response, Nona entered the room.

"Hey, sweetheart, I'm home."

Kelly was stretched across the canopy bed, lying on her stomach with her legs hanging over the edge. Even though the headphones covered her ears, Nona could still hear a bit of Usher coming through the plugs.

She walked over to the bed and tapped her daughter's shoulder.

Kelly rolled over and smiled. "Hi, Mommy," she said. Her tone was casual, as if she'd seen her mother that morning. She took off the headphones.

Nona held her. "Your music was so loud, you didn't hear me come in," she said. "I keep telling you that you shouldn't play . . ." Nona paused as the smile vanished from Kelly's face. "So, how have you been, sweetie? I missed you so much." She squeezed Kelly's hand.

"Fine."

"And how's school?"

"Fine."

"Did you do anything special while I was away?"

"No."

Nona lightly bit the corner of her lip. "What are you listening to?" She lifted the CD case from the bed.

"Nothing."

"Since when did Usher become 'nothing'?"

Kelly shrugged.

"I guess you don't feel like talking tonight, huh?"

Kelly shook her head. "I talked to you last night on the phone."

Nona kept her sigh inside and stood. "Well, I had a good trip, but I'm so glad to be home with you."

Kelly glanced at her mother, then looked down. "When are you leaving again?"

Her daughter's eyes saddened her, and Nona lowered herself back onto the bed. She pulled Kelly into her arms. "I'm going to be home for a while, honey. Isn't that great? We'll be able to spend quite a bit of time together."

Kelly leaned away from Nona, but she was smiling. "Really? Do you think you'll be home for my play? I got the part of Lady Macbeth. Remember, I told you?"

"Of course I remember." Nona tried to recall the date that Kelly had told her and at the same time review her own schedule in her mind. But then she shook her head. "And I'll be there."

Kelly grinned. "That's great. I can't wait for you to see me. Macbeth, that's Shakespeare, you know."

Nona tugged at her daughter's thick ponytail. "Maybe I can help you practice some of your lines."

"Really? Will you have time?"

Nona smiled. "We're going to have a lot of time together from now on." She paused. Kelly had heard those words from her many times. "I promise," Nona added. "And we can start with dinner. Odessa will have everything ready in about thirty minutes or so."

"Okay, but—" Kelly stopped for a moment, letting go of her smile. "What is Odessa fixing?"

"I told her to broil some chicken."

Kelly leaned against the bed's headboard. "I'm not hungry, Mom."

"You have to eat, sweetheart."

"But I've been on a diet while you were away and I don't want to break it."

Nona wanted to scream every time she heard Kelly say the word "diet," a word that had been coming from her daughter's mouth since she was five. There was so much that she wanted to say, but Kelly had heard it all from her before.

Nona said, "Well, broiled chicken and a salad is very healthy." She stopped as if she had a new idea. "You know what? I'll have Odessa chop up the chicken into the salad. That'll fit right into your . . . diet. Okay?"

It took only a moment for Kelly's cheer to return. She nodded, then put the headphones back over her ears. "Call me when dinner's ready," she shouted.

Nona turned toward the door, but just as she put her hand on the doorknob, Kelly called out.

"Mommy." She took off the headphones. "I'm glad you're home," she said softly before she returned the music to her ears.

Nona blew Kelly a kiss. God surely answered prayers.

# two

The three louder-than-life voices of Destiny's Child blared through the thousand-square-foot room, made to look even larger by the floor-to-ceiling mirrors that covered three walls.

But still, it wasn't enough space for the one hundred bodies that packed the floor this Saturday morning. It was like this for every Brickhouse class that Nona led.

"Okay, now, kick," Nona exclaimed, her voice loud through the microphone headset. "Kick, kick, kick . . ." She sang her instructions to the music's beat.

"What . . . the hell . . . is her . . . problem?" Leila puffed to Anna, who was pounding the hardwood floor next to her. "She's never pushed us this hard."

"Yes, she has. You just don't remember. She's been gone for so long."

"I don't remember any pain like this."

"Well, remember this is what we're here for," Anna panted. "And remember, this is a privilege, sweetie. Nona only tortures a special few." Anna winked at her friend as she twisted her periwinkle leotard-clad torso, imitating the double side kick that Nona was doing on the raised platform in the front.

"Aren't we the lucky ones?" Leila groaned, but then she smiled when she peeked at her reflection in the mirror. She knew she looked good in her black unitard that didn't leave room for flaws. She twisted so that she could see herself better. Her boobs were still high, her behind, lifted, her stomach flatter than it was before she had two children. And her beauty was still natural. She hadn't had to go under the knife—not yet.

People always gasped when they found out her real age. And they should, she thought. It took commitment to keep her thirty-one-year-old figure looking as if she were hovering closer to twenty-one. Besides her starvation methods, it was Nona's Brickhouse techniques that kept Leila's picture next to "svelte" in the dictionary.

It was work, but it was necessary. Marriage did not provide an exemption from having to look a certain way. In fact, being married to the New York Knicks star player, Shawn Lomax, made it worse. Leila had to compete with the groupies who swarmed her husband after every Knicks game. In bed, she often searched Shawn's eyes, wondering if he was comparing her to the numerous women that he had screwed while married to her.

Her light green eyes moved to the mirror again. She'd always been aware of her looks. From when the girls in fifth grade chased her home because they said, "She thinks she's cute," until her days in high school when she had her choice of any male she wanted. Her cinnamon-tanned skin, almond-shaped eyes, and curly bronze-colored hair that fell to the middle of her back provided many benefits— including an introduction, and eventual marriage to the multimillionaire basketball superstar Shawn Lomax. But not too long after they said, "I do," Leila discovered that it was going to take much more than her trophy-wife looks to keep her man faithful to his marriage vows. The accoutrements of the NBA lifestyle did not exactly fit with what Leila had dreamed would be her traditional marriage. She wanted a union filled with morals and values. But the money, sex, and power that came with being a famous basketball player made it almost impossible for any professional athlete to sustain a committed relationship. And Leila Lomax had seen many a marriage come and go during her wifely tenure with the Knicks.

"Come on, Leila," Nona yelled, pulling Leila's eyes away from the mirror and her thoughts back to the workout.

Leila sucked her teeth, but smiled inside. She knew she was blessed to be in Nona Simms's class, even if they were best friends. Brickhouse was the only gym in the country where members were on a waiting list to renew their membership. And only members with three years' good standing were given the chance to stand in line for Nona's Saturday morning class.

"Come on, y'all." Nona clapped her hands and hollered as she paced the floor, challenging her clients. "Push it."

Leila kicked her leg higher. Her eyes roamed through the room, looking at the other gleaming bodies. She wasn't sure if people were shimmering from sweat or from the diamonds that adorned almost every ear and most ring fingers.

Leila smiled when she saw Toni Lee planted in her usual front and center spot, with pure concentration etched on her face. Her perspiration-soaked, leopard-print midriff top and matching Daisy Duke spandex shorts fit better than her own skin. Even with her ponytail bouncing and loose strands of hair plastered to her neck, Toni looked as if she could stop at a second's notice and pose for a layout in *Playboy*. After staring at her, Leila strained to kick her leg two inches higher.

"Okay, people. Hit the floor."

Moans followed Nona's demand—the same ones that always came when Nona's signature abdominal drills were about to begin. Brickhouse's theme song played loudly through the Bose speakers.

Leila grunted as she fell to the floor, humming along with the song. "She's a brick . . . house. She's mighty, mighty just lettin' it all hang out . . ."

This was her world—at least five times a week—with other flawless bodies looking to achieve a higher level of perfection—looking to gain the Nona Simms athletic yet curvy body.

She grumbled through the forty-five minutes of crunches, leg lifts and overall pain. Her body screamed, but Leila pushed harder as she remembered the Knick's City Dancer she'd caught chilling out with Shawn in a rear booth at her favorite Houston's restaurant two weeks before.

Even the warm-down hurt, and when Leila completed her last stretch, she let out a deep breath. She didn't have the strength to clap with the others when Nona yelled, "That's a wrap."

Leila lay on her back—spread eagle—as others moved toward the locker area.

"Are you going to stay there for the rest of the day?" Anna stood above her with her arms crossed. Her stance made her petite, five-foot-four frame look much taller.

Leila didn't move, not even as people stepped over her, and not even when Toni wandered over to the two of them.

"What are you guys up to?" Toni asked, still breathing as if she hadn't stopped working out.

"Well, first I have to get Leila up from this floor." Anna laughed.

"I don't plan on moving . . . ever."

They all laughed.

Anna said, "Since I have the two of you together, let me ask you something."

Leila struggled to sit up as Toni joined her on the floor. "Sounds serious," Leila said, looking up at her friend.

"Oh, no." Anna waved her hand in the air. "I just wanted to invite you to lunch at my house next Thursday. I'm starting a new foundation—a literacy program for children—and I need your ideas." She paused and smiled. "So, as the mayor's very significant other, can I bribe you ladies with a wonderful lunch at Gracie Mansion—low calorie, of course."

"Count me in," Leila said. It was always a reality check to Leila whenever she was reminded that her fun and humble friend and workout buddy was New York City royalty.

"Me too." Toni glanced at her watch and jumped up. "I've got an interview with *People*." She glanced at Nona, who was talking to a client. "Our leader is still holding court. Tell her I'll catch her later," Toni said before she rushed from the room.

A moment later Nona glided toward them, and Leila shook her head. "You just taught this class, and there's not a sweat gland on you that's been used."

Nona took a swallow from the water bottle she carried, then chuckled.

"It's not fair," Leila whined.

"Get over it." Nona tapped her friend playfully on top of her head. "Anyway, are you guys having lunch here?"

Anna said, "That's a good idea. There's something I want to talk to you about anyway."

Nona turned to Leila.

Leila stood, shaking her head at the same time. "Can't do it today. I've got to . . . get home. The kids . . . I planned to do . . . something with them," she stammered.

"Hey, I wish you'd told me," Nona said. "I would have loved to have seen Steph and Shawn Jr. You know what? Kelly is coming down in a little while. She's supposed to go to the movies, but she'd love to get together with you and the kids . . ."

"Oh, no," Leila said before Nona could finish. "We couldn't do a group thing today." She lowered her eyes and spoke to the floor. "What we're going to do . . . it's been planned for a while. And I don't want you to have to drive all the way out to Jersey . . . you know."

Nona squinted. "Okay. We'll do it some other time." She stared at Leila. "I guess it's just you and me." She spoke to Anna, but her eyes were still on Leila.

Leila looked up. "We'll get together soon. Next weekend, maybe. Let's check our calendars."

Nona nodded.

Leila said, "Well, I have to get out of here." She took only a few steps before she turned back. "Nona, what's up with Allen?"

There was silence for a moment, before Anna strolled away from her friends, to the other side of the studio. Both Nona and Leila followed Anna with their eyes. When Nona finally turned to Leila, she grimaced.

*I'm sorry,* Leila mouthed.

"What do you mean, what's wrong with Allen?" Nona whispered.

Leila exhaled. She was glad Nona wasn't going to lecture her about mentioning Allen in front of Anna. It was so hard, since they'd all been friends and spent so much time at Brickhouse.

Leila said, "Allen seems different. I worked weights with him yesterday and he was . . . I don't know . . . weird."

"He's fine. There's just a lot of business stuff going on right now."

"I know, but this seemed . . . personal for some reason. Like something is really bothering him."

Nona frowned. "He hasn't mentioned anything to me."

Leila shrugged. "Okay. Maybe he was just having a bad day. I'll see you on Monday." She paused and glanced at Anna, who stood waiting across the room. "See you, Anna."

Anna waved without a smile.

Leila glanced at Nona before she dashed from the studio. She felt bad for Anna, but she couldn't spend this time thinking about her friend. She had big plans for today.

In the locker room, as the heat of the shower's water hit her, Leila thought about lingering, but she stepped from the stall after just a few minutes, knowing that sometime this afternoon, she'd be back in the shower again. The warm, titillating thoughts of the afternoon delight that lay ahead brought goose bumps to her skin. She dressed and hurried outside, through the full parking lot. As she put her key in her car, her eyes wandered to the Lexus SUV parked next to her. A man and woman were tangled in the backseat, but suddenly dipped from her view.

Her face warmed with the rush of blood, and she looked away. She hated seeing that. It only reminded her of the times she might have been seen. In the same parking lot. In the same position.

She swerved from the parking lot and pushed thoughts of the couple in the car, and Anna, and Allen, and Nona from her mind. Most importantly, she pressed thoughts of her husband, Shawn Lomax, far away. She turned her G500 Mercedes truck down Second Avenue, driving in the opposite direction of her Alpine, New Jersey, home and grinning as she fantasized about the time that awaited her.

# *three*

Allen leaned against the edge of his black lacquer desk. "I really like these ideas, Isaac." He flipped through the pages of the proposal for the Golden Citizens Health Guild. "You put a lot of thought into this."

Isaac grinned.

"I particularly like the health screenings. Anything we can do to educate our people." Allen tossed the proposal onto his desk. "Black people just don't have access to the medical information we need."

Isaac nodded and leaned his broad shoulders against the back of the chair. "I want to teach some of the senior citizen exercise classes."

Allen laughed as he looked at the bulky trainer. His black T-shirt made his already bulging biceps protrude more. Isaac was the only trainer at Brickhouse who was bigger than Allen. "Man, you'll hurt those ladies. They may save money with the free classes, but they'll make up for it when they go running to their doctors with aching muscles."

Isaac chuckled with his boss. "No, man. I know what to do." He crossed his legs. "Anyway, I want to run one last thing past you. When I speak to the churches about advertising in their bulletins, I want to also see about using their facilities."

Allen frowned. "I thought we'd have all the classes here."

"Yeah, but I really want as many people as possible to attend these outreach programs. And, as I thought about it, I began thinking about my grandmother. She doesn't like going to unfamiliar places. But her church? Man, she'll hang out there all day and night."

Allen nodded.

"So I was thinking," Isaac continued, "that the churches would be a good place to do these classes. Make these folks feel comfortable and they'll be more likely to attend."

Allen smiled as he thought back to the beginning—he and Nona had started in a church basement.

Isaac stood. "So think about it and let me know."

Suddenly Allen closed his eyes.

"Hey, man." Isaac rested his hand on Allen's shoulder. "Are you all right?"

Allen rubbed his fingers between his eyes. "Yeah, I'm fine. Just tired."

He opened his eyes, and it took a moment for him to focus on Isaac's concerned face.

Allen walked around his desk. "I've just been keeping long hours while Nona was away. Not to mention the extra stress with the rezoning issue."

Isaac shook his head. "Man, I try not to think about that. What would happen to Brickhouse . . . and to all of us if this place were closed?" He continued to shake his head as his own words began to sink in.

"That's not going to happen," Allen said, pointing his finger at the trainer. "Nona and I have a plan, and when we're finished, Brickhouse will still be here."

Isaac smiled. "Maybe we should get some of the clients involved too. Many of the people who come in here have major pull."

Allen held up his hand. "No. Even though I know everyone has heard, I don't want us talking about it around here. No need to have the clients panic."

Isaac nodded.

"We don't want to get anyone excited." Allen paused. "And speaking of excited, do you have a minute?"

Isaac glanced at his watch. "I have a session in fifteen minutes."

"I'll make this quick. You need to talk to Eric."

Isaac chuckled as if he knew what Allen was going to say.

"I don't understand him," Allen continued. "The Brickhouse parking lot is not lover's lane for the social elite."

Isaac laughed. "That's a good one, man."

"This isn't funny," Allen responded, although he couldn't keep the smile from his lips. "It's getting ridiculous."

"I know, but Eric isn't the only one," Isaac said, trying to defend one of his top clients.

"That's my point. The parking lot needs an X-rating. Look, just tell Eric that he needs to curb his sextracurricular parking lot activities. The guy is an MBA with IBM. Surely he can afford a hotel room."

Isaac smiled. "True, but I don't think I should be the one to handle this with Eric. What about if I call a couple of my friends on the force? We could have them cruise the lot for a while. You know, nothing serious. Just enough to put a scare into Eric."

"No," Allen exclaimed. "New York's Finest is the last thing we need, especially with all of this rezoning stuff going on. We'll handle this. You just talk to Eric."

"Okay." Isaac shrugged. "But you need to talk to your clients too."

Allen's eyes widened. "Like who?"

"Leila Lomax."

"Get out of here."

"You didn't know?"

"Obviously not. Who is she doing in the parking lot?"

Isaac shrugged. "I don't know . . . it's been a while since I saw her. But some jock, and it's not her almost-seven-foot-tall, basketball-dunking husband." He laughed and tapped his watch. "I've got to get to my client."

Allen frowned as he watched Isaac rush from the office. He wanted to go after him and ask more about Leila, but he didn't have the strength. He rested his head in his hands and rubbed his temples. Maybe if he had something to eat. He reached for the salmon wrap that had been delivered from the gym's restaurant. But the moment his hand touched the wax paper, he drew back. It had returned—the dizziness, the nausea, the pain in his abdomen.

He closed his eyes and took a breath. "I've got to eat." When he opened his eyes, he dragged the sandwich to the center of the desk. It took only a few seconds for the blend of smells of mayonnaise, cream cheese, onions, green peppers, fish, and cheese to reach his nose. A tidal wave of bile rolled through his stomach, and he shoved the salmon wrap into the trash can.

"Damn," he muttered. Perspiration sprinkled his forehead.

What would Nona say if she knew? he wondered. But he already knew the answer. "She would kill me."

They'd been through this before, and he sighed as he remembered the look of disappointment in her eyes every time she looked at him during that time.

"You're risking everything that we've worked to build, Allen," she had said to him. "If anyone finds out about this, we could lose Brickhouse. I won't allow you to do that to me."

"I promise, Nona. This will never happen again." He had repeated those words a thousand times, trying to get her to trust him as she had in the beginning. He had meant every word of that vow six years ago. But here he was again—breaking his word, and risking their operation when Nona needed him the most.

He slammed his fist against the desk. "I can't do this," he scolded himself. "If anyone finds out, it'll be over."

Allen wiped the water from his brow. He had to stop—Nona needed him, and he needed to protect her. But on top of those thoughts, another one more menacing entered his mind—while he was the only one who could protect Nona, he was also the only one who could bring her down. Because of him, she could very well lose Brickhouse.

# four

Nona sauntered into the restaurant packed with patrons as if it were a five-star eatery. But even though it was part of Brickhouse, many Harlem residents came just to partake of the healthy, yet delicious dishes that rivaled those of some of New York's finest restaurants.

She spotted Anna at the table reserved for her and her guests.

"Hello, Ms. Simms."

The greetings followed her as she made her way through the room. She waved, but didn't stop to talk. It was an unspoken rule—she was not to be disturbed in the restaurant.

"Hey, hey. Sorry it took me so long," Nona said in her sister-girl voice. Even though Anna Leone was the first lady of New York City, Nona still considered this woman whom she'd known since her college days her homegirl. Anna was a graduate teacher's assistant in the English department during Nona's sophomore year. They met at a nearby Thai restaurant they both frequented during their lunch breaks. Recognizing one another from campus, the two women bonded quickly. They'd been close at Barnard—becoming known as Ebony and Ivory. When Anna left Barnard to go on to Fordham law school, the two friends didn't let a day pass without a phone call, email, or coffee break.

"No problem." Anna smiled. "I was looking over the menu. I don't know how you do it. On top of everything, you've added all of these new items."

Nona chuckled. "Like you didn't know."

"I didn't. I wasn't here at all while you were away." Anna's eyes scanned the menu. "There's so much, it's hard to decide."

Nona watched as Anna studied the five-page booklet, and she beamed. Her friend was looking good. Anna had added mahogany tints to her shoulder-length brown hair, and although she'd always been small, she looked especially fit now with the muscle definition she'd added to her arms and legs. But the best part was that the glow that Anna had when they first met was back—after its five-year absence. It seemed that Anna had finally found a way to accept the curveball life had thrown her.

Anna looked up. "Why are you staring at me?"

"Do you know how good you look?"

"I work out with you. I pay you a lot of money. I'd better look good."

"You know what I mean."

Anna lowered her eyes. "I'm trying, Nona."

"You're doing great." Anna covered her friend's hand with her own. "It's good to have you back."

"Well, one can't grieve forever."

"There's no expiration date on mourning. You did it in your own time." Nona opened her napkin and placed it on her lap. "But I know Todd would be happy to know that you're back in your groove," she said softly.

It seemed to Nona that Anna almost smiled at the mention of her son's name. It was the first time she'd mentioned Todd and not seen tears come to her friend's eyes. "And I'm sure that Anthony is glad to have his wife back."

Anna shook her head. "He hardly notices that he has a wife."

"That's not true. He just has a lot on his shoulders. Running this city is more than a full-time job."

"I know, but still, ever since he became mayor, I feel something's missing from our marriage. It's like he's distracted by more than his job." She paused. "But complaining does nothing. That's why I'm going to do something about it. And that's what I wanted to talk to you about." Anna moved to the edge of her chair. "I want to tell you about a program I'm putting together, and I need your support."

"Whatever it is, I'll do it."

"No." Anna shook her head. "I don't want this to be a friendship thing."

"I won't do it because of that."

"Good."

"I'll do it because you're the mayor's wife."

Nona laughed, but Anna rolled her eyes.

Nona said, "Okay, honey. What do you need?"

Anna leaned forward as if she couldn't wait to get the words out. "I've come up with an idea. A Children's Literacy Outreach program."

"What's that?"

"It'll be a children's foundation that encourages reading. But it will be more than just a message or commercials on television. I'm thinking of tools like mobile libraries . . ."

As Anna continued, Nona rested her chin in the palm of her hand and watched her friend. Anna was the mature, intellectual, intense one in their friendship circle. Even now, she looked as if she were making a presentation to a corporate board—reviewing her objectives, detailing every point, outlining the entire program.

Nona nodded as if she were listening intently, but her mind wandered as she recalled her friend's journey.

Five years ago when Todd, Anna's son, died, Nona had doubts whether her friend would ever recover. She had never witnessed a person overcome with such sorrow. At the funeral, it took three men to pull Anna back from Todd's coffin when she tried to climb in.

As Nona watched Anna, she had sobbed until her chest ached. Her cries came from more than just empathizing with her friend. It was the mental anguish that twisted Nona's guts at the thought of what she'd do if she lost Kelly.

For weeks after the funeral, it was as if Anna's soul had been buried with Todd. She disappeared from life, leaving her husband and friends feeling powerless to help.

Nona had visited Anna daily, but besides hello and good-bye, Anna spoke no words in between. Nona would sit with her friend for hours as Anna gripped her son's picture, thrusting it into her chest as if the act would bring him back to life.

"There's nothing I can do for her," Anthony had grumbled to Nona at the time. "I don't know how much more I can take."

"She's grieving," Nona tried to explain.

"So am I, but who's here for me?"

Nona had tried to console Anthony too, but her concern was for Anna.

Then almost six weeks after Todd's death, Anna appeared at the gym.

"I'm so glad to see you," Nona had said, squeezing her friend in a hug.

Anna had even tried to smile. "I have to do something." Her words sounded as if they were coming from a robot.

"Good. Are you here to take my class?"

Anna nodded and turned toward the locker rooms. As she walked, she talked over her shoulder. "Nona, I need a new trainer," she had said without emotion. "If I'm going to stay at Brickhouse, I don't want Allen anymore."

Nona had wanted to convince Anna to stay with Allen. She was sure that if the two continued to work together, they'd be able to wade through the issues that hung between them like a guillotine.

But Nona could tell that her friend was teetering on a thin emotional cord, and she wasn't going to be the one to tear the rope. "Let me work on that for you," she said just before Anna reached the double smoked-glass doors that led to the dressing area.

Anna nodded as she held the door handle. "Tell Allen to stay away from me." This time, emotion oozed from each word. She spewed so much hate that Nona had to take a step backward.

Nona remembered she had simply nodded as tears burned her eyes. She couldn't believe Anna still blamed Allen for Todd's death; however, there was no way she could convince her friend.

But now as she looked at Anna, with her fingers fluttering with the words she spoke, there was no sadness in her.

"So what do you think, Nona?"

Nona blinked, trying to focus on Anna's words. "It sounds good. You know I'm behind anything you do." Nona meant those words. She would do anything for her friends, but this was also coming at the perfect time—it could be an opportunity for positive exposure, right during the zoning hearings.

Nona continued, "What made you think of this?"

Anna shrugged. "Maybe I'm ready to be more than the mayor's wife. Lord knows there's not much to do in that position besides hobnobbing with the socialites." She sighed. "And this would be my project. I plan on doing everything from selecting the board to being involved in all the fund-raising."

"That's terrific."

"And maybe I'll get the chance to actually use my degree."

"I don't know why you say that, Anna. You do a lot with—"

"Everything I've done in the past few years has been in the name of getting Anthony elected or in the name of being the mayor's wife. This will be for me."

Nona nodded. She knew more than anyone how important it was to have your own thing. "I understand. Now, I have something to ask you. How involved is Anthony with all of this rezoning stuff going on in Harlem?"

Anna shrugged. "He's mentioned it; I know he's on the committee, but I don't know much about it." She leaned forward. "It's not really going to affect Brickhouse, is it?"

It was Nona's turn to shrug. "We're trying to make sure it doesn't."

"The rumor is they might close down . . ." She paused and looked around the restaurant. "I don't even want to say it."

Nona waved her hand in the air, dismissing Anna's words. "Don't worry. But do you think you can toss a letter from me on top of Anthony's in-box?" Nona laughed, but she was only half joking.

"Let me see what I can do. I'll talk to Anthony, see where he stands, and get back to you." Anna squeezed Nona's hand. "This is the reason you have friends in high places."

Nona smiled. "Let's hope that'll be enough. Now, didn't we come here to eat?"

"Yeah, but you know what? Now that you're on board, I could use this time to make some calls." She looked at Nona beseechingly. "Would you mind if I took a rain check?"

"Go ahead," Nona said, waving her hand. "Get busy and keep me posted."

Anna air-kissed Nona's cheek. "I'll see you on Monday. If I find out anything about the rezoning before then, I'll call."

Nona grinned as Anna glided toward the front of the restaurant, her stride filled with her newfound passion.

But suddenly Nona frowned when she saw Allen appear at the café's entrance. She jumped from her chair. "Anna," Nona called, even though she knew her friend wouldn't hear her over the blend of conversation and background music that mixed to compose a melodic hum in the air.

Nona lowered herself back into her chair and watched Anna engineer her way through the maze of tables. She held her breath as Anna's path came closer to colliding with Allen. A second later, they were face to face. They both paused. Nona couldn't tell if words were exchanged, although she was sure they didn't speak. They hadn't in five years.

Anna rushed away, out of Nona's view. Nona stood again, but Allen's eyes told her to sit as he moved toward her table.

"I'm sorry about that," he said, his eyes filled with the same sadness Nona saw every time Allen and Anna met.

"Don't apologize. You didn't know—"

"It's hard to time these things. I thought Anna had left a long time ago." He shook his head. "I want it to be over. Hell, I never wanted it to start." Allen lowered his eyes.

"Sometimes I wonder . . . maybe Anna's right. Maybe Todd's death is my fault."

"Stop it, Allen." She covered his hand with hers. "How were you supposed to know that Todd was taking steroids?" she asked him the way she always did when she saw the shroud of guilt blanket him. "My goodness, after all you'd been through with that terrible stuff." She shook her head. "There was nothing you could do."

Allen held her gaze for a moment, then looked away.

"It wasn't like you were his supplier or encouraged him. You were just training him. You know how dangerous . . ." Nona sighed. "Anyway, Anna just needs more time. She wishes that you had been able to stop him from taking those damn steroids."

When he turned back to her, his eyes spoke for him. *Isn't five years enough?*

"She lost her son—her only child," Nona said, answering his unasked question. "Everyone handles grief differently. She'll come around."

The way Allen nodded his head let Nona know that he wanted to believe her words. She wanted to believe them too.

Allen stood. "Anyway, I came in here for some juice."

"Are you all right?" she asked, taking his hand.

"I will be as soon as I can convince Anna—"

"I'm not talking about that. Leila asked me if there was something going on with you, and I told her no. But now that I look at you, you seem kind of . . . I don't know . . . flushed. Like you're not feeling well." She tilted her head. "I noticed it yesterday too, but I thought you were just tired."

He shook his head. "I'm fine. It's just Anna. And you're right. I am a bit tired." He forced himself to smile. "You know, I've been doing double duty around here."

"And I hope you know how much I appreciate it."

"I know. But you know I'd do anything for you, Nona."

"Hey, Mom."

They both glanced up to see Kelly approaching the table.

"Hey, sweetie." Nona hugged her.

Allen tugged at Kelly's ponytail. "How're you doing, kid?" He stepped back and smiled. "You look sharp," he said, admiring her studded Rocawear denim jacket. "You must have a hot date."

"I do." Kelly giggled. "With you. We're still going to the movies?"

"You know it. I have some things I have to clear up in my office, and we'll be on our way."

"Are you sure, Allen?" Nona asked. "If you're tired, Kelly won't mind."

"No way. My girl and I have a date, and I'm never too tired for that."

Nona smiled. For years Allen had been filling in some of the missing pieces in Kelly's life.

"I'll be right back, kiddo."

Kelly sat down with Nona as Allen dashed from the restaurant.

"This is perfect," Nona said. "You're just in time to have lunch with me."

Kelly shook her head. "I ate already. I'll just have something to drink."

Nona motioned to Gail, who, next to Allen, had been with her the longest. From girl Friday, to administrative assistant, and now catering manager, Gail was invaluable. As she approached the table, Nona thought of how the rezoning would affect so many people. Gail was the single mother of three boys, one of whom was a freshman at Columbia University. Brickhouse had become a career for

Gail. She had helped to develop Brickhouse's catering program, and on Saturdays she filled in as a waitress to earn extra money. She was determined that it wouldn't be for lack of funds that her children didn't get a college education. What would Gail do if she lost the gym?

"Hey, Miss Thang," Gail said, leaning over to kiss Kelly on the cheek.

Nona smiled. This was a family, and Brickhouse was their home. Kelly was part of this too. Everyone embraced her, as if she were a younger sibling. In a small way, it made up for some of what Nona believed Kelly missed at home. And then the thoughts that seemed to haunt Nona daily returned—about how she just didn't have enough time. About how her focus on her career was robbing Kelly of a normal family life. About how her daughter had only one parent, who was hardly ever around. Sometimes Nona believed that she had dealt Kelly an unfair hand.

Yet in a small way, the "family" at Brickhouse made Nona feel a bit better. But now, Reverend Watkins threatened that. His plans would destroy this family. Without his even being aware of it, Reverend Watkins's destructive tentacles reached far beyond this building, although Nona knew that the reverend and his cronies would never care even if they knew.

But he had never met anyone like her before. There was no way he was going to win.

"So, Nona, do you want to order anything?" Gail asked, interrupting her thoughts.

"The vegetable burrito. And Kelly will have a hot chocolate with lots of whipped cream."

Kelly said, "Could you please change that to a cup of green chai?"

"Sure," Gail responded as Nona frowned.

Kelly waited until Gail moved away before she said, "Mom, you know I'm trying to cut out sweets," she whined.

Nona cringed, knowing what her daughter was thinking. But before she could respond, Kelly said the dreaded words, "How else am I going to look like you?"

"Honey, I love the way you look. That's all you need to do. Be the best that you can be."

"That's what I'm trying to do." Kelly stood. "I'm going to the bathroom. I'll be right back, Mom."

As Nona watched Kelly work her way through the restaurant, she wanted to stand up and scream—to convince Kelly that she was fine the way she was. Yes, she was a bit overweight, but it was mostly baby fat. Nona had been the same way when she was Kelly's age.

The challenge was, Kelly would never be a small girl—not with the genes she carried. Her father was six-three, and over 230 pounds. Nona herself worked hard to maintain her size six. Without a healthy diet and almost daily exercise, she would easily edge up to a size twelve or fourteen.

But Nona maintained her figure for a healthy lifestyle and a healthy business. She was her best advertisement, but that was the problem. Ever since Nona's face and body became plastered on billboards and bus placards across the city, Kelly's self-image had suffered. She'd never forget the first time Kelly had shocked her with her words.

"Mommy, can I go on a diet?"

Nona had stopped moving as she and Kelly were walking to kindergarten class at the day care center around the corner from their apartment.

"Kelly, do you know what a diet is?"

"Yes, Mommy. A diet is for fat people."

That was the starting line. For years Kelly's weight had

been the subject of an unending tug-of-war—Kelly insisting that she had to lose pounds and Nona, on the other end, assuring her daughter she was fine the way she was.

In the last months, the battle had escalated.

First, Odessa had found dozens of empty wrappers and boxes crammed in the back of Kelly's closet.

"I don't know, Ms. Nona." Odessa's French-Caribbean accent turned thicker with her concern. "I don't know what this means."

Nona had sorted through the shopping bag stuffed with loose cellophane. Marshmallow pies, coffee cakes, honey buns, potato chips . . . she couldn't count the number of empty packages.

Odessa said, "Kelly always tells me that she doesn't want any snacks and now I find all of this. I don't know what this means," she repeated.

Nona knew exactly what it meant. And what was worse, she feared that there might have been more than just the secret binging. What if her daughter was purging?

"Odessa, it's normal for girls Kelly's age to sneak a few snacks." Nona tried to keep her tone casual, even though every organ inside her trembled. "There's nothing to worry about. I'll handle this."

But Nona hadn't known what to do. She considered confronting her daughter, even bringing Ronald, Kelly's father, into this matter. But in the end, she decided to wait and watch, praying that Kelly had gone through a fleeting phase that had already passed.

Two weeks later, Nona discovered her strategy was not going to work when the headmaster at South Chester Prep called her into the school.

"Ms. Simms, I don't know if you're aware, but Kelly has had a bit of trouble." Mr. Howell, the headmaster, sat sternly straight, with his gold-framed bifocals lowered to the tip of his nose.

Nona had frowned. "Trouble? I don't understand. I go over her homework every night, and her last progress report said she was doing well. I'm surprised—"

Mr. Howell stopped Nona. "Obviously, your daughter hasn't talked to you," he said in his English accent, sounding as if he was chastising her.

Nona wanted to stand, walk behind Mr. Howell's desk, and tip over one of the heavy mahogany bookcases that lined the wall behind him. Instead she slumped a bit in her chair. "Kelly and I talk every day."

"Has she told you about this?" Mr. Howell slid the single page from the *New York Post* across the desk. It took less than a second for Nona's blood to freeze.

Two weeks before, this front-page Sunday edition story had thrilled her. When the calendar section editor of the *New York Post* called and asked about Kelly appearing with her, Nona had agreed. This was the solution she'd been searching for. She would bring Kelly into the business. Then she and Kelly would be closer. Kelly would feel loved and necessary . . . and would be less likely to sneak food in the middle of the night.

The picture had been taken at Nona's book signing at the Fifth Avenue Barnes & Noble. Nona was dressed in a black and white midriff top with black leggings that hugged like skin. Kelly, holding her mother's hand, was dressed in a top that matched Nona's, but with black shorts. The two-inch headline read, "Body Beautiful."

But right underneath, the words "And Fatty Daughter" had been scrawled in red marker.

"One of the teachers found it on the mirror in the girls' locker room," Mr. Howell said.

"This is horrible."

Mr. Howell nodded. "The student responsible has been reprimanded. But I called you because I had a feeling that Kelly had not shared this with you."

Nona tried to swallow the lump that clogged her throat. "No, she hadn't."

"Ms. Simms, I also called because Kelly has endured relentless teasing. I know this is part of growing up, but frankly, the situation with Kelly concerns me. The girls in her grade taunt her in class. And during recess and in the cafeteria, she's often alone. When she's teased about her weight, she doesn't even fight back. When her teachers or the guidance counselor try to talk to her, she says she's fine. And now that I know that she doesn't even talk about it to you . . ." He shook his head.

"I think she will now."

Mr. Howell shrugged. "That's possible, but I'd like to make a suggestion. Kelly is holding so much inside, and that worries me. I believe she should see a therapist." It was the dismay in Nona's eyes that made Mr. Howell add, "Kelly needs to talk to someone. I believe there is a lot festering under the surface. And with all that is going on in schools these days . . ."

His unfinished sentence daunted her. It was a subtle warning.

"You don't think it's enough for her to talk to me?"

Mr. Howell had looked down his nose as he said, "Ms. Simms, has she talked to you yet?"

Nona had left that meeting with a miscellany of emotions. She was horrified at what Kelly had endured. And she was overflowing with sadness because her daughter had not felt secure enough to bring her despair home.

That night after she checked Kelly's homework, Nona had approached her.

"Hey, Kelly, why don't you sit in here with me for a little while." Nona patted a spot next to her on her king-sized bed.

Kelly had shaken her head. "No, I wanna watch TV in my room."

"You can watch it in here." Nona punched the Crestron remote, turning on the plasma television. "What do you want to see?"

Kelly sighed as she slumped onto the bed. "I don't know."

She handed Kelly the remote and watched as she flipped through the channels. "How's school?"

"Okay."

"Anything special going on?"

"No."

Nona took a deep breath. "Kelly, I spoke to Mr. Howell today."

Kelly sat up and stared at her mother. "Why? I haven't done anything wrong."

Nona clicked off the TV. "I know, honey. He just wanted me to know what's been going on with you." She paused. "He showed me that picture the teacher found in the locker room."

Kelly jumped from the bed. "Mom, it's no big deal."

"Why didn't you tell me about it?"

"Because it's no big deal." She folded her arms and fought to hold back the tears that sprang to her eyes.

Nona reached for her daughter, but Kelly stepped back. "Sweetheart, I don't mean to upset you, but we have to talk about this."

Kelly wiped a single tear that rolled down her cheek.

This time when Nona reached for her, she didn't back away. Nona took her hand and pulled her onto the bed. She put her arm around Kelly and lowered Kelly's head onto her shoulder. It was then that Kelly freed the hurt she'd been holding.

Nona hugged her daughter in silence. She treasured the moments, although she could feel Kelly's pain through every tremble of her body. Nona wished she could take the sting of the hurt from her and exchange it for the strength that she'd gained through the wisdom of her years. But Nona knew that some of what Kelly was going through was a rite of passage—strength was an asset that she'd have to earn herself.

After a few minutes, Kelly said, "Mom, it was awful when I saw that picture. Everyone was laughing at me."

Nona closed her eyes, forcing back tears of her own, and squeezed her daughter tighter. "I know, sweetie."

"They always bother me and I wish they would just leave me alone. I don't know why they don't like me."

Nona wished she could find the words to explain it to her child. In an instant, the times she'd been teased and bullied as a child sparked through her mind. Her heart ached as if the torment had happened only yesterday. But even today, with time behind her and wisdom beside her, she still couldn't explain why. There never seemed to be a logical explanation for why people act upon their own jealousies and insecurities. Like Kelly, she had no idea why she'd been shunned by her classmates.

"Kelly, I think there is something we can do about everything you've been going through."

Kelly lifted her head from her mother's shoulder and looked at her with hopeful eyes. "Really?"

Nona nodded and took Kelly's hands into hers. "Mr.

Howell asked me to speak to a Dr. Gibbs. I called him today."

Kelly frowned.

"Dr. Gibbs is a therapist . . ."

Kelly's eyes widened as she snatched her hand away. "I'm not seeing any shrink," she yelled as she drew back.

"Kelly, wait—"

"Mom, if people are teasing me now, just wait until they hear that I'm seeing a doctor because of them."

"Sweetheart, I just want you to have someone to talk to, and no one at your school will know."

"Mom, everybody knows everybody's business at school. They'll call me a freak. It'll be worse for me if those girls found out that I had to get checked out because of them."

"Kelly, I can make sure that no one knows. I can protect you—"

"You haven't protected me yet. Why should I believe you now?" Kelly screamed.

Time froze. The seconds stretched in silence.

Finally Kelly said, "I'm sorry, Mom." She wiped the tears from her face. "But I'm not going to any freak doctor." She ran from the room, leaving Nona with no words to say and no idea what to do.

That had happened almost two months ago, at the beginning of the school year, and since then, Kelly refused to talk to Nona about school, answering all Nona's inquiries with only single-syllable words.

"Mom?"

Kelly's voice brought Nona back to the present, and Gail stood next to her with the vegetable burrito and green chai.

After Gail walked away, Kelly sat down and asked, "Mom, you looked like you were daydreaming. What were you thinking about?"

Nona smiled. "I was just thinking about how we're going to have a great weekend. Maybe after you get back from the movies, you and I can do some shopping."

Kelly's smile matched Nona's. "That sounds good, Mom. Where do you want to go?"

"I'll leave that up to you."

Kelly lowered her eyes, then raised them slowly. "Can we go to Saks? I saw in the paper that they were having a sale."

"Sounds good to me. We'll tell Allen to take you to a short movie."

Kelly laughed.

Nona took a bite of her burrito and looked at her daughter with her hands wrapped around the mug. "Why don't you have something to eat before you go to the movies, since we're going shopping afterward?"

"No, Mom." She took a small sip of tea as if she were savoring each calorie in every swallow.

Nona nodded but remained silent. How could she force Kelly to eat? She was trying to be careful. Nona had read numerous articles that advised parents not to push their daughters in situations such as this. Many advised that parents often made too big a deal out of what was just a phase, and Nona wanted to make sure she wasn't doing that.

If she played this right, Nona believed that one day Kelly would move on. One day her daughter would look in the mirror and see only her reflection—absent her mother, the girls at school, or the images that magazines delivered as truth. And when that day came, Nona knew that Kelly would recognize and accept her beauty—both inside and out. In the meantime, Nona would continue to watch her daughter and pray.

## five

Allen stopped at the large oval reception desk. The circular lobby buzzed with the sounds of the Saturday afternoon workout crowd as clients and staff greeted one another. Brickhouse boasted more than three thousand members, many of whom had been coming to the gym since before Nona had moved into this building. More than half of the staff had been with Nona for more than four years, which was considered an eternity in the industry.

Allen leaned against the Lucite top and checked the sign-in sheets as the two employees assigned to the front desk swiped clients' membership cards as they entered.

"Hey, Allen," a woman who had been coming to the club for more than five years greeted him. "When are you going to have time for me on your schedule? And I'm not talking about working out."

He smiled, waved, and returned to the sheets in front of him. No time for conversation. He wanted to finish. He loved the time he spent with Kelly, but the break today was as much for him as it was for her. He hoped the fresh air would make him feel better.

"Are you teaching tonight's class, Allen?" This time it was a male client addressing him.

"No, but I'll be back in front of the room on Monday."

The greetings and questions bombarded him, and within minutes he realized standing in the reception area wasn't a good idea. He picked up the prospective members' folders, then moved toward his office. As he walked, he scanned the thick pile of applications. He wanted to begin working on these right away. Some people had waited for more than two years to become members of Brickhouse because of the long waiting list; he wanted to bring in as many as he could as soon as possible.

He paused outside his office, glanced up the long hall, and listened to the Saturday afternoon hum of the gym. This was the sound of success; he couldn't have imagined any of this when he first joined Nona.

When he began working for her, he was impressed with her idea to bring a complete gym to Harlem. He was pleased to help her get started, although he expected he wouldn't be staying very long. Working with Nona would be good experience before he moved on to a more visible and lucrative position.

But somehow the years had passed, and before he knew it, Nona was talking to him about plans to open up a forty-thousand-square-foot facility.

"And I want you to be part of it," Nona had said to him then. "I want you to have a financial interest."

Allen had tried in every way he could to tell her that her plans would never work. It was too much of an undertaking. Sure, they were bursting out of the building they were in, but Nona's plans rivaled the health club facilities that were thriving south of Ninety-sixth Street. There was no way a gym like what Nona had in mind could survive in Harlem.

It wasn't that Allen had accepted the stereotypes like many of the trainers in the city. The running joke among his peers was that blacks and Latinos ate all the fried chicken and burritos 125th Street had to offer, but wouldn't dream of going to any gym to work off the greasy, fattening food. Allen realized that these poor eating habits existed, but he believed it was because people were creatures of habit and convenience. People didn't work out because they had never had the convenience of a gym in their area. Still, this was too much of a risk for Nona to take—he just wasn't sure how a full-fledged gym would do in Harlem.

But Nona moved forward as if she didn't hear what he said or as if he didn't know what he was talking about— Allen was never sure which. So he did the only thing he could do—he followed.

It was a good thing that Nona's capacity to dream was large enough for both of them. She shared her meteoric rise with him, often telling others that she would be nowhere without him. Allen accepted her compliments, but he knew the truth. Nothing would have stopped her. This miracle that surrounded him was Nona's baby—a seed in her mind that blossomed into a vision, that metamorphosed into reality.

But the dream had not come without its nightmares. There were weeks when they weren't sure they'd make payroll. There were days when they'd prayed the lights would stay on until the last class ended. Yet they had scrounged through.

Allen knew that, in his small way, he provided Nona with stability. That's why he'd ignored offers to bring a replica of the Brickhouse Technique to other gyms or requests to work with America's famous and infamous.

He shook his head. He didn't have time to linger with these memories. He stepped into his office and dragged himself to the desk. All he wanted to do was run home and fall into bed. But he had promised Kelly a movie.

He slumped into his chair. When was he going to get his energy back? He had to figure out a way. Nona didn't realize it yet, but he was falling behind in work, canceling classes. He even felt as if the rezoning issue was his fault. If he had been on top of his game, he would have known about it sooner, giving them more time to prepare.

And now his challenges were overflowing to his clients. He didn't want people running to Nona as Leila apparently had. Although he couldn't blame Leila—not the way he had treated her yesterday.

Allen and Leila had been working on the chest-press machine, and Leila was whining as she always did.

"Damn, Allen," Leila had exclaimed. "I've never lifted this heavy before. How much weight do you have on this dang machine?"

He had taken a deep breath as he spotted her, giving her more assistance as she pulled the bar to her chest.

But his silence did not silence her.

"I don't know why I torture myself with this every day. When is someone going to come out with a pill? Just pop one a day into my mouth and bam. You've got the perfect J-Lo body. Whoever comes up with that product will make a fortune. I'd pay a million of Shawn's dollars for that."

Her voice went up an octave with each sentence, and he pressed his lips together, trying to hold back his annoyance that was twisting into anger.

"I don't know why we do this," Leila continued her complaint rampage. "And it's mostly women, trying to stay in shape for men who don't appreciate anything we do—"

"Come on, Leila. You're not concentrating. Stop wasting energy talking and push." He held his hands under the bar, giving her more support than usual and hoping that would get her to shut up.

As Leila raised the bar above her head, Allen squinted against the glare of Leila's five-carat pear-shaped diamond ring, and that annoyed him more. He took a quick glance around the massive room. Women were spinning on stationary bikes, trotting on treadmills, and scaling stair climbers. Yet there were more platinum and diamonds in that room than graced the red carpet at the Academy Awards.

He shook his head. What made women wear their finest jewels and blanket their faces with layers of makeup, just to work up a sweat at the gym?

"I can't believe I'm paying you one hundred and fifty dollars an hour for this torture."

Her voice pricked his skin like a sharp pin.

She continued, "I don't know how much more of this I can take."

*Just what I was thinking,* he thought.

Leila exhaled and dropped the weighted bar onto the rack with a loud clang.

Allen flinched but said nothing. He grabbed his clipboard and motioned for Leila to follow him to the next machine.

"Just ten more pounds and I'll be happy." Leila sighed. She paused, looking Allen up and down. "You know, it's people like you who kill me."

Allen looked at Leila. Her long bronze curls were pulled high atop her head in a ponytail. In her black workout bra and Capri-length leggings, she looked almost perfect. There wasn't much more he could do to help her, even if he took a surgical knife and sculpted her body himself. Her desire was unattainable. There was no way she could look like a sixteen-year-old.

"Looking at you makes me almost hate you," Leila whined.

"What are you talking about?" He didn't really want an answer; he just wanted to finish the workout. He looked down at the chart and checked off the machine and repetitions Leila had just completed.

"Come on, don't think it's not noticeable. You've lost how much now?" Her practiced eye rose up and down her trainer's body. "At least five pounds, probably closer to ten . . . and that's just in the last month. Tell me I'm wrong."

Allen squeezed the edge of the clipboard.

"And what makes it worse," Leila continued, "is that you don't even need to lose weight. You already have the perfect body, the perfect face. You're a hunk." Leila laughed and winked. "So tell me, what's your secret?"

He slammed the clipboard onto the floor. "Mind your own business, Leila," he said through clenched teeth. "I'm here to train you, this is not about me."

"Allen—"

He held up his hand. "I want to work, not talk."

Silently Leila lowered her body onto the leg-press machine. She opened her mouth, but when she glanced at him, she pressed her lips together.

"Okay," Allen whispered. "Let's go. I have another client in ten minutes. One . . . two . . . three."

He didn't have to hear her murmurs to know that Leila was cursing under her breath. He felt bad then and even worse now as he remembered their session.

Leila was one of his favorites—ever since he'd inherited her as a client from Nona's A-list, when Nona had to end her one-on-one client sessions because of her schedule. Allen worked hard with every client, but he befriended few. Leila was one that he called a friend.

That's why he was surprised by his own outburst. His

friend had made a simple comment about his body—
something he was certainly used to. Since he began lifting
weights as a teenager and had shaped his body into this top
form, he had been confronted with open stares and forward
comments all the time. Most men even stopped to suck in
their stomachs before approaching him. He knew he was a
good-looking man; he wasn't modest in that sense, although he kept a tight rein on his ego. But he never wanted
to be just another fine-ass gym rat.

With all he'd helped Nona accomplish, Allen knew that
he was much more than that, although he didn't feel like it
today. He was moving from the asset to the liability side of
Nona's friendship sheet. But if he worked hard, he could be
back in top shape before Nona noticed that he'd been gone.

He ticked off a plan in his mind: He'd force himself to
eat. And he'd get more rest. But would that be enough to
take away the pain?

His eyes moved to the telephone. He stared at the black
instrument for several minutes before he lifted the handset
and dialed the number that was embedded in his memory.
He pressed the numbers before he could change his mind.

As the phone on the other end rang, Allen closed his
eyes. This wasn't the solution, but he had no other answers.

"Hello," the baritone voice came through the phone.

Allen rubbed his still-closed eyes, trying to soothe the
sudden ache in his head. "Hey, man, it's me. Allen Wade."

He heard the man chuckle. "It's been a long time."

His pulsing temple throbbed more. "Yeah . . ." Allen
paused and took a deep breath. It took just a few moments
to make the arrangements. When he hung up, he didn't feel
any better, but he knew soon he would. He'd have the medicine he needed, even though it wasn't at all what the doctor ordered.

# six

"Mom, what is this?"

Nona turned from the chrome double sink, letting the water continue to run over the head of lettuce. She squinted at the envelope Kelly held in her hand. "You're holding it. You tell me."

Kelly flopped into one of the four chairs at the round glass dinette table. "It looks like an invitation to a premiere—Toni Lee's premiere."

Nona rolled her eyes, but smiled when her face was out of Kelly's view. She loved these times—when it was just the two of them. It was a rarity, but today she'd come home early, taking advantage of her light Tuesday schedule, and Odessa had gone for an overnight visit to her nephew in Queens. So it was just mother and daughter—precious moments to deposit into her memory.

"Mom, I think you're ignoring me."

"What would make you think that, sweetie?"

"Because you haven't said anything about the premiere."

Nona twisted the water knob and turned around. The setting sun filtered through the window and shined atop

Kelly's head. It seemed to form a halo, and Nona smiled—
her daughter, the angel.

"Mom . . ." Kelly whined. She shifted in her chair, making her crown of light disappear.

"What do you want me to say? You saw the invitation.
I'm sure it's going to be nice."

"Nice?" Kelly exclaimed as if her mother didn't have a
clue. "It's going to be much better than that. Mom, can I
please go with you?"

"You're kidding, right?" Nona asked, wiping her hands
on the dish towel.

"I'm not. Mom, I would love to go to a Toni Lee premiere." Kelly fondled the invitation as if it were a five-
hundred-dollar gift certificate to Saks. "Do you know what
the kids at school would say?"

"Give me one good reason why I should take you to a
Toni Lee movie. Just the title *Love's Desires* should let you
know how I feel about that."

"But, Mom. I'm eleven and three-quarters. I'm practically
grown. I've been to R-rated movies before. Plus I know Toni."

Nona raised her eyebrows, and Kelly giggled, holding
her hands in front of her face.

Kelly said, "Okay, so maybe I don't know her. But I met
her at Brickhouse. Remember you introduced us. She's
really cool." She paused. "And remember what you said
when you wanted to meet my friends?"

Nona shook her head.

"You said that any friend of mine was a friend of yours.
So shouldn't it work the other way too?" Kelly laughed.

Nona pulled a salad bowl from the cabinet and began
breaking apart the lettuce. "That's true, Ms. Smarty Pants.
But there is no way I'm going to let my child go to a movie
with the title *Love's Desires*."

"Why not?" Kelly straightened up in her chair as if that would add sophistication to her words. "I'm mature enough to separate fantasy from reality. I know that a movie is just a product of creative minds."

Nona raised her eyebrows higher.

Kelly continued, "That's what you told me when we watched *The Exorcist*. It's true about all movies."

Nona had to force herself not to smile at the smirk on Kelly's face. "First of all, Kelly . . ." Nona paused. This was one of those moments when she sounded just like her own mother. And she didn't mind at all. "Toni is an adult, so she is Ms. Lee to you."

Kelly lowered her eyes.

"Second, you and I both know that Ms. Lee's movies can be sexually explicit, which is something that at your tender, precious age, I must be mindful of."

Kelly sighed.

"And last, Li'l Miss Thang, you and I watching *The Exorcist* one night when it just happened to be on television is different than you traipsing into a theater with a whole bunch of grown-up, overheated bodies to see *Love's Desires*."

"Mom, all movies are the same. Whether it's sex, horror, science fiction, fantasy, it doesn't matter," Kelly said, continuing her argument as if she were a lawyer. Clearly, she was her father's child. She continued, "I could understand your concern if we were discussing a documentary, but a movie is just a movie. Even I'm smart enough to know the difference."

Nona smiled, first at the thought of her sexy friend Toni Lee in a documentary. Like that would ever happen. But she smiled wider at her daughter. It was obvious that she wasn't wasting the eighteen grand a year she paid South Chester Prep.

It had been a struggle to get Kelly into the school last year. Not only was there a seven-hundred-name waiting list for the fifth grade, but the waiting children had parents who filled the pages of *Who's Who in New York Society*. It was the school's reputation that made Nona ignore the odds and find a way to move Kelly's name to the top. Though her method was not at the top of her ethics list, the two years of free personal training sessions that she'd given the headmaster and his wife was a very small price to pay to make sure her daughter had the best education.

"All right, Kelly," Nona finally said. "I'll think about it. Let me talk to Toni and find out more about the story line . . ."

"Mom, you know what the movie's about." Kelly sighed. "The TV trailers have been running for three weeks." She paused. "But I know what you really want to know. You're going to ask Miss Lee how much haggity-ga-ga there's going to be, right?"

Nona laughed. She hadn't heard Kelly use that term in a long time—the one she'd invented when Kelly was just a toddler to refer to sex.

Even though Nona was laughing, Kelly didn't end her assault. "Plus, Mommy, this is something we can do together. You and me, me and you, right? You said we were going to spend more time together."

Nona's chuckles disappeared, and she turned so that Kelly wouldn't see the way her words pricked Nona's heart.

*Something we can do together.*

Kelly's words played over in her mind, and the guilt filled her once again. Yes, she was home tonight, but when was the last time she'd left work on a weekday before eight or nine o'clock? Usually she barely made it home with enough time to check Kelly's homework before she went to bed.

Her life pulled her heart apart. She was exhilarated by all that she'd accomplished, and she wrapped herself in a cloak of euphoria, basking in the knowledge that she could give Kelly anything that she wanted. But the cost was that she couldn't seem to give Kelly what she needed.

It had been so different in the beginning. When she held the tiny six-pound, ninety-second-old infant in her arms, she had made promises.

"I'll always be here for you," she had whispered in her baby's ear. "I will be a good mother."

For the first two years of Kelly's life, Nona had fulfilled that promise. But as the years passed, she began to ask herself what being a good mother meant. Didn't it mean fulfilling your dreams and desires so that you could pass that happiness on to your child?

Nona couldn't pinpoint the exact time when her nine-to-five days had been traded for twelve-to-fourteen-hour ones, and her five-day work weeks for seven-day ones, with prayers that somehow God would give her an extra twenty-four hours.

At that time, her mother had been concerned.

"You can't leave this child alone so much," Jacqueline, her mother, had commented after Brickhouse had been open for a year.

"Mama, she's not alone. That's why I hired Odessa."

Jacqueline shook her head. "That's not what I'm talking about. Kelly needs to be with kin. She needs to be with you."

"I'll only be working like this for a little while longer, Mama. As soon as Brickhouse is off the ground and running . . ."

"Let her move in with me until then."

Nona had been shocked by her mother's words. "Absolutely not, Mama. Kelly's my child, and I can take care of her."

"Well, you're not doing a good job, are you?"

Her mother's words had stunned her. She wouldn't do anything to hurt her child—after all, she was working as hard for Kelly as she was for herself. But her mother's verbal assault opened her eyes to what others were seeing. She was an absentee mother, raising her child in a single-parent household.

That was when she had her first dose of guilt."Mom," Kelly brought her back to their conversation. "We could do this together, right?"

Nona turned on the water full blast. "I said I'll think about it, sweetie, okay?" She blinked back tears. "Enough's enough, and it's way past your bedtime anyway."

Kelly frowned. "Mom, it's only seven o'clock and we haven't eaten yet." She stood and walked over to the sink. "Is something wrong?"

Nona shook her head and faced Kelly. "No, sweetie." She forced herself to smile. "I'm just tired. Can you set the table for me, please?"

Kelly nodded, and pulled the place mats from the drawer. But she kept her eyes on Nona as she pulled the salmon steaks from the range-top grill and mixed tomatoes, celery, and mushrooms into the salad.

Kelly placed the plates on the table. "Don't worry, Mommy. Allen's not going to let anyone destroy Brickhouse," she said softly. "He's got it under control."

Nona looked up and stared into the serious green eyes of her daughter, and she saw nothing but love. In that moment, she wanted to pull Kelly into her arms and kill Allen at the same time. Why had he said anything? How could he put this burden on her child?

"Mom, I know he wasn't supposed to tell me," Kelly said as if reading Nona's mind. "But I'm not a baby. I could tell that something was bothering you ever since you came back from your trip. So when Allen took me to the movies on Saturday, I asked him what was going on. It's no big deal, though. I can handle it." She smiled. "I want to be here for you, Mommy, and I can pray."

Nona ran her hand over her daughter's hair. "Thank you, sweetheart, but I don't want you to handle anything except for school and your friends and all your activities. Leave Brickhouse to me, okay?"

Kelly nodded and wrapped her arms around Nona's neck. They held each other for a long moment.

"Enough of this mushy stuff," Nona said, reluctantly letting Kelly from her arms. "Let's eat."

"Can I say grace tonight?"

Nona nodded, and after Kelly blessed their dinner, she began chatting about the play that she'd be performing with the Harlem Cultural Arts Center.

"I love playing Lady Macbeth," Kelly said as she stuffed salad into her mouth. "But I don't like Robert. He's Macbeth, and never in a million years would I marry a man like him."

Nona sighed inside. A child's wisdom. Too bad she hadn't been as wise in her twenties. With a little judgment, maybe she wouldn't have fallen for the first jive-talking, slick-walking man who came her way.

Ronald Simms had been the first person she met at New York University's Graduate School of Business. She was sitting in the student lounge when a deep voice addressed her.

"Is this seat taken?"

Her head rose, her eyes settling on the eyes of the six-foot-three supreme being. It was the first time she understood how one's breath could be taken away. She stared.

The green-eyed Adonis repeated his question, but he was already sitting in the seat across from her. With a smile, he revealed teeth that had obviously been cared for by an orthodontist.

He extended his hand. "My name is Ronald Simms."

Nona slowly lifted her hand. "No."

He frowned. "No?"

Damn, she thought. Her mouth was just catching up with her brain. "I mean, no, that seat isn't taken."

He smiled and stared at her, aware of his effect. "It is now."

That first meeting had lasted almost two hours as he asked her questions about herself. In between, he told her why he was getting a JD/MBA.

"I want to be an entertainment attorney. I tried my hand at acting, but was smart enough to heed my high school guidance counselor's advice and find another career."

He laughed at his words, and she savored the sweet sound in her ears.

"So now I know what I want to be when I grow up," he continued.

She had taken a sip of her tea. "Would you have to move to Los Angeles to do that?"

"No, New York is fine. In fact, I'm interning this summer at one of the largest firms in the country right here in the city."

She had sighed, relieved although she didn't know why. Three hours ago, she didn't even know this man. Yet now she wanted to spend the rest of her life with him. Right there, she said a silent prayer that somehow their paths would cross again—even if it was just a sighting on campus.

That night Ronald had called the two-bedroom apartment in Lenox Terrace that she shared with three other girls.

"How did you get my number?" she asked, surprised, but pleased.

"I'm going to be an attorney. I have my ways when I want to spend time with a beautiful woman."

They had talked well past midnight, until she struggled to keep her eyes open and her lips moving. That call led to their meeting the next night at a Mexican restaurant on West Fourth Street. That date led to a year's worth of togetherness.

Nona had been fascinated by Ronald's drive. He'd study in the library for hours, focused on his goal of graduating at the top of his class. But during their summer break, his attention shifted. After work, he concentrated on having a good time.

"I want you to show me New York," the native Virginian told Nona. "I want to see this city through you."

Nona had taken him to all the standard sites, and many only New Yorkers knew. They strolled through the summer street fairs and went to off-off-Broadway plays. And then there were the days when she took him to the part of New York she loved the most—Harlem.

But Ronald didn't share her love for uptown.

"You like hanging out there, don't you?" he asked one night after she told him she had tickets to a play at the Harlem Cultural Arts Center.

"It's my home. I love it."

He shook his head. "I don't know why. You're getting your MBA. You can rise above Harlem now."

She had turned away from him, tears stinging her eyes

and an ache filling her heart. But she excused his words, attributing them to his ignorance. After all, she'd heard much dumber statements from others.

It's probably all the negative things he's heard about Harlem, she thought as she pushed the hurt from his words aside.

That should have been her first sign.

Months later at graduation, Ronald had met her and with his cap and gown still in place, in front of friends and family, he proposed to her on bended knee.

Their first year of marriage had been beyond bliss. Ronald put in long hours at the William Morris Agency, where he had worked as an intern. Nona began her career as a marketing assistant with the New York Fitness Club.

Only her beloved Harlem was missing from her life. When they married, Ronald had insisted on moving into a downtown apartment. For the seventeen-hundred-dollars-a-month rent they were paying, Nona knew they could have much more than the cramped one-bedroom. But she didn't push it. One day she'd convince Ronald, and they'd move back to Harlem.

On their first anniversary, Ronald took Nona to Tavern on the Green. When she announced that she was pregnant, tears filled his eyes.

"You're going to have my baby?" his voice trembled. "I can't believe this." He kissed her, and Nona knew their happiness would last forever.

But "forever" came to an end the next week when she received a letter in the mail fashioned from cut-out magazine letters.

*Your husband is the best lay I've ever had.*

If someone had kicked her in the stomach, it wouldn't have matched the pain she felt as she read those words. She had met Ronald at the front door when he'd come home that night—just after midnight.

"Hey, honey. What are you doing up?"

Nona wiped her tear-streaked face. "What is this?"

He frowned and took the paper from her. He scanned the letter, looked at her, and shook his head. Without a word, he walked into the living room and dropped his briefcase.

"Well?" she said, following him.

"Nona, I don't know what this is."

"Who sent it?"

"Baby, I don't know."

"It has to be someone who knows us, Ronald. How else would they have our address?"

He chuckled. "Sweetheart, sometimes you are so naïve. This person could have gotten our address any number of ways. It's not like we're unlisted. And everyone who works with us knows where we live." He had taken her hand and pulled her into his arms. "Honey, it's just someone who is jealous. They don't want to see us happy. And we're happy, right?"

He kissed her nose, and Nona melted in his arms. In her head, she believed his words. In her heart, she knew the truth.

For the next few months, she ignored the nagging doubts that throbbed inside her. It was easy as she focused on preparations for their baby. And Ronald was finding his way home much earlier each night than he had in their entire year of marriage.

But after Kelly was born, it was hard for Nona not to accept that her marriage was in trouble. It was more than just the late hours and lack of attentiveness toward her. It wasn't even the constant telephone hang-ups or the letters that she still received, but hid from Ronald. It was his lack of interest in their baby. Ronald lived as if she and Kelly didn't exist—attending late dinners, red carpet parties, and movie premieres without her.

"It's all for business," he told her when she complained.

Soon her complaints stopped, and she accepted the inevitable.

Before Kelly was even two, Nona and Ronald divorced, and in a surprise move, Ronald relocated to Los Angeles. Ever since, he played father once a year—for fourteen days and not an hour longer.

"Asshole" was the best way to describe him, although she had to admit that she was luckier than most women— he was a paying asshole. His child support checks came on time, showing that he was much more committed to their divorce than he ever was to their marriage.

But Nona did a good job of keeping her descriptive adjectives about the green-eyed bandit to herself. Kelly loved her father and lived for the annual two weeks that he gave her. And despite what Nona thought of Ronald Simms, he had given her the precious gift of Kelly.

"So what do you think, Mom?"

Nona shook her head slightly, trying to focus on what Kelly was saying. She stared at her daughter, and in Kelly's green eyes, she saw Ronald. *Why doesn't Kelly look more like my side of the family?* Nona thought as she often did when she looked at her child.

"I'm sorry, sweetie, what did you say?"

"I was asking if I could go to the movies with Allen again on Saturday. He said he would take me if it was all right with you."

Nona nodded, and inside thanked God that Allen was in Kelly's life. "It's fine with me. What are you guys planning on seeing?"

Kelly grinned. "Thug Life. It's supposed to be good. You should see it, Mom. All the new rappers are in it."

Nona frowned. She'd heard about all the cursing and violence. What was Allen thinking, planning to take Kelly to an R-rated movie? No wonder Kelly was begging to go to Toni's premiere. Allen had her in training. She'd have to talk to him.

"I hope you decide that we can go to Toni's movie . . . together." Kelly stood and began to clear off the table.

Nona took a deep breath. Yes, she would definitely have to talk to Allen first thing in the morning.

## seven

"Okay, people, that's a wrap," Nona yelled through her wireless headphones.

Before Nelly belted out the last word to the song, Leila bounced onto the carpeted floor as if her one-hundred-and-nineteen-pound figure was too heavy to hold up a moment longer.

"It's always the same thing with you." Anna laughed. "I'd think your stamina would be better by now." She wiped her neck with a towel that lay against her floor mat.

Leila opened one eye and moaned. "It never gets better with Nona. She's always trying to kill us, but today was worse. She has to be PMSing." She sat up.

"What's up, girlfriends?" Toni asked as she sauntered toward them.

Lifting her head, Leila opened her eyes and looked at Toni. Her black unitard made her already lithe figure seem slimmer. Leila groaned again and dropped back onto the carpet.

In one movement, Toni lowered herself into the lotus position. "What's wrong with her?" she asked Anna.

"Leila thinks Nona is trying to kill her." Anna laughed.

"Why would you think that?" Nona said, joining the group and breathing as if she'd been relaxing under a palm tree.

Leila groaned again.

Toni said, "Anyway, I wanted to make sure that all of you were going to be at my premiere."

Leila opened one eye again. "After what Nona just put us through, is that all you can think about?"

Toni glanced down at her form-fitting leotard. "That's why I do all of this. So, can I count on my best friends in the world being there?"

"Anthony and I will be there," Anna said.

"You can count me in, too," Nona added. "By the way, I was thinking about bringing a guest."

Leila sprang straight up from her prostrate position as if she hadn't been stricken with pain just moments before. "You're bringing someone?" she said and scooted closer to Nona. "Do tell."

"Yes." Toni smiled. "I didn't know you were . . . seeing anyone."

Nona glanced at her circle of friends, their eyes brimming with curiosity. Even Anna, the one who stayed away from gossip and idle chatter, appeared overcome with interest. "I wasn't going to say anything, but . . ." She paused and ran her hands over her slicked-back hair. "I was thinking about bringing . . . Kelly."

It took seconds for her words to reach their brains. Nona laughed at their momentarily puzzled expressions. "So, Toni, do you think *Love's Desires* is too sexy for my daughter?"

Leila bounced back against the carpet, and Anna laughed.

Toni said, "Kelly? I thought . . ." She shook her head. "Anyway, it would be great if Kelly came."

"That's not what I asked. You only do R-rated movies. Is *Love's Desires* too much for Kelly?"

Toni waved her hand, dismissing her friend's words. "Nona, you're too conservative. Kids are exposed to much more today than what's in my little movie." Nona's sigh made Toni continue. "Okay, so there's a little sex, and some nudity, but nothing Kelly can't handle."

Nona twisted her lips in doubt.

"Come on, it's nothing worse than all of that booty shakin' she sees on BET and MTV."

They all laughed.

"And think about it," Toni continued. "If Kelly is seeing this stuff on TV and in videos and in movies, it's better if you're sitting next to her to explain it . . . you know what I mean?"

Nona paused for a second. "I'll think about Kelly. I'm still not sure that she's ready for something like this. But you can count me in."

"Okay, that's two of my friends," Toni said as she nudged Leila.

Leila raised an arm up from the carpet and groaned. The other three laughed.

"I'll take that as a yes," Toni said.

"Well, I have an appointment," Anna said, folding her mat under her arm. "I'll see you guys later."

As Anna moved toward the locker room doors, Allen entered the gym from the other side. Nona watched Allen's eyes scan the room among the stragglers who remained, chatting with one another or stretching in front of the mirrors. She knew he was searching to make sure that the room was clear—of Anna.

Allen strolled to the group. "What's up, ladies?"

Toni lifted herself from the floor in one motion. "Are you coming to the premiere?" she asked in a businesslike tone.

"I'll be there."

"Great, my entourage is complete." Toni clapped her hands.

Allen turned to Nona. "I wanted to remind you—Derrick will be here in twenty minutes."

His words made Leila sit up. "You're meeting with Derrick Carter?" She smiled.

Nona shook her head. "Believe me, it's not pleasure."

Toni folded her arms across her chest.

Nona continued, "It's business. Something I'm forced to do."

The tip of Toni's Ralph Lauren sport shoe tapped against the gym's carpet.

"Well, force me." Leila laughed.

Toni held up her hands, stopping the conversation. "I've got to go." Her words were terse. "I'll see you guys later." She stomped away from her friends.

Allen frowned as he watched Toni move with haste toward the locker room.

"So tell me," Leila said to Nona. "What's really going on with you and Derrick?"

"Exactly what I said. Business. He's producing the Central Park video."

Leila sucked her teeth. "That's not juicy."

Nona sighed. "Allen, I'll be in my office. See you, Leila."

Leila nodded at Nona, smiled at Allen, but as she turned toward the locker room, he stopped her.

"Leila, I wanted to talk to you."

"Sure."

"I'm sorry about . . . what happened at our last session."

Leila paused a moment. "That's okay. I was worried about you."

"No need. I'm fine."

"Good," Leila said as she turned away.

"I promise our next session will be much better," he said.

Leila waved her good-bye. She stepped into the locker room and nodded mindlessly at the women who had spent the last hour in Nona's torture chamber with her and who still lingered in the tranquillity of the locker-room oasis Nona had made with the overstuffed down chairs and chaises.

As Leila punched the combination on her locker, she thought about what Allen had said. She was glad he was well, but it was his words that made her smile. He promised their next session would be better. But nothing would surpass the last session she'd spent with her other friend. Just the memories of that time, just days before, made goose pimples rise on her skin. Her thighs were still a bit sore from the positions she'd assumed, and Nona's class didn't help. But it was worth it. Her goal was to turn him out. In a few months he'd be doing more than screaming her name. If it all went the way she planned, there'd be several carats set in a platinum band on her left hand in her future. She looked at the ring that graced her finger now. She couldn't wait to replace these five carats that Shawn had given her. She couldn't wait to replace Shawn. Her new ring would probably be a bit smaller, but that didn't matter.

Leila smiled as she peeled the leotards and tights from her body, leaving the items crumpled in a ball at the foot of her locker. As she passed the mirrors that lined the walls on the way to the showers, her smile faded when she glanced at her image. She turned away, making sure she didn't look into her eyes. She didn't want to see the concern she tried to bolt deep inside. The concern that came from the fact that if she were to get what she wanted, people she cared about would be hurt. She couldn't worry about that. She couldn't worry about Shawn or her children or her friends. She'd learned over these years that if she didn't look out for herself, who would?

Leila raised her chin inches higher and sauntered toward the shower with nothing more than a towel draped over her shoulder.

# eight

"I'm glad we finally have this time together," Derrick said as he unbuttoned one of three buttons on his single-breasted jacket and moved toward the round conference table.

"Let's sit over here." Nona pointed to the chair in front of her desk as she lowered herself into her executive's chair. With its high back, her seat was raised so Nona was always just a bit higher than anyone across from her.

Derrick glanced at the conference table, then back at Nona. He hesitated for only a moment before he smiled and moved toward her.

Her trained eye roamed twice over his body before he sank into the chair. It took only seconds for her to assess his suit. Armani for sure. Years had passed since she'd divorced Ron and since then she'd had little reason to study men's clothing. Still, she was a fashion connoisseur, attending the designer shows in Europe and setting aside the week in September each year to attend New York's fashion extravaganza.

It was the last thing she wanted to admit, but this six-two, chocolate man looked good. Just as he always did. That revelation annoyed her even more.

"I was pleased when I got the call that you'd accepted my bid for the Central Park production. After our last project, I wasn't sure . . ."

It was hard for Nona to concentrate on his words when his past spoke louder than anything he could say. Whenever she saw him, she was taken back in time. To the days when Toni was overcome with sorrow because of this man. Even now, Nona almost shuddered as she recalled how Toni had been suicidal after Derrick's rejection. For months Nona had lived in fear of receiving that call announcing Toni's demise—that is, until Toni slipped into the arms of Lorenzo Vespucci, a B-actor who was known more for his biceps and pectorals than his acting skills. Toni drowned her tears in the dark-haired Italian's chest, and Nona had been overcome with relief when her friend appeared to put every thought of Derrick Carter behind her. But although Toni had long ago forgiven Derrick, it was difficult for Nona to forget that this man had driven one of her best friends to the edge of life.

Derrick leaned forward and laid a folder on Nona's desk. "The first thing I wanted to go over was the objective and then the timetable. Just make sure that we have our goals lined up."

Nona blinked, allowing her mind to return to the meeting.

"What I'm most excited about is that this production is going to allow you to step into mainstream, Nona, like never before. If you think fifteen million copies was good last time—" He stopped and shook his head as if the vision overwhelmed him. "You will no longer be just a gym rat."

"Is that what you think of me?"

"Oh, no," he said, crossing his legs. "Don't be offended. I

don't mean that the way it sounded. I'm just saying that this production can take you out of the gym and into millions of homes."

Derrick was a Yale graduate, very articulate, but he might as well have been saying, "Blah, blah, blah." Having to work with him was the only factor that dampened her excitement about this Central Park production. But since HBO was the major sponsor, she'd had to accept their strong recommendation that Derrick lead the project.

But no matter who he was, she wasn't going to let anyone forget that this was her idea, her vision. It would play out the way she wanted it to.

He said, "We're going to make this more than just an exercise video."

To Nona, he spoke the last four words with disdain.

"It won't be like the last time," he continued. "This is almost going to be a tribute to New York. So far, the mayor has agreed to attend the filming, and we have invitations out to other city dignitaries. It's going to be a major event. When I get through, you're going to be bigger than big."

She pressed her lips together to hold back the first words that came to mind. "You know I'm not really concerned about that, Derrick," she said finally. "What's most important to me is that the point of the video is not lost—this is about leading a healthy life through exercise. That's what I'm about."

"And if that were true, Nona, your last video wouldn't have sold fifteen million copies."

She knew he didn't say the words that surely burned on his tongue—that her video success was because of him.

Nona was smart enough to realize that was true. Before Derrick Carter, Nona had produced five workout videos, all filmed within the walls of Brickhouse. With two cameras, ten of her trainers, and overhead fluorescent lighting, the tapes looked more like good college productions than professional creations, Nona had to admit. But it was the message that Nona wanted to deliver, and her last pre–Derrick Carter video had sold almost a million copies.

Then Derrick stepped in, and with one production, increased her sales fifteen-fold. She gave him credit—he had created a Hollywood-quality production that looked more like a film than a workout video.

But she had learned a few things herself. Although she was aware that the glitz of the video helped with sales, she knew much of the demand came because of her name. And because her videos were different. There was thirty minutes of exercise routines, complemented by thirty minutes of discussion on how to maintain a healthy lifestyle. She was about substance—Derrick was about style. Glitter was good, but she would not allow her message to be lost.

"Well, I'll be anxious to see the storyboards," she said, deciding to sidestep all arguments now. There would be many debates in the days to come. She opened the folder and glanced at the timetable. "This seems rather aggressive. Do you think we can have the production ready to go in less than six weeks? Before Thanksgiving?"

His grin was filled with confidence. "I wouldn't have given you this schedule if I didn't know we could make it. And Thanksgiving is a key time. We could cash in on those early holiday sales." He paused. "Of course, this is contingent on me being able to handle my business." He paused as if he wanted her to hear all that he wasn't saying. "If I can proceed without too many disturbances, without too many delays, without too many opinions; if everyone remembers that I'm the expert, then we'll meet this deadline with no problem."

She paused for a beat. "Just say what you need to say, Derrick." She'd tossed thoughts of not battling to the side. But before he could respond, she held up her hands. "Never mind. We need to just move forward. But before you go," she said, standing, "I want to know what you're going to do about the bootleg problems we had last time. You know, we lost a lot of sales because of that. Those pirated tapes were being sold right in front of Brickhouse."

He shrugged, not moving from his seat. "I'm not sure what I can do."

"Well, I would think with all of your . . . expertise, you'd have some suggestions, some idea of how to make sure it doesn't happen again." She folded her arms across her chest.

Derrick smirked. "I'll get back to you with some plans, but my responsibility is to deliver the video that will make you a star."

"I told you, I'm not concerned about that."

He stared at her for a moment, and she wondered what she saw in his eyes. Annoyance? Disappointment? She wasn't sure, and it irritated her that she even cared.

"Do me a favor," he finally said as he stood. His six-foot-two frame allowed him to look down on her. "Just let me be me. I'll make sure that you get everything you want, but please don't try to turn this into some kind of . . . black thang."

She didn't know if it was his tone or his choice of ghetto jargon that made her want to deliver one of the right upper-cuts that she taught in her Brickhouse classes. But instead she inhaled and pressed down her rising rage.

Wordlessly she watched as he lifted his briefcase, buttoned his jacket, and then smiled with teeth that had probably been shaped with expensive metal braces before he even reached puberty. "By the way, our next meeting is scheduled for the day after Toni Lee's premiere. I assume that still works for you." Nona gritted her teeth together and nodded.

Even seconds after she was alone, she stood at the side of the desk, in the same place where he'd told her not to turn this project into a "black thang."

She took another breath and sat behind her desk. No matter how much she disliked Derrick, she couldn't let her disdain for him get in the way of what she had to do. There were enough battles in front of her. She needed her energy to save Brickhouse, not fight Derrick Carter. She would do everything she could to remember that. She just hoped she could do it.

Allen glanced at his watch. It had been forty-five minutes, and Nona had not yet burst through his door sputtering complaints about Derrick Carter. He chuckled as he thought about the two of them behind closed doors. *I should offer Derrick some private workouts,* he thought. That would at least give him half a chance if Nona decided to beat him down. He chuckled again at that thought.

It was the sharp jolt of pain to his left side that ripped his smile away. Allen grabbed the edge of his desk, holding himself up. He took deep breaths, trying to ease the contractions in his stomach. Almost a minute passed before his breathing returned to normal.

*I can't do this,* he thought as he lowered himself slowly in his chair, praying that the cramps didn't return. A second later he reached for the telephone, but then dropped the receiver back into the cradle. It had been more than a week since he'd made the call and three days since his last fix. With each passing minute he'd gained confidence that he could get through this without any help. He had to keep it up. The longer he stayed away from the drugs, the better. He could kick this, with just a little time. He had to because this was killing him. And it would surely kill Nona.

He lifted himself from the chair, grasping the edge of the desk, just in case. When he felt steady, he moved forward, but he'd taken only two steps before the pain punched. him. He reached for the frame of the chair, but collapsed to the floor. It took minutes for him to rise to his knees, then to a complete stand. Using the back of his hand, he wiped the saliva that seeped from the corners of his mouth.

There was no way he could do this without help. He needed the drugs. He'd take them, just a little bit at a time, until he was well.

"This is best," he said as he grabbed the telephone. He repeated that thought over and over as he dialed, then listened to the ringing on the other end.

"It's me," Allen said when the phone was answered. The baritone snicker that came from the other end made Allen want to slam down the phone. But the ache that held its place in his side kept his grip on the receiver.

"So what is it this time?" the voice asked.

Allen took a deep breath. "I need—"

"I know what you need." The chuckles continued. "Drop by this afternoon. What time—"

"Allen." Nona swept into his office with only a perfunctory knock on his door.

He slammed down the phone without saying good-bye. "Uh, I was just making a call," he stammered.

Nona frowned.

"I mean, I'm finished now."

He could see the questions in her eyes. The way she

tilted her head, he knew she was wondering why he was explaining.

"I'm sorry, do you want me to come back?" she asked.

"No," he said, waving his hand. "Come on in." He hoped she didn't notice the tentative steps he took around his desk before he sat. "How did the meeting go with Derrick?"

She sighed as she slumped into one of the chairs in front of him. "Painful." She shook her head. "The video is supposed to be a good thing. But working with Derrick is no different than working with those assholes that we have to face from the Harlem Empowerment Office."

"Maybe he'll be good practice for facing those assholes," Allen said.

It took a moment for the ends of Nona's lips to slip into a smile. "You're right about that." But a second later, her smile faded, replaced by a grimace of apprehension.

Allen took a breath before he stood and moved to sit next to Nona. "You know we're gonna win this, right?"

She shook her head. "I'm gonna fight, but—"

He squeezed her hand, stopping her. "Don't even think about anything except winning. I promise you, Brickhouse will be standing and you'll be victorious. No matter what I have to do."

The return of her smile made his return too. She leaned over and kissed him on the cheek. "Do you know how much I depend on you?"

He hugged her. "I'll always be here, Nona. I'll never let you down." He closed his eyes and prayed that the words he uttered were true.

# nine

The grandfather clock in the corner of the office chimed twelve times. Anna raised her glasses from the bridge of her nose and rubbed her eyes. She couldn't believe she'd been working for six hours. She'd risen with the sun, expecting to be finished by nine so that she could dash to Nona's Saturday class. But she hadn't lifted her head from the Children's Literacy Outreach proposal until now.

She squeezed her eyes tight, and smiled. It felt good to have this kind of passion back in her heart. The ends of her lips turned down just a bit at that thought. Much of her love of life had died with Todd. But as each month passed nudging her into the future, the past didn't hurt as much. She felt as if she were being slowly resurrected. It was time for her to rejoin life in every way, and with this program, she'd be making a difference in the lives of the most important people on earth—the children.

She slipped her eyeglasses back in place and glanced through the pages of notes she'd written with the input she received from Nona, Leila, and Toni last week. "Okay," she said, pléased. "All I need to do now is make suggestions for the board."

She pushed aside the papers on the desk, searching for another notepad. Not finding one, she stood and walked across the room. She couldn't remember the last time she'd worked in Anthony's office. The room was gloomy and heavy with the dark oak, oversized desk, credenza, and file cabinets. And Anthony always kept the window blinds closed. It was the most depressing space in Gracie Mansion.

But today this was paradise. Far away from Anthony, who always used Saturdays as his days to sleep in—and then requested that she service him, demanding either their once-a-week sex session or a three-course breakfast.

But she didn't feel like being a wife in either way this morning. The literacy proposal had to be complete today so that she could begin sending out the corporate letters Monday.

Anna slid open the cabinet where Anthony kept his supplies. She pushed aside the file that sat atop the pile of notepads, but then frowned as she noticed "Harlem" scribbled across the folder's width. Leaving the drawer open, she took the file with her to the desk. She sat as she glanced through the papers, her eyes widening with each turn of the page.

"This is what Nona was asking me about," she whispered.

Her eyes scanned the pages, moving at a rapid pace. Each page was a shocker, but it was the letter at the back that left her with her mouth open.

"Reverend Watkins?" she said aloud. She read the letter twice. "Oh, my God."

"Anna, where are you?"

She jumped at her husband's voice, then stuffed the papers she held back inside the folder.

"Anna."

Anthony's voice was getting closer. She didn't have time to return the folder to the cabinet. She pushed the manila file underneath the pad with her notes.

"Anna."

"I'm in the office," she yelled out.

A few seconds later, he appeared at the door. "Didn't you hear me calling you?"

She shook her head. "No," she said, hoping he didn't notice the squeak in her voice.

He squinted before he stepped into the office. "What are you doing in here?"

"Working." She paused and noticed the file cabinet drawer she'd left open. "On my proposal," she added quickly.

He was still frowning when he handed her the cordless phone. "It's Nona."

"Okay," she said, taking the phone with trembling hands. "Thanks." She waited until he stepped out of the office before she breathed. It took a few more breaths before she lifted the receiver to her ear.

"Hello," she said as she exhaled and rushed to the file cabinet.

"Hey, girl. Just checking on you. Missed you this morning."

"I was working on the literacy proposal." Anna slammed the file cabinet shut and then slumped into the chair behind the desk.

"That's great. I can look over the proposal for you, if you'd like."

"That would be terrific."

"By the way, did you ask Anthony about the rezoning project?"

Anna sat up and glanced at the folder on the desk filled

with pages of information—everything that Nona needed. "No, I haven't had the chance to talk to him."

"I don't mean to be a pest, it's just that the first public meeting is on Monday."

"Really?" Anna said, fondling the folder between her fingers. "I didn't realize it was that soon."

Nona sighed. "Reverend Watkins is rushing this through, and I'm going to need all the help I can get."

Anna paused. "Nona, do you really think you could lose Brickhouse?" she asked, staring at the folder in her hand.

"I don't know, Anna. I'm trying my best to fight this . . . and to keep a positive attitude at the same time."

Anna slipped the last page from inside the folder and scanned the letter. "I promise, I'll talk to Anthony."

"Thanks, Anna."

"And, Nona . . ." She paused as she stared at the paper in front of her. "I have a feeling that you're going to be fine."

"Can I get that in writing and then send it up to God?" Nona chuckled.

"You never know. I just might be able to get that in writing for you. I'll speak to you later."

Anna read through the pages once again before she replaced the folder. She'd wait for Anthony to leave the house on his way to one of his many meetings or whatever he did to fill his day. Once he was gone, she'd make copies. Then she'd plan her strategy.

It wasn't even a choice for her. Anna knew who held her loyalty. When she went to Nona, and when she gave her friend what she needed, Anna was going to make sure that Nona had a fully loaded gun.

# *ten*

"Promise you'll call the moment you get out of the meeting," Anna said.

Nona smiled. She really did have good friends. Toni and Leila had both phoned this morning with the same request.

"I will."

"I mean it, Nona," Anna urged. "I need to know everything that happens in there."

Nona's eyebrows rose in surprise at her friend's tone. "What's going on, Anna? Has Anthony told you something?"

"No, no," her denial came quickly. "It's just that I'm praying for you and want to know everything so that . . . I can know what to say to Anthony."

Nona frowned, only half believing her friend. "Okay, I'll call you when I get out."

It still took a few minutes for Nona to reassure Anna, and when Nona hung up, she wondered what was behind the stress she heard in Anna's voice.

By the time Nona walked downstairs and into the kitchen, her thoughts about Anna's phone call had been replaced with thoughts about the meeting. She'd been to public hearings before, but never one that affected her so personally. She couldn't imagine what this meeting would yield. There would be only two meetings for the public—a month apart. Today was the first one, but she knew very well the stage could be set. Today could be the beginning of her losing everything—everything that was important to her.

"Morning, Mom," Kelly chirped with a smile that stretched to her ears. She was sitting at the kitchen table with Odessa.

"Good morning, sweetheart." Nona kissed her daughter's forehead and eyed the small bowl of half-eaten oatmeal that sat in front of her.

"I was just telling Odessa about Ms. Lee's movie. It'll be my first premiere, you know."

Nona laughed. "Well, how do you know I'm going to let you go?"

Kelly stood up and wrapped her arms around her mother's waist. "Because you're the best mother in the whole world. And almost two weeks have passed and you haven't said no. And you know that I can handle this. And you're the best mother in the whole world."

This time Odessa joined in the laughter. "Well, you're right . . ." Nona said.

"Yippee." Kelly cheered and jumped in the air as if she were an NBA cheerleader.

"I am the best mother in the whole world."

Kelly paused. "But what about the premiere? Can I go, Mom . . . please?"

The skin in Nona's forehead creased as if she were in deep thought. She lowered her eyes. "Well . . . I've decided . . ." She paused and looked at her daughter through her long lashes. "You can go to the premiere."

Kelly's cheers returned, and even Odessa clapped.

"I love you so much, Mommy." Kelly hugged Nona.

"I love you too, baby. Now finish your breakfast so that you can get to school."

"Okay, Mom," she said, returning to the table. She stirred the oatmeal in the bowl. "I am so excited."

As Kelly chatted about the premiere with Odessa, Nona filled a bowl with granola. She smiled as she sat at the table with Odessa and Kelly, but her face belied the thoughts in her head.

What would she do if she lost Brickhouse? It was as much a part of her as the blood that coursed through her veins. Brickhouse kept her alive.

"Mom, do you think I could have a new dress for the premiere?"

Nona nodded as she took a sip of her juice. "Of course; we'll go shopping for both of us."

She spoke as if she were listening, but she couldn't shake the overwhelming thoughts that rattled inside her head. She didn't know what she was going to say at this meeting. Over the last two weeks, she'd contacted other Harlem businesses that would be affected. But no one shared her concern.

"Oh, Ms. Nona," the lady who owned the Orient Express, the largest Chinese restaurant in Harlem, exclaimed. "I'm so happy to go into the mall. They said I could have six months' free rent. Lots of people will come and I will make lots of money."

Mr. Robertson, whose family had owned the cleaners on Frederick Douglass Boulevard for more than fifty years, told her, "I'm going to take the buy-out package, Nona. I'm seventy years old and this is perfect timing. My wife and I are headed down to Florida."

And B.J., the owner of the most popular soul food restaurant in the city, had said, "Girlfriend, I couldn't believe the tax break they're offering. And did you know I'd been thinking about buying my building? Girl, I'm so glad that I just sat still and waited on the Lord because clearly this rezoning is a blessing straight from Reverend Watkins and heaven."

Nona had almost choked after B.J.'s comments. But by the time she spoke to other retailers, she was gagging. The moving incentives, plans for residential redevelopment, buy-out packages, and tax incentives had Harlem's business owners leaping as if they'd won the lottery. But maybe that was because no one else was losing a forty-thousand-square-foot facility.

Her next step was to approach the politicians she'd worked with over the years, but not one had returned her calls.

"They know why you're calling," Allen had said. "Everyone believes Harlem East is going to mean big things for Harlem. The word is Harlem East is going to revitalize this area in a way nothing else can."

What was she supposed to do?

All she had were a few friends and a few thousand members of Brickhouse—half of whom didn't even live in Harlem. How was she supposed to stop Reverend Watkins's speeding locomotive? A sudden vision hit her. In her mind, she saw a train, Reverend Watkins, train tracks, and thick braided rope, the kind that was used to anchor a boat—or strap someone down. She smiled.

"Mom, can I?"

It took a couple of seconds for Nona to mentally return to the kitchen. "I'm sorry, honey, what did you say?"

"I said some of my friends are taking the train home from school today. Can I ride with them?"

Horror contorted her face. She shook her head to erase the image that just seconds ago she had enjoyed. "No. Odessa will pick you up."

"Oh, Mom," Kelly whined. "It's just a couple of train stops."

Nona held up her hand. "Remember the premiere."

Her mouth had been open, ready for her next protest, but Kelly locked her lips together and smiled. She leaned over and kissed Nona's cheek.

"Have a good day," Nona said. "I'll see you tonight."

"Mom," Kelly began softly. "I can tell that you're really worried, but you don't have to be. I prayed a lot last night, and everything is going to be all right."

Nona dropped her spoon into her bowl, then hugged her daughter. She never wanted Kelly exposed to the challenges of her business, but she couldn't imagine anything better this morning than having those words from her daughter.

"Thank you, sweetie." She hugged Kelly as if she didn't want to let go.

When she leaned back, Kelly grinned. "You'll get this over with today, and then it'll be all about you and me and the premiere."

Nona laughed. It could never be that simple. But maybe, just maybe, with Kelly's prayers, it would be.

Nona stood at the top of the concrete steps and took a quick glance at her watch again. When she looked up, she exhaled as Allen sprinted toward her.

"Sorry I'm late," he said, breathing as if he'd just run ten miles.

"That's okay." Nona smiled, but as she stared at her friend, her grin disappeared. She rested her hand on his arm. "Are you all right?"

"Yeah." He wiped the sweat from his forehead and loosened the blue paisley-print tie that choked his neck. "It's just this suit and being late. Sorry."

She nodded. "I guess you just look like I feel." She smiled and leaned over as if she were about to share a secret. "But don't worry. We have Kelly's prayers."

Allen chuckled and put his arm around Nona's shoulders. But their fleeting cheer dissipated the moment they stepped through the oversized glass doors of the 125th Street building. The Harlem Empowerment section of the New York City Zoning Commission had moved from the Empire State Building offices into this building that was best known for housing former President Clinton.

As soon as she stepped off the elevator on the sixth floor, the dull ache began at the edges of her brain. With each passing second the pounding increased until even her toes pulsed. She closed her eyes for a moment as they approached the zoning offices that occupied almost half of the floor. At the doors with the gold letters that read "Harlem Empowerment," Allen squeezed Nona's hand. "Let's do this."

"I almost feel like we need to pray first."

Allen chuckled and opened the door. Inside, the receptionist led them to the conference room.

Nona had been in these offices for other hearings when the room was packed. Today the seven chairs around the conference table were occupied by the committee members, but the seats that had been set up for the interested public were empty—except for one, where a single reporter from the *Amsterdam News* slouched in one of the folding chairs.

Nona sighed. It was worse than she expected. With no time to garner support from the community and little chance of any businesses coming to her side, she hoped there was a miracle waiting inside Kelly's prayers.

"Don't worry," Allen said as if he could feel her waning confidence.

"Well, Ms. Simms." Reverend Watkins stood as they entered the room. "A surprise, but a pleasant one. I'm glad you decided to join us."

She remained stiff, her face stretched with seriousness as the reverend reached for her hand. "I'm sure you realize I have a special interest in this meeting . . ." She glanced down at her hand, which was still gripped inside his. She looked back at the reverend and raised her eyebrows.

He smiled as his thumb caressed her fingers.

Nona shivered as she snatched her hand from his grasp. In that moment, she wondered how the reverend kept his twenty-five-year-old Jheri curl so shiny.

Reverend Watkins grinned, then nodded at Allen. "Please have a seat. We were just about to get started since we didn't really expect anyone." The reverend returned to his place at the head of the conference table. "No need to waste time; everyone knows how good this plan is for Harlem." Reverend Watkins chuckled, and the men around the table joined him.

Nona sat in one of the front-row seats and glanced at the participants. She knew everyone—the congressman whose district included Harlem; the councilman; the assemblyman; a community leader who had made his name as one of the cochairs for the Harlem Welcomes Former President Clinton Committee; the commissioner for the New York City Zoning Commission; and the mayor.

Nona paused when she looked at the mayor. Anthony Leone gave her a quick nod, then lowered his glance to notes that rested in front of him. She frowned. Anna was her friend, but over the years, she'd come to think of Anthony the same way. But today the mayor didn't seem friendly at all.

She shook that thought away. This meeting was driving her into a sensitive emotional zone, and she didn't need that. She needed to be aware, watch every move, study every gesture. Her instincts were screaming—something was going on here, and if she was going to win, she had to find out what it was.

"Well, let's get started." The reverend leaned back and adjusted the pants legs of his light blue suit. "Obviously, this meeting is just a formality. Everything's set. I'm going to review—"

Nona raised her hand, but began speaking at the same time. "I didn't realize that anything had been decided. I thought the reason for this meeting was to hear from those who are affected by having Harlem rezoned. To discuss the issues."

Reverend Watkins frowned and looked around the table as if he didn't understand what language Nona was speaking. "Ms. Simms," he began, not even looking at her, "what issues need to be discussed? It's a known fact, the whole world agrees . . . this rezoning, as well as Harlem East, is wonderful for our community."

Nona stood. In her mind, she fast-forwarded through the words she'd rehearsed this morning in front of the mirror in her bedroom. She eased her knee-length suit skirt down a bit as the reverend's eyes roamed up her legs. She took a deep breath. "I agree that Harlem East is a good thing for this community, but what I don't understand is why rezoning has been added to this project. Three years ago when Harlem East was just a concept, I was one of the first people to support the plan because it was going to build, not destroy. But this plan now . . . to move every business into the mall—I don't understand how this is good for the community."

"Oh, Ms. Simms." The reverend chuckled as if he'd just

heard a comical statement from a child. "Didn't you have a chance to read the proposal?" He put on his glasses and glanced at a folder in front of him. "I know you were sent a package."

"I've read through everything—"

"Then you know that this is a two-hundred-and-fifty-million-dollar project designed to bring more corporate business into Harlem and as a by-product will create jobs, better housing—"

"You do not need to review the benefits of Harlem East."

"Well, I thought I had to since you mentioned building our community. That's what we're doing." Reverend Watkins finally looked at her.

"I'm not talking about Harlem East as a project. I'm talking about forcing all businesses into the mall. It doesn't make sense—expecting every Harlem resident to shop in one place." Nona looked around the table, hoping to draw a response from someone other than the reverend. But every committee member's eyes were focused on Reverend Watkins—as if it had been decided he was their only mouthpiece. James Pace, the *Amsterdam News* reporter, remained as bored as when she'd first entered the room.

"It may not make sense to you, Ms. Simms, but it is clear to everyone else." He paused and glanced around the table. The other members nodded in agreement. "The only reason we've been able to attract companies like IBM and Disney and major retailers like Macy's, Sears, and Old Navy is because we have designed this project to draw people to Harlem East. We are getting the support of major corporations because we're rezoning to bring businesses, and thereby more traffic, into the mall."

"Even if I were to buy that, what does this have to do with Brickhouse? Why would you need to close my business? Shutting me down is not going to increase business for Harlem East."

"Ah, now I see." Reverend Watkins chuckled and looked around the table as if he'd finally understood the punch line of a joke. "This is personal for you, Ms. Simms."

"No, not personal. I'm just asking—"

"You're not thinking about what's good for Harlem. You're only concerned about yourself."

"I'm asking the question—"

"Nona . . . may I call you Nona?"

"No."

"Nona, there are many who are giving up something because our community means so much. You've got to see past Brickhouse and stop looking at just yourself."

"That's not what I'm doing. I'm—"

Reverend Watkins held up his hands. "You've made this all about you."

Nona took a step toward the conference table. "If you would just let me finish—"

"There's nothing for you to say. This is about the greater good—"

"The greater good, my ass—" Nona almost screamed. From the corner of her eye, she saw James Pace perched on the edge of his chair, his pen racing across his reporter's notepad.

"Whoa, let's not let this get out of hand." The mayor's voice was a welcome reprieve from the reverend's.

Allen stood and rested his hand on Nona's shoulder, urging her back into her seat.

"Now, the purpose of this hearing," the mayor continued, "is to hear all positions."

"I agree, Anthony," the reverend said to the man he saw

more as his buddy than as the leader of New York City. "But we can see just by the attendance at this meeting that the community agrees with us. We've had larger turnouts when we were nominating the dog-catching committee." He was the only one who chuckled.

Nona took a deep breath. "I don't care who's at this meeting and who's not. I need to understand why Brick-house has to be destroyed. For goodness' sakes, *my* business is good for Harlem. I employ almost one hundred people, I pay more taxes, I support any cause that will build this community."

"But you've decided to end your support here." The reverend smirked.

"If you're defining my support as closing down my business, then my support stops here."

Seconds later, the commissioner turned to Nona.

"I don't understand." The commissioner frowned. "I thought you were in total agreement with this, Ms. Simms. I have to admit that I was surprised when I heard you had agreed—"

The reverend coughed, then stood. "Listen everyone, we don't need to get into details. It's under control."

It was Nona's turn to frown. What was the commissioner going to say? Her eyes moved between the commissioner and the reverend. She leaned back in her chair. Now she was sure. This smelled like one of the reverend's schemes.

The reverend turned to Nona. "Ms. Simms, I'm sure you can understand that we can't stop the progress of an entire community for you. Now, we're prepared to give you a buy-out as well as incentives for the restaurant you're opening in the mall. And don't worry . . . no one is planning on tearing down your precious Brickhouse. A real estate developer on the board believes we can turn that building into some jazzy condos." The reverend looked at his watch. "This has gone on far longer than expected."

Nona sat still as the mumbles of agreement rose from the table. She felt as if she were in the twilight zone. Turn her gym into condos?

"Unless there is any . . ." The reverend paused and looked at Nona. "Unless there is any *new* business, we need to review the financial packages that have been accepted with Harlem East."

Nona stood. "I'm putting every one of you on notice now," she began, making eye contact with each man at the table. She'd worked with most on one committee or another. They all knew her commitment to Harlem. But they also knew that she was a fighter. "I've worked too hard to build a business to now lose it just because some . . ." She paused and looked at the reverend. "Because someone believes that closing my business is good for Harlem. I will not let that happen. Just understand that every company, every business that has committed to the mall will hear about this." She grabbed her briefcase and stomped from the room, with Allen following her. In the silent instant that followed, the *Amsterdam News* reporter shot out of the room. He couldn't wait to go to press with his latest scoop.

Just before the conference room door closed behind them, Nona heard the mayor say, "Reverend Watkins, I think we have a problem."

Nona slammed her hand against the elevator button. She pressed it again and then turned toward the door marked "Exit." Without a word, she trotted down the stairs.

"Nona, slow down." Allen puffed trying to keep up.

She didn't stop until they reached the lobby. "You know

this is not about helping Harlem or anything else. This is only about benefiting that bootleg preacher up there."

Allen rested his hands on his knees, trying to catch his breath.

"I don't know if this is about money, or power, or what. But I swear, Allen," Nona said as she paced in front of the staircase door, "I'm going to stop that curl-wearing, polyester suit–loving excuse for a pastor." The heels of her pumps clicked against the marble floor, accentuating each syllable as she spoke.

"You're . . . right," Allen breathed. "I know . . . they're up to something. Don't worry; we'll figure it out." He paused as a wave of heat washed over his body. "Let's talk about this at the office, but first I've got to find a restroom."

"Okay, are you riding back with me?"

Allen nodded. "I took a cab over. I'll meet you outside." He watched as Nona dialed Ray from her cell phone to bring the Escalade around. The lobby security guard pointed him to the restroom.

Allen sighed as he looked at himself in the bathroom mirror. Beads of perspiration spotted his face like chicken pox. He turned on the faucet, allowing the water to get as cold as possible as he took off his tie. Then he lowered his head and splashed the water onto his face. He kept the water coming until he couldn't stand the ice-cold fluid anymore.

His eyes were closed as he reached for a paper towel and was surprised when one was handed to him.

"Oh . . . thanks," he said wiping the water away. When he opened his eyes, the reverend stood, leaning against the adjacent sink.

"Not feeling well, Allen?"

He looked at the reverend for a moment, then turned back to the mirror. "What can I do for you, Watkins?"

"Ah, a man who gets straight to the point. I like you."

Allen thought of a million retorts, but stayed silent. He dried his hands, then turned to the door. "Have a good day, Reverend."

"We have a mutual friend."

Allen shook his head. There was no way he shared any associates with the reverend. He reached for the doorknob.

"Talmadge."

Allen stopped.

"Talmadge Williams."

He felt as if he were being swallowed by the air.

"You know who I'm talking about, don't you?" the reverend queried.

The reverend repeated the name, and each time, Allen felt as if he lost four beats of his heart. He finally faced the reverend.

Reverend Watkins had been standing with his arms crossed, but now he took a step toward Allen. "I thought that would get your attention."

Allen felt as if his tonsils had swollen, blocking his ability to speak. It took seconds for him to say, "What do you want?"

"Well, first, tell our friend Talmadge I said hello."

"I don't know who you're talking about."

The reverend gave a short chortle, then looked at his watch. "I don't have time to play chicken with you, so here's what I know. Talmadge is your long-term drug supplier. I wonder what Nona would think about that."

Allen hoped his face didn't show his relief. This was nothing new. Everyone knew that he had had a problem once. But it was long gone—at least in the minds of everyone else.

"Watkins, Nona knows what I did years ago. But she

also knows that I've worked long and hard to break that addiction."

"So Nona knows that you were late to this meeting because you were filling up on your supply?"

The room was now airless, and Allen felt as if he were spinning with the questions that swirled in his mind. How did the reverend know where he'd been? How did he know that Allen was running late? What else did he know?

As if reading his thoughts, the reverend continued, "The rest of the world might think you're a recovered steroid abuser, but I know the truth. You're back on that stuff again, Allen." He paused. "And by the looks of you, I won't have any problem proving it."

Allen used the back of his hand to wipe the sweat from his forehead.

The reverend continued, "If the police were standing outside that door right now, could you guarantee that you'd be free after a body search?"

Before he could think about it, Allen tapped the pocket inside his jacket, then pulled his hand away as the reverend laughed.

"I wonder what would happen to Nona if it was revealed that drugs were being supplied through Brickhouse."

"That's not true," Allen yelled, then lowered his voice. "No one is selling drugs out of Brickhouse."

"Oh, really. What about Todd, the mayor's son? Where did he get the drugs that killed him?"

Allen had to hold on to the wall to steady himself.

The reverend said, "Oh, yes. This could be interesting news for the mayor."

"You could never prove anything."

"You know what's great about this, Allen? I don't have to prove anything. Just a few phone calls to the right people will have this city buzzing. I may even be able to get a criminal investigation started. Doesn't Nona have a daughter? What would happen to her if her mother ended up in jail?"

He snatched the reverend's polyester lapels before he could stop himself. "Nona has nothing to do with this," he growled.

"I . . . know . . . that." Reverend Watkins shook himself free from Allen's grasp and shoved him aside. "But it doesn't have to be true. I need to place just enough innuendos to keep this in the news until the rezoning is complete . . . and Brickhouse is gone."

Allen squeezed his hands into fists.

"Now the way I want to do this, Nona would walk away with quite a package. She'd get compensation for her club . . ." He paused and held up his hands, stopping Allen from speaking. "I know it's a pittance compared to what she'd earn, but she'll still have her restaurant in the mall." He paused again and snapped his fingers as if he had a sudden thought. "And you know what I'll do? To show you the kind of man I am, I'll throw in a bonus. I'll rent Nona an additional space in the mall. She can open . . . a juice bar or something."

"Nona doesn't want the pennies you're throwing at her. And she doesn't want a juice bar. She's worked hard to build Brickhouse," Allen said through clenched teeth. "We're going to fight for that."

"I don't think so." The reverend shook his head. "I have enough on you to shut Brickhouse down, and then Nona won't get a thing."

"You won't be able to do that," Allen said, although his strength and his conviction were fading.

"Oh, Allen, I've taken down men much greater than you.

Do you really want to take that chance? Nona could lose her business and her reputation."

"You are a—"

"Whatever you call me, it's nothing compared to what you are." The reverend took a step closer. "You're a stone-cold murderer. And that alone will bring Nona, and her business, and her family, all tumbling down. And you, my friend, will be the cause of Nona Simms's great fall."

Allen pressed his lips together.

"So do you want to test me?" When Allen stayed quiet, the reverend said, "I didn't think so."

"What do you want?"

His laugh lasted for long seconds. "Nothing much. Just convince Nona to move Brickhouse somewhere else. Far, far away from Harlem. I don't want her taking her clients with her."

Allen frowned. "Why would you care about her clients?"

The smirk disappeared from Reverend Watkins' face. "You've got your own business to worry about. Stay out of mine. Just do what I told you to do . . . or else." He turned to the mirror and straightened the collar on his jacket before he walked toward the door. "And one last thing. Don't you ever put your hands on me again." He brushed past Allen, leaving him trembling in the middle of the public bathroom.

Nona clicked off her cell phone the moment Allen climbed into the SUV. "What took you so long? Was there a line in the men's room?"

"Yeah." Allen leaned back against the soft leather seat as the Escalade rolled away from the curb and turned south onto Frederick Douglass Boulevard.

Nona laughed, but then eyed Allen. "What's wrong?"

He shook his head. "Nothing."

"It's Reverend Watkins, isn't it?"

Allen's eyes widened. "What . . . do you mean?"

"He got to me too." Nona bounced back against the seat. "I need to speak to the commissioner. I need to know what he was starting to say when Reverend Watkins stopped him cold. There's something going on." She turned away from Allen and stared out the window as if what she needed was just beyond the glass. "I called the commissioner's office to get his cell number, but his assistant wasn't giving up any information."

"Do you think the commissioner will tell you anything?"

She shook her head. "I don't know. But I have to try." She faced him. "I won't lose Brickhouse. I'm ready to go toe-to-toe with Reverend Watkins. We'll see who's standing at the end of this fight."

In his chest, his heart pounded faster. In his mind, images played forward like a movie—images of what would happen if Reverend Watkins carried through his threats. It would begin with the media—newspapers and possibly even television—with the sensational story: Popular Health Club Under Investigation for Drug Trafficking.

Then the police would come. The visions were clear—Nona being dragged down the brick steps of her club and weeping as they twisted her wrists into the handcuffs, and Kelly standing behind her mother, screeching, "Please don't take my Mommy away . . ."

"Nona." He almost screamed her name and she frowned. "I'm sorry," he continued. "But I was just thinking. Maybe we shouldn't do this. Maybe we shouldn't fight."

"You've got to be kidding."

"I know how you feel. I didn't say anything in the meeting, but I was fuming. I wanted to strangle that man."

"So what are you saying now?"

He twisted in the seat to look into her eyes, but he couldn't. Instead he focused on the space over her shoulder. "We've known for a long time that Reverend Watkins has some kind of political machine behind him. He will fight you—"

"I'm a fighter too."

"But Reverend Watkins plays dirty."

Nona shrugged. "So what? It's not like he has anything on me."

Allen swallowed. "He doesn't need anything. You know how he operates. He didn't have anything on Yellowstone Cable, yet he organized that boycott by saying they didn't employ blacks. Even with proof, they couldn't *prove* it to the community because of what Watkins said. It cost Yellowstone millions. And he didn't back off until they paid him."

"That's why we have to fight. Because of the type of man he is. You know there's more to this than a mall and rezoning. I'd bet all my bank accounts that there's something big in this for that son of a—"

"Nona," he interrupted her. "I agree with everything you're saying, and I would encourage you to go all the way if I thought we stood a chance. But going against Reverend Watkins, even if we win, we could lose."

"What do you mean?"

He took a breath, hating his next words. Knowing that if it wasn't for him, Nona could stand and fight and keep her business. But the truth was, she'd never be able to win this battle, not with what the reverend had on him. He exhaled. "Reverend Watkins is all about dirty tricks. I can't imagine what he'd do, but I don't want anything to affect . . . Kelly."

Her eyes widened. He had hit his mark—point blank. If he were playing darts, he'd have won the game. But he had never felt more like a loser.

"What could he possibly do?" she whispered.

He kept his eyes away from her. "I can't even imagine, but you know the reverend . . ."

In their silence, he prayed that her imagination would take her to the worst places. He hoped she'd remember the newspaper headlines involving the reverend and his scandalous behavior in the past and how he always used the lowest common denominator to his advantage.

He kept his eyes straight ahead, staring at the back of the front seat. "Nona, you don't have to lose everything. If we walk away, maybe we can negotiate a better deal—with enough money for you to open another Brickhouse someplace else." He paused. "Like maybe in Los Angeles. The West Coast is fitness-crazed. Brickhouse would be huge out there."

Her eyes were wide. "You're talking about starting all over . . . in Los Angeles . . . just because Reverend Watkins wants me out of here?"

"Harlem East was his plan. He's going to do whatever he has to do to make it work. He's going to stop whomever he has to stop to get his way. Think about the policemen he's had fired, or the city officials who have fallen because of him, or the men who've dared to go against his candidates in elections."

Nona closed her eyes. "This is unbelievable."

For the first time, he looked at her. "Staying here in a fight with Reverend Watkins won't be good for Kelly, but Los Angeles could be. She'd be closer . . . to her father."

Nona's groan twisted his insides. Only the image of Reverend Watkins in his light blue suit, leaning against the bathroom sink with a smirk on his acne-covered face, forced him to continue. "Think about it, Nona. LA would be a great market for us. It's the fitness capital of the universe and the top market for your books and tapes. And as Kelly approaches her teenage years, it will be good for her to be closer to her father."

Allen leaned back in the seat, praying that he'd said enough.

He waited for Nona to speak, but she stared out the window. He wanted to know what she was thinking. He needed to know that he'd ended her battle cry. But he remained silent, allowing his words to marinate in her mind.

The SUV slowed in the Brickhouse parking lot and had barely stopped before Nona leaped from the car. He almost ran behind her, but then relaxed as he shut the car door. Allen stayed on the club steps and watched Ray drive the car to the side of the building. Then he lumbered inside. He wanted to go to Nona, to calm her down, to assure her. But staying away was best right now.

Inside, Allen swept past the patrons and staff members who waved or asked for a moment of his time. He rushed to his office and leaned against the closed door.

His nightmare had come to life. He had destroyed Nona. Even if none of Reverend Watkins's threats came to fruition, even if Nona decided she wouldn't fight, her business as it was today would never be the same. Because of him.

His heart wanted to cry, but his eyes were dry with the painful knowledge that he was the bullet Reverend Watkins would shoot through Nona's heart. He reached inside his suit jacket and pulled out the Ziploc bag filled with pills.

He hated these drugs. He shook one of the red capsules from the package.

He hated the reverend. He twirled the capsule between his fingers.

He hated himself. He swallowed the capsule without water—over the years, he'd become good at that.

He sat at the desk and closed his eyes. The seconds ticked to minutes. The contents of the red pill flowed into his blood, easing the aches, relieving the pain. His body was free from the hurt. It was only then that his heart released his tears.

# *eleven*

Leila glanced at the telephone again and bounced onto the couch. "What is taking Nona so long to call?" She couldn't wait to hear how the zoning meeting had gone.

She sorted through the mail—the bunch of catalogues on the foyer table. Shawn had all their bills and important papers sent to accountants and lawyers. In the beginning of their marriage, she'd thought it was so sweet when Shawn said he didn't want her bothered with anything more than being his wife. But in the passing years that had spread the wedge between them, Leila realized just how precarious a situation this put her in.

Leila pulled out the Victoria's Secret catalogue and flipped through the pages. She stopped at the centerfold. The model stood, stretched across the two pages, in red stilettos, legs spread wide and hands on her hips, in a red lace and leather half-cup bra and matching garter thong.

Leila smiled. The photo transported her back to the time when she'd bought a similar set at Bloomingdale's. Her grin widened—she'd never be able to wear that outfit again. Not after the way it had been ripped from her body.

She sank into the full cushions on the family room couch and shivered when she recalled the moments of that day, two years ago. She had taken a chance, showing up at her friend's apartment unannounced and unplanned. She'd never done that before, but on that day, she needed him.

"Leila, how did you get up here?" he had said, his lips stiff with annoyance. "We weren't supposed to meet today."

She tightened the belt of her Burberry trench coat. "I know we didn't plan this, honey, but I was dying to see you." Then she lowered her voice. "You're not going to leave me standing in the hallway, are you?"

"I don't like surprises."

"I know." She tried to peek inside his penthouse apartment through the barely opened door. She was relieved; if he had company, he would have never answered. "I'm sorry. It's just that I've been shopping at Bloomingdale's and I bought something I wanted to show you. Come on, let me in," she whispered. "Someone might see us and then . . . what would Shawn say?"

He rolled his eyes but stepped aside, allowing her to saunter into the apartment. The heels of her pumps sank into the deep pile of the carpet.

"I don't like this, Leila."

"I'm sorry."

"I could have been . . . busy."

"You're not going to stay mad, are you?" She followed him into the living room and stood as he flopped onto the white leather couch. He tossed the newspaper he'd had in his hand onto the table.

"Oh, come on. I'm here now." She looked around the massive space that combined his living and dining room areas. The apartment was much neater than last time—no clothes strewn across the chairs, every trinket and ornament selected by his designer in its proper place. "And it doesn't look like I interrupted anything."

He grunted as he picked up the remote and switched on the plasma television that covered the wall above the fireplace. P. Diddy filled the screen, and music blasted through the room's surround-sound speakers.

"Well, if you're going to ignore me . . ."

He kept his eyes plastered on the TV.

"Okay, I'll leave. But first I want you to see this." She untied the belt on her trench coat, opened it wide, positioned her hands on her waist, and sucked in her stomach until every one of her ribs poked through her skin. "Do you still want me to leave?"

He struggled to hold back his surprise, but it didn't work. Leila smiled with him as she looked at his lap and noticed his growing sign of pleasure. "I told you—I bought something that I wanted to show you."

He laughed as he jumped up, stripped the coat from her, and tossed it onto the floor. "You want to show me something? Baby, now I got something to show you."

She giggled in the seconds it took him to drop his sweat pants to his ankles and reach for one of the condoms that he kept in the crystal candy dish on the side table. A moment later he had her bent over the couch and pushed her thong aside before he entered her.

"You wanna show me something, baby?" he asked as he squeezed her breasts through the leather and lace.

"Oh, yes," she moaned.

"Show me."

She shuddered as he pounded against her, squeezing her, awakening every nerve inside. She tried to crawl from his grasp, but he pulled her closer. Her groans grew louder as she matched his rhythm. He gripped her waist tighter—she moaned. He moved faster—she screamed. When he leaned over and sucked on the tip of her ear, she called out his name.

Her cries filled the room and mixed with the music still bellowing from the television. She glanced at the screen, and Ludacris moved toward her, bending down as if he were speaking to her.

"When I move you move, just like that . . ." Leila sang to herself.

She almost laughed, but couldn't. She was traveling to the edge of ecstasy. She squeezed her eyes and tried to hold her breath, wanting to savor every feeling in that moment.

It was always a wonder to her—the way they shrieked together. She never finished this way with her husband.

"Oh, my," Leila had said over and over. But before she could catch her breath, he lifted her above his shoulder. With just two steps, they reached the balcony, and he slid open the door.

The October wind whipped across the twenty-sixth floor space. "It's a bit chilly out here," she said as pimples rose on her skin.

"Don't worry, baby, you'll be hot in a minute." He unhooked her bra and then tossed it over the railing.

"Hey."

He laughed. "What's wrong, baby?" He smashed his mouth against hers, bruising her bottom lip. When he pulled back, he said, "I'll buy you another one if that's what you're worried about."

"I'm not worried about anything." She wrapped her arms around his neck.

He pushed her against the balcony's banister and lifted her legs. In one motion, he yanked the garter thong from around her, ripping it into two pieces.

She grabbed the thong before he could toss it over the side. "I'll keep this. A memento."

He twisted her around, and she clutched the railing as he smashed against her back. They moved together as if they were meant to be.

Below, Central Park sat in its grandeur, and she smiled even wider between her mutters of pleasure. Shawn had taken the kids to Central Park that afternoon. It had been scheduled—their one family afternoon a month to keep up appearances for the children. But fifteen minutes before they'd planned to leave, she'd told Shawn he'd have to take the kids alone—she had important plans. He'd argued— she'd done what he'd always done . . . she stomped out in the middle of his words. As she raced her Mercedes into the city, there was only one word to describe what she felt— power.

Now she whimpered with glee at that memory and what her friend was doing to her. She searched the hundreds of ant-sized humans that scampered through Central Park below. Of course, she wouldn't be able to see Shawn and her children this high above the city's oasis. But still, she entertained the vision that Shawn would somehow look up and see his wife being taken by his teammate, his partner, his boy. One of his best friends making his wife have orgasm after orgasm. Those thoughts quickened the spasms that began in her center and released her into the arms of bliss.

They had finished that afternoon in his two-person steam shower. She could almost feel the body glove he had used to massage the Pearblossom soap into her skin until every inch of her was covered in lather. It had felt so good, he felt so good . . .

"Leila, what are you doing?"

It took her a moment to drag back to the present, to leave the Fifth Avenue penthouse, to return to Alpine, New Jersey, and to remember the eyes staring at her—the eyes of Shawn Lomax. She wanted to close her eyes and return to that day, the last time she'd been with him. Her husband's teammate had left Leila and New York without even a phone call when the Knicks traded him one week later.

"I said, what are you doing?" he repeated in the tone that reminded her of someone dragging their fingernails across a chalkboard.

"I was resting."

His eyes moved from her face past her torso to her crotch, where her hand rested inside her jeans. He shook his head. "Whatever."

Years ago, she would have been embarrassed, her husband finding her like this. But the years of tears that she'd poured into her pillow made her apologize for very little these days.

"Have you seen my keys?" he asked.

"No, but where are you going? We have Shawn Jr.'s parent-teacher conference this evening."

"Oh, I forgot."

"I scheduled it around you. You said you'd be free tonight."

The way he glared at her, she wondered if he remembered any of the reasons that they'd married. But the disgust that contorted his face reminded her that he had long ago forgotten.

He said, "You're going to have to cover for me."

"I always cover for you."

"So then you know how to do it."

She slammed the pillow against the couch. "Damn it, Shawn, I am so tired of—"

"What are you tired of, Leila? Tired of living larger than a queen? Tired of sitting on your butt all day while I work?"

"Work? You play with a basketball all day, Shawn. Don't get it twisted."

"I don't see you adding any dollars to our bank account."

"Shawn, I don't want to fight with you." She inhaled. "I've been trying—"

"You've been trying to do what?"

"I've been trying," she began slowly, "to make things better between us. Shawn, I want our marriage to be better." She reached for his hand, but he pulled away. "I just want to talk."

"I don't have anything to say, and I know you won't say anything I want to hear." He held up his hand, stopping her protest. "Look, I don't have time. I've got to go."

She lifted herself from the couch. "Where are you going?"

"I'm a grown man, Leila."

"You're a married man, Shawn." She felt like a silly hypocrite before the words could even fall off her tongue.

He rattled the keys he found on the entertainment center. "I'm outta here." He didn't look her way as he trotted from the room.

She sat and held her head in her hands as she heard the garage door open. She stayed in place as the engine on the Hummer roared when he pulled it out onto the street and then away . . . away from her.

She rammed her fist against her leg. She had shown herself weak. She didn't know why she'd said that she was trying. Shawn didn't care about her. She had served her purpose—helped to set him up as the family man when he entered the NBA. She was the requisite gorgeous wife, who later delivered two children for him, and stood by his side whenever the portrait of the perfect family was called for.

But now that he was in his thirteenth year and still holding a multimillion dollar contract, her role had diminished—to almost nothing, as far as Shawn was concerned. She was still around, living in this house as his wife because it was cheaper for him that way.

Leila didn't feel her tears until a small ring of water had gathered on her knees. She reached for the telephone and dialed through the emotions that she was trying to hold back. As the phone rang, she prayed it would be answered and she would get what she needed.

"Hello."

"It's me," she said, hoping she was hiding her tears.

"Well, it's good to hear from you, baby."

She closed her eyes and squeezed more water from her eyes. Relief washed through her. She was wanted.

"I've been thinking about you." His sweetness poured through the telephone. "When can we get together? I need you, baby."

Her tears still flowed, but not because she wasn't wanted. He said he needed her. And that's what she needed. "I had an appointment tonight, but I can cancel it," she said.

If Shawn didn't care about their son's teacher conference, why should she? She was more than Shawn's wife. She was more than a mother. She was a desirable woman. And the man on the other end of the phone purring sweet sounds into her ear proved it.

# *twelve*

"Okay, this is the last one, Leila." Allen stood at the foot of the quadriceps machine ready to assist with the last rep.

"I'm so sore." She moaned.

"Come on, girl." He chuckled. "You've been saying that all morning. What were *you* doing last night?"

Leila released a stream of breath as she returned the machine to the starting position. She tried not to smile. It had been a week since she'd seen her lover after Shawn ran off, but the things they'd done together . . . She'd probably be sore for a few more days. "I think you're getting a bit too personal, Mr. Wade." She stood and wiped her neck with her towel. In the mirror, she could see the entire workout floor behind her, and her smile widened.

Allen marked Leila's chart and looked up. He followed her glance to a guy dressed in black workout pants and a matching tank top lifting himself on the pull-up bar. Allen frowned. He recognized Leila's husband's teammate and wondered if this was the jock Leila was allegedly doing in the parking lot. That would be some mess—Leila being caught with one of her husband's friends—even worse, his teammate.

"Did you hear what I said, Allen?"

"Uh, no. Sorry."

"I said, I'll share my bedroom secrets if you'll share yours." She laughed, but he didn't join her.

"Leila," he began, leaning closer to her, "I don't want to get into your business, but you need to be careful . . . before everyone is in your business."

She turned away from the man in the mirror and looked at him. "What do you mean?"

Allen motioned his chin toward the man Leila had been watching. "There are some rumors going around."

"About what?" She followed his glance in the mirror. "You're not saying that people think . . . me and him? Please."

He shrugged. "All I'm saying, Leila, is be careful. And go easy on those public displays of affection—especially the ones . . . in the parking lot."

She lowered her eyes. Someone had seen her—damn it. Good thing those days were long over. She was with a real man now, and he damn sure wasn't anybody's basketball player. "I don't know what you're talking about. Anyway, I'll see you tomorrow at Toni's premiere. You'll be there, right?"

He nodded, but she never saw him as she rushed toward the locker room. He shook his head. That was good advice he'd just passed on—keep your personal business private. If he'd been more careful, he wouldn't be feeling as if he were staggering on a balance beam a thousand feet above the earth. And he would be able to sleep more than two hours every night, rather than pacing the wooden planks of his bedroom floor trying to figure out how he was going to convince Nona to desert Brickhouse and Harlem.

As he turned to the workout room doors, he swayed. He leaned against the mirrored wall and closed his eyes.

"Allen, are you okay?"

He nodded. "Yeah," he said, glad it wasn't Nona, or Leila, or Toni catching him in this state. "Just didn't eat this morning."

The woman in the lime-green spandex shorts and matching bra top smiled. "I know how that is." She paused. "Maybe we can grab something to eat now? Are you free?"

He shook his head and hurried to his office. He never mixed with the clients, although he was bombarded with propositions. But that wasn't the reason for his rudeness. Dizziness was the first sign. Nausea and abdominal cramps were sure to follow.

He breathed deeply when he closed his office door. Since he had become a regular partaker of these drugs again, he'd learned to time his episodes. He had to reschedule many clients and even cancel a few, but for the last week he had been a functional addict.

At his desk, he opened one of the drawers and pulled out the small metal box. Then he used the key he kept in his pocket, not taking the chance of anyone stumbling on his stash.

Inside the box was the bag. Inside the bag were two capsules. Inside the capsules was his relief.

He glanced at his watch. Five hours had passed. He would have to take one capsule if he wanted to work through the afternoon. But then he'd have only one pill left—and he'd have to do what he'd been trying to avoid. He'd have to make contact.

He looked at the telephone and then he heard it.

*Talmadge Williams.*

The scratchy hoarseness of the reverend's voice had stayed with him for the entire week.

Allen turned away from the phone. Maybe he could

wean himself off the steroids. Maybe there was enough in his system to go the rest of the way on his own. Maybe he would never have to make that call again.

Yes, he thought. Except for that spell of dizziness he'd just had, he'd been fine for most of the week. He could do this.

He glanced at his watch and jumped from his chair. It was time to meet Isaac for the first Golden Citizens Health Guild session.

"Argh," he yelled before he had taken his second step. He clutched the desk, trying to keep himself from collapsing completely. He fought to keep his cries of agony inside, but the pain stabbed him with such severity that he was sure this was his time to die.

"Please, God. Please, God. Please, God," he whispered between the cramps that gripped his intestines with a force that hammered him to his knees.

Minutes later when the pain subsided, he stayed crouching, afraid that even a deep breath could bring back the wicked spasms. He wasn't sure how much time had passed before he accepted that death hadn't come to him—this time.

He pushed himself back into the chair. So much for thinking he could do this on his own. And who was he protecting by not making the call? It was too late to protect Nona. Because of him, Nona was laid out like a Butterball turkey at Thanksgiving. Reverend Watkins was going to have his way with her, carve her any which way he wanted—all because of him.

Allen poured one of the capsules into his hand and then remembered the pain. He dumped the last one into his hand and swallowed both. This was a first—taking two at one time.

In moments, pleasure flowed through him. At least six free hours. He shook his head at that thought. He'd never be free again.

With no more thought, Allen picked up the phone.

"Talmadge, it's me."

The man on the other end chuckled. Allen hated that chortle. In that sound, he heard all of that man's thoughts—that he knew Allen would call, that he knew Allen was weak, that he knew Allen would be calling him for the rest of his days.

They made their deal, and then Allen grabbed his portfolio. He had to get to Morningside Church. He was the keynote speaker, ready to address the hundreds of senior citizens on how a healthy lifestyle could add years to their lives. As he thought about the words he was about to say, he was grateful for the few acting classes he'd taken in college because today was going to be one of the greatest performances of his life.

## *thirteen*

Even before they were close to Times Square Kelly spotted the streaks of light that flashed through the dusk sky from the strobes in front of the Ziegfeld Theatre.

From that moment, Nona had heard the same question every five minutes: "Mom, how much longer?"

And Nona continued to give the same answer. "Not much longer."

"You said that last time."

"So why do you keep asking me?"

Kelly bounced back into the leather of the rented Town Car seat, and then smoothed the satin skirt of her dress. "Do you think we'll see Ms. Lee?"

"Of course." Nona patted her daughter's hand. "Calm down, Kelly. There's nothing to be excited about . . . yet."

Kelly took a deep breath and folded her hands on her lap. Nona smiled. All those lessons—ballet, piano, acting—gave her eleven-year-old the grace of one several years older. She was pleased she'd made the decision to share this night with Kelly. She prayed this was a new beginning for them that could end some of Kelly's challenges.

Nona's smile faded when she looked up at Allen sitting across from her. It didn't seem he had heard any of her exchange with Kelly. He was staring out the window, as he had been doing since the beginning of the ride.

She was more than surprised when Allen had called that morning and asked if he could ride with them; and her surprise escalated when she'd said yes. She was so afraid he'd bring it up again. It wasn't an unusual request; he usually escorted her everywhere. But for the last week, they'd shared the same space, but not their usual lives. Their conversations were polite, forced, not the exchanges of best friends who'd been through so much together. And neither dared broach the subject of the love they shared—Brickhouse—or the rezoning issues. There was no way she'd survive a replay of their last discussion. Even now, the memory of his words pleading with her to quit made her nauseated. It was a conversation with Allen that Nona never wanted to have again.

"We're here."

Nona fluttered her fingers through her head, making sure that the front of her spiked style was in place. She smiled as she thought about the night ahead. This was what she needed. A time of celebration with her friends to take her away from thoughts about business.

Ray slowed the car, and before he rolled to a stop, Kelly had her hand on the doorknob.

"Wait, sweetheart," Nona said, putting her hand on Kelly's shoulder. "Ray will open the door for you."

"Oh, I forgot."

Kelly stepped out first. As Nona leaned forward, Allen caught her elbow, assisting her.

She paused. "Thank you."

He nodded. In the dimness of the limousine, she stared

into his eyes. There was a message in the misery that veiled his face. But a moment later, it was gone when they stepped from the car.

"Mom, this is a real red carpet."

Nona took Kelly's hand as they stepped onto the scarlet walkway. While women dressed in designer gowns and men garbed in expensive tuxedos stopped to greet the press, Nona pulled Kelly toward her protectively past the professional celebrity watchers waiting with their microphones and cameras. She shielded her daughter's face with her hand.

"Nona Simms, look this way." A camera flashed.

"Nona, over here." Another bulb exploded.

"Nona, we're with *Access Hollywood.* Can we get just a moment?"

The shouted requests continued, but Nona smiled, waved, and walked without stopping.

"Mom, don't you want to talk to any of them?"

"No, sweetheart," she said, wrapping her arm around Kelly's waist. "Tonight is all about you."

"Me and Ms. Lee." Kelly beamed.

Nona laughed, and she knew she'd made the right decision. No family photo ops tonight. She wasn't sure, but after that last photo session she'd shared with Kelly, she wasn't taking any chances of her daughter being hurt again.

"Nona, it's good to see you."

Before she had a chance to step inside the theater, Derrick greeted them.

Oh, God, she thought, swallowing her cheer. This was supposed to be a good night. "Hello, Derrick."

His eyes passed over her as if he were admiring a piece of art. "You look beautiful tonight, Nona."

She didn't know why, but some of the joy she'd lost when she first saw him returned. "Thank you," she said, feeling for a moment like a teenager.

Derrick shook hands with Allen before he said, "Who is this lovely young lady?"

Nona didn't think it was possible, but the smile that had filled Kelly's face widened. "This is my daughter, Kelly."

Derrick took Kelly's hand. "It's a pleasure to meet you. I didn't know your mother was going to have such a beautiful date."

"Thank you," Kelly said through giggles.

Nona expected Derrick to turn away then, but he kept his focus on Kelly, asking how old she was, where she went to school, complimenting her on how mature she was.

Nona raised her eyebrows as she watched. Allen stood to the side, like a proud father, while Derrick's questions went beyond polite inquiries. He seemed genuinely interested as he talked and listened to Kelly.

Nona's eyes roamed over Derrick. It was an involuntary action, she decided. Something she did whenever she saw him. He seemed to have a penchant for Armani—this time it was formal wear. She might have hated the man, but she loved his affection for well-designed clothes, and enjoyed studying the way well-designed clothes loved him back. The black and white combination—the white single-button, notched-lapel jacket, with the black tuxedo pants—was an outfit she would have picked out for him.

She shook her head before a smile could fill her face. He got her every time—with his looks.

"Nona, you have a wonderful daughter." He leaned closer and pretended to whisper, "If I were just a little younger . . ."

When Kelly giggled again, Nona had to smile. It wasn't

often that she saw her daughter totally happy, and she had to admit she was pleased that Derrick had made Kelly laugh. Nona allowed her glance to pass over Derrick again, and she inhaled the slight scent of Versace Man that wafted to her nose as he stood so close. She loved that fragrance; she'd purchased a bottle for Allen last Christmas. She closed her eyes and breathed in . . .

"Hey, girl."

Leila's voice dragged Nona from the vision she was about to imagine, and she was relieved. What had she been thinking? This was Derrick Carter. She had to remember that she couldn't stand the man. Although tonight he was making it a bit difficult for her to keep that in mind.

Nona hugged Leila.

"You look beautiful." Leila stepped back and admired the Versace backless gown that Nona wore. "I love your hair," she said.

"You look mighty good yourself." Nona turned to Shawn. "And you are quite handsome tonight, Mr. Lomax."

"Yeah," he grunted and took a sip of the golden liquid inside the glass he held.

Nona tried not to show her surprise as Shawn turned his back on his wife. "So, did you guys just get here?"

Leila nodded as if she were weary. "But we've been here long enough for Shawn to already be drinking."

He rolled his eyes. "I'm going over there," he said, motioning with his chin toward a group of men chatting and laughing at the bar. Nona recognized several of the Knicks. "I'll catch you later."

"Shawn, the movie is going to begin . . ." He moved fast enough and far enough to not hear the rest of her words.

"Oh, sweetie," Nona said and took her friend's hand. For the first time since she'd arrived, she was glad that

Derrick Carter had stepped into her space. He still had Kelly's attention.

Leila blinked to keep the water from her eyes. "Don't say anything, Nona. I'm just trying to hold on. Tonight should be about Toni anyway." She squeezed Nona's hand. "And if I can't have my husband, at least I have my friends." She took a breath. "And here are two more of them now."

"Hello, ladies," Anna said as she joined Nona and Leila. The mayor followed behind her. "Looks like this is going to be quite a festive affair."

"Aren't all of Toni's premieres wonderful?" Leila laughed.

Nona smiled. Just seconds ago, she was sure that Leila was going to fall apart in the middle of this lobby, but Anna's presence had cheered her up.

"How are you, Mayor Leone?" Leila asked Anthony.

"Just fine, Leila." He turned to Nona. "And how are you doing?"

"I'm hanging in there. Doing my best to salvage my business." She held up her hand. "But I don't want to talk about this now. No business tonight, just fun."

"That's what I'm talking about." Toni laughed, joining the group in her sheer, curve-hugging Vera Wang gown that matched the color of her eyes and left little for one to imagine. "This is wonderful. The gang's all here. Now, I have the best seats in the house reserved for all of you," Toni said, tossing her hair over her shoulder. "Go to row BB when you get inside." Toni's eyes roamed to where Kelly and Derrick stood. "Well, look who's here. Kelly, it is so good to see you again."

"Hi, Ms. Lee. Thank you for having me."

Toni hugged Kelly. She turned to Derrick. "And how are you, Mr. Carter?" she asked through half-closed eyelids.

"Good, Toni." He greeted the rest of the group before he

said to Nona, "Thank you for sharing your daughter with me. We're still on for tomorrow afternoon?"

"Definitely," Nona said with more cheer in her voice than she'd planned.

Toni stared at Nona for a moment, then stepped away without a word. Seconds later, Derrick excused himself from the group.

Anna said, "I know you don't want to talk about business, but I want you to know—the Central Park video . . . I want to help you with that."

"Excuse me," the mayor said, walking away before Nona could respond.

"What's going on?" Nona asked. "In just five seconds, we've driven all the men from our group." She laughed.

"I'm still here," Allen said.

"And you're all we need," Leila said.

"You got that right," Anna added. She took Leila's hand. "Come on, let's get a drink before the movie begins."

When Nona, Allen, and Kelly stood alone, Allen leaned close to Nona. "Did you notice the way Toni reacted to Derrick mentioning your meeting?"

"What do you mean?"

"I don't know. She doesn't seem to like the idea of you working with Derrick. I think she might be jealous."

"First of all, Allen, any time I spend with Derrick is just about business—"

"I know that, Nona, but—"

"And secondly, this is not the time to be discussing this. Tonight we should be celebrating Toni."

Allen held up his hands. "I didn't mean anything. I didn't think—"

"Maybe that's the problem, Allen. Maybe you should start thinking."

"Mom."

It was the look on Kelly's face—excitement mixed with confusion—that made Nona remember where she was. In that instant, the lobby lights flashed and Nona took Kelly's hand, returning her daughter's smile. It took a moment for her to look at Allen. *I'm sorry,* she mouthed.

He shrugged as if it were okay, but Nona knew she'd wounded her friend, and that was not what she'd wanted to do. Even though she knew where her words had come from—from that place inside her that had not forgotten his warnings after the zoning meeting. From that place that kept her awake at night telling her that Allen might just be right.

She'd go to him later, apologize, explain . . . and beg for the fight that he'd always had in him to return. His fight was contagious. It was what she always held on to. It was what she needed now to win against Reverend Watkins.

The marble-adorned lobby was crammed with many of the hundreds who had been invited to this premiere and they began to push their way toward one set of the double doors leading to the theater. In the crowd, Nona spotted her friends.

Leila walked alone, just a few steps ahead of Anna and the mayor, while Shawn stayed in a circle near the bar with his friends.

Nona shook her head. With all that she had to face, she knew one thing for sure. She put her arms around Kelly's shoulders. There was definitely no place like home.

# fourteen

Nona dashed down the staircase, but then paused at the bottom.

"And, Odessa, there were so many beautiful women. And they were all dressed in designer gowns. And I got to meet Ms. Lee again and she gave me a hug. It was great."

"Well, what about the movie?" Odessa's accent floated into the hallway, where Nona waited. "Did you enjoy the movie?"

"It was all right," Kelly said just as Nona entered the kitchen.

"All right?" Nona and Odessa said at the same time.

Kelly shrugged. "Everybody knows that premieres are all about being seen."

"Oh, really," Nona said.

"Yeah. Seeing all of those famous people was much better than the movie. The girls at school are going to be so jealous."

Nona filled a cup with coffee that Odessa kept brewing until she had her fill.

"Well, I'm glad you had a good time, sweetie."

"I sure did. And, Odessa, afterward Mom took me to Jean-Georges for dessert, even though it was a school night. And then she said I didn't have to go to school until third period today." She sighed as if she had lived a wonderful dream. "I wish every day was like yesterday. It was great hanging out with you, Mom."

Nona smiled. Her desire to just grab her coffee, rush back upstairs, and jump into her clothes faded with Kelly's words. She really did enjoy this time—breakfast was the only meal that she rarely missed sharing with Kelly.

She took a deep breath, buttered two pieces of toast, and joined Kelly at the table. She glanced at the apple-shaped clock that Kelly had made in third grade. Ray would be coming to take Kelly to school in less than thirty minutes. She could certainly give her daughter that much time.

As Kelly continued her play-by-play commentary on the premiere, Nona rolled over the idea that had come to her that morning. She didn't know why she hadn't thought of it before. But it was more than luck that had made her turn over this morning and click on the television to *Good Morning America*. And Charlie Gibson. And Alicia Keyes. And the mini-concert in Marcus Garvey Park.

"Mommy, who's Mr. Carter?"

Nona blinked. "He's a friend of Toni's and he's worked with me on my videos."

"Really? What type of work does he do?"

Nona wanted to say that Derrick Carter worked to get on her nerves. "He's a producer, which means that he puts together everything to make a video or movie come together."

"He told me he worked with Steven Spielberg on Ms. Lee's movie, and he said that one day he wanted to get together and show me what he did. I hope he calls soon. I really liked him."

Nona wished she'd felt the same way. But if she thought her time with Derrick had been difficult in the past, it was nothing compared to what would happen when they met today. Even now, hours before their meeting, she could hear his words of disgust, see his look of disdain. But it didn't matter.

When the doorbell rang, Kelly jumped up. "Oh, that's Ray." Kelly kissed Nona. "Bye, Mom, and thanks for a terrific night."

"You're welcome, sweetie. Have a good day."

Kelly smiled. "Oh, I know I will," she said as she grabbed her backpack and dashed to the door.

"I haven't seen her this happy in quite some time." Odessa chuckled as she reached for Kelly's plate.

Nona nodded, then noticed the plate in Odessa's hand. "What did Kelly have for breakfast?"

Odessa glanced at the slice of bread with just a few bites missing from the corners. "She only wanted a piece of toast and juice."

"That's all she had?" Nona asked as if she couldn't believe Odessa's words.

"I'm sorry, Ms. Nona. I thought she wasn't hungry because I assumed you had a late dinner. I figured Kelly was still full."

Nona sighed. Yes, they'd stopped by Jean-Georges, and she'd been pleased when Kelly ordered a slice of raspberry swirl cheesecake. But Kelly had taken only one bite. Nona tried to convince herself it was the excitement of the evening that kept Kelly from eating, but now as she stared at the toast that Odessa still held over the table in her trembling hands, Nona realized it was going to take much more than a night at a premiere to get Kelly's eating on track.

"That's okay, Odessa." Nona placed her hand on her

housekeeper's shoulder. "We just have to be more aware—watch what she's eating . . . or not eating."

"Yes, Ms. Nona." Odessa turned toward the sink.

Nona sighed. She was sure she'd made a few inroads with Kelly. And maybe she had. It was just going to take a bit more. No problem, she was up to it. She would do anything for her daughter—just as she would do anything for her other baby. She had the perfect solution for Brickhouse. All she had to do was get Derrick Carter to understand this was how it would be.

"You have quite a daughter," Derrick said after he and Nona exchanged greetings. "I really enjoyed talking to her last night."

His words made her proud although she dreaded what would happen in the next minutes. While he continued to chat about the premiere, Nona sat behind her desk and took in the sight in front of her.

As usual, Derrick was dressed impeccably, although much more casually. Not Armani this time; she guessed Ralph Lauren—a navy blazer with tan pants. Although the suit was different, his scent was not, and she inhaled, loving his fragrance.

Today was the first time she noticed his hair—the way it glistened under her office lights. As if it had just been washed, but without time to dry, and his short cut swirled with curls cropped close to his head.

"Maybe," he continued as Nona studied his full lips as they moved, "I'll get a chance to see Kelly again one day."

Nona took a deep breath. She couldn't explain why her heart was pounding as if she cared what Derrick would think. After all, she didn't really like him. At least that was what she kept telling herself. "Derrick," she began, hoping that he'd remember she was the mother of the young girl he seemed so fond of.

"Okay, let's get to work," he said, pulling a file from his briefcase. "It's all finalized," he said with excitement. "The dignitaries, the special guests, the dancers, all of the production equipment from the lighting to the music. My team has been working. I got the final permits for Central Park this morning."

"I want to change the venue."

"What?"

"Marcus Garvey Park."

"What?"

"It should have always been at Marcus Garvey Park. I don't know what I was thinking, but Brickhouse is in Harlem and Marcus Garvey is the Central Park of Harlem."

She breathed, allowing the silence of passing seconds to let her words settle between them.

"Nona," he started, his bass-tone voice filled with forced patience, "we are too far into this. It was an aggressive schedule to begin with and you want to change the venue at the last minute when it makes no sense. Central Park is the perfect venue."

"But when you think about it, Derrick, it makes much more sense to do the video where I live and work."

"You live in Manhattan. You work in Manhattan."

"I live and work in Harlem."

He threw up his hands. "Here we go again. You and Harlem."

She waited, half expecting him to call her video a "black thang" again. His words reminded her of all the comments she'd heard through the years. And he affected her the same way all those other people did. Didn't matter.

"Nona," he said, leaning forward, his hands flat on her desk. "Please rethink this."

"I have. And my only regret is that I didn't plan it in Marcus Garvey in the first place. Not only for all the reasons I've told you, but have you heard what's going on with Brickhouse and the Harlem Empowerment Office?"

"I've heard rumors."

She stood. "It's more than neighborhood gossip," she said, pacing behind her desk. "There's a real chance that Brickhouse could be closed."

"Okay," he said as if he had a solution. "Now I understand where you're coming from. And I pray that it all works out for you. In fact, you have my support, and I'll do whatever I can to support you. But this has nothing to do with the video."

"Yes, it does. See, not only does it show everyone in Harlem how committed I am to this community, but it gives me a chance to employ people who live here and showcase the place where I live and that I love."

"So you're trying to impress a few politicians?"

Nona almost laughed as she thought of the seven men in the Harlem Empowerment Office, sitting around the conference table, unable to utter any words until they received direction from Reverend Watkins. "I don't care about the politicians," she said, remembering that even after all her calls, she still hadn't heard from the commissioner. "I care about the people. I need the people behind me." She returned to the chair, her voice high with excitement. "We can invite the residents of Harlem to somehow participate in the video. And at the same time, I can turn it into a rally to keep Brickhouse. I haven't thought it all through yet—"

"Obviously."

She ignored his interruption. "Maybe I can have petitions, maybe I can organize a rally at the Harlem Empowerment Office, maybe I can just get a few hundred Harlem
folk upset."

Derrick took a breath. "Nona, I understand your
dilemma, but please don't get it twisted. One is about keeping your business, and like I said, I'll do anything I can to
help you do that. But the other—this video is about building your business."

"It's the same thing to me, Derrick."

He sat back in the chair, pressed his lips together, and stared
at her for a moment. "What can I say to change your mind?"

She hoped her smile would diffuse his anger, but she
shook her head solidly. "Nothing."

"What if I tell you that it's the biggest mistake you'll ever
make? People across the country will buy this video when
they hear it's been filmed in Central Park. But no one will
be impressed with it being in Harlem. Who's ever heard of
Marcus Garvey?"

Nona wondered who he saw when he looked in the mirror. "Well, maybe we can teach a few people a few things."

"I don't know." He shook his head. "This is probably
going to push back the video date several weeks. We'll miss
the important holiday sales."

"That's fine."

"I don't even know if it can be done."

"I'm sure you'll figure out a way."

"And the dignitaries . . . I can't promise who will attend
now that you want it . . . in Harlem."

"It never was about them."

"I still want it to be a diverse crowd. I don't want all
black faces." He paused when Nona raised her eyebrows.
"I'm just thinking about marketing."

"That's your job, Derrick. I'm just doing mine."

More silent seconds passed. He stood. "Well, there's no need for this meeting. I have to get to work. Start over." He tossed the file back into his briefcase. "You know this is going to cost more money," he said as if that was the final ace that could change her mind.

"I understand. If you can fax me a new budget as soon as you have one, I'd appreciate it. And of course, you'll be paid for all of your time."

"There was never a doubt about that." Derrick snapped the lock on his briefcase. Nona stayed in place, her hands folded on her desk. He didn't even look at her before he stomped from the office and shut the door without another word, leaving the delicate scent of Versace Man to remind her that he'd been there. Nona held her breath until she was sure he was out of the building.

It was a certainty now. There was no way Derrick Carter would ever work with her on another project. After this video, she'd never have to see him again. *And that's just fine with me,* she thought, although she couldn't explain the slight ache that she felt in her heart.

# fifteen

They collapsed onto the down-filled pillows on the king-sized feather bed at the same time, their heavy breathing the only sound that filled the space.

It was a minute before he said, "Leila, Leila, Leila."

She rose up and laid her head on her lover's chest, feeling his heart still racing.

He kissed her forehead. "You're fantastic, sweetheart." He was still panting. "I swear you're going to make this old man have a heart attack."

She giggled. "You're hardly old."

He wrapped his arms around her, holding her tight. "I love spending time with you."

She snuggled deeper into his arms. These days were the best of her life. She'd never felt so cherished.

"Did I make you happy, Leila?"

She smiled. "Of course." She gave the answer she always did when he asked. Her physical release wasn't what was important. It was the way he made her feel—inside and out. His words were so different from her husband's. Shawn never asked. Shawn never cared.

"That's good," he said, kissing her forehead. "You know that's all I want to do. Make you happy."

She laid her thigh over his. She wanted to be one with him again.

He continued, "You looked beautiful at the premiere last night."

She sat up. "Did you really think so?"

"Of course." He wiggled his fingers through the curls of her hair. "I wanted to grab you right there in front of everyone."

She sighed. His words were pure poetry.

"I'm telling you, I had to control every bone within my body to keep my hands off you. There was not a woman in that place who could rival you. That's why I called you this morning."

"Really?"

"I had to see you. I couldn't wait to be with you."

It didn't matter to Leila that she didn't believe what he said—she was sure he believed it. He was the first man who'd ever spoken to her that way, and it made her shudder with joy. His words wiped away the ones that Shawn used to torture her. This man wanted her, needed her.

"I just wished . . ."

Her eyes widened at his words. "You wished what?" she asked.

He smiled at her. "Nothing."

"No, please, sweetie. Tell me what you were going to say."

He sat up and leaned on his elbow. "So, what's on your schedule for the rest of the day, besides maybe a little more of this?" He flicked her nipple with his finger.

She pouted inside, wanting to know what he wished. Did he have the same wishes and hopes that she did? She stared at him, and his smile widened. Of course he did. His words were proof. He wanted everything that she wanted.

"Sweetheart, do you think we could ever get married?" she blurted before she could think through the thought.

It took a moment, but then he leaped from the bed, dragging the heavy comforter to the floor with him. "What are you talking about? Asking me if we could ever get married. Are you crazy? You're married to Shawn Lomax, for God's sake."

"I know, but I was just thinking—"

"Don't think, Leila. That's not why I'm with you."

She pulled the sheets up to her chest, covering herself. She was shocked into silence. Where were the words that he was whispering to her just moments ago?

"Look," he said, grabbing his pants. "You knew from the beginning that this was just about fun and games."

He was almost completely dressed before she could command her mouth to move. "I'm sorry . . . I just thought—" She stopped when he glared at her. "I don't know what I was thinking." She scooted from the bed and stood in front of him, letting him soak in her nakedness.

He looked at her for a moment, but she knew trouble was ahead when he turned away.

"Please don't leave." She put her arms around his neck. "I'm sorry."

"Leila, I can't afford you thinking this is any more than it is."

"It's just the things you said to me."

He wrestled her hands free from his neck and laughed. She heard the pity inside his chortle. "Get real, Leila, it's part of the game."

"I know," she whispered her lie. She hadn't known. She'd believed every wonderful syllable that had surged through his lips.

"Well, I hope you'll think about this because if we ever get together again—"

"If we ever get together again?" Panic covered each word as she spoke them.

"If we ever get together again," he repeated. "I don't want a repeat of this. You know who I am, Leila. I can't afford the drama."

She swallowed as he shrugged his shoulders into his jacket. "I don't want any drama either, sweetie. I just want you."

He grunted.

"When are we going to get together again?" It was a plea more than a question.

"I don't know."

"I thought we were going to spend the entire afternoon together today. Where are you going now?"

He looked at her as if she'd just landed from Mars. "I'm a grown-ass man, Leila. And we're not married. Take that mess home to your husband." He was gone before she could say anything else.

It took several moments before the numbness that had shielded her began to drip away, and then tears rolled down her cheeks. It was the first time he'd ever walked out on her, but she was well acquainted with this scene. He spoke to her the way Shawn always did. He left the way Shawn always had.

Within minutes, her tears turned to sobs. She fell onto the bed, grabbing a pillow and holding it as if it were her lover. She cried until her head throbbed and her stomach ached.

She had to talk to someone. She reached for her cell phone. "Nona will know what to do," she said aloud. But before she dialed the first number, she turned off her phone. She couldn't talk to Nona. She couldn't talk to Nona or Toni or Allen or Anna. The only people who could help her could never know about this. Because if any of them ever found out, she'd lose much more than their friendship.

She was alone.

Leila grabbed the comforter from the floor and wrapped herself inside the luxurious quilt. Then in the middle of the cosmopolitan elegance that only the Ritz-Carlton could provide, Leila cried until the sun's light bowed to the night's darkness.

## sixteen

Nona hardly looked up when she heard the knock on the door, but when she did, she was surprised to see Allen.

"Hey, you," he said.

She smiled. Even though they saw each other every day, their contact had been only formal in the two weeks since the zoning meeting. She missed him. "Come on in."

They sat in the middle of a strangers' kind of silence before Allen said, "I don't like what's been going on between us."

"I know, Allen, I'm sorry."

He leaned forward. "I'm sorry too, Nona. I hope you know I only want what's best for you."

"I know. That's why I was surprised when you said I should give up. We both know that's not at all what's best."

He nodded.

She continued, "You're usually such a fighter. We've won so many battles together."

"I know, but Reverend Watkins—"

"We can beat him too, I promise."

He shook his head, and Nona saw the doubt in his eyes.

"I've been working on something for the last week," she said as she stood and joined him on the other side of her desk. "You know we're moving the video to Marcus Garvey Park."

"I got the e-mail."

She touched his hand and they both smiled. "Sorry about that. I didn't want you trying to talk me out of it. Anyway, I'm moving it to get community support. I've got our publicist, Terrie Williams, on it, and of course, my good friend and editor-in-chief of the *Amsterdam News*, Elinor Tatum, is on our side. Anna's been working with me and we're not sure what to do, but I'm going to make some kind of announcement at the taping about Brickhouse closing . . . about being pushed out of Harlem . . . about all of Reverend Watkins ideas."

Nona frowned when Allen sat still, as if her good news didn't faze him.

She continued, "Now, how do you think several hundred Harlem residents are going to react to that news?"

He shrugged. "It could work."

"You betcha it could. It's my last hope, Allen."

The buzz on the intercom stopped them both, and Sarah's voice floated into the office. "Nona, Odessa's on the line."

"Let me take this." Nona picked up the phone. "Odessa?"

"Ms. Nona, I just want you to know that I picked Kelly up from school. The nurse sent her home."

"Why? What's wrong with her?"

"I don't know. The nurse said Kelly had an upset stomach all morning," Odessa said. "But I wonder if it's her not eating. She's been complaining about her stomach hurting for the last week or two. But now I think it's much more than that."

"Odessa, why didn't you tell me Kelly hadn't been feeling well?" Nona asked, raising her voice slightly.

Allen stood and walked to her side.

"I wanted to but every night that I tried to wait up for you, I fell asleep. And then in the mornings, you seemed so preoccupied with Brickhouse and the video and the rezoning. You haven't even had breakfast with us in a week. I didn't know what to do."

"You could have called me," Nona said, now standing. She shook her head slightly to keep away the guilt she felt building. The guilt that told her if she wasn't so busy with her business, she would have noticed that Kelly wasn't feeling well. "You could have left me a note, Odessa," she said, wanting to shift her guilt.

"I'm sorry. I didn't think about that. And I thought Kelly just had a little stomach flu," Odessa explained. "I didn't want to bother you with everything you have going on if that's all it was."

"Odessa, there is nothing more important than Kelly."

"I know. I'm sorry I didn't tell you."

"Well, I'm on my way home. Please keep checking on Kelly." She hung up.

"What's wrong?" Allen asked.

Nona sighed and tried to answer that question. But she wasn't sure. Was this just a stomach flu or did this have something to do with Kelly's eating habits? "I'm not sure."

"Is Kelly all right?"

Nona shook her head, hoping that would keep away the guilt and the tears she felt burning her eyes. "I don't know. Let's just pray that she is." She grabbed her purse.

"Do you want me to drive you home?"

"No, Ray's here. I'll call later."

She was out the door and past Sarah before anyone could

ask any more questions. It took almost half an hour for Ray to drive her the twenty blocks in the afternoon traffic. Nona's mind was jumbled with thoughts. She wanted to believe that Kelly just had a stomach bug, and after a few days of rest, she would be back to her normal self. But the sinking feeling in Nona's stomach told her that this was something more.

Ray had barely stopped the Escalade before she jumped out and hurried up the steps to her brownstone. "Kelly," she yelled when she opened the front door.

Odessa rushed to meet her. "She's in her room, Ms. Nona. She's been resting."

"Is she still throwing up?" Nona asked as she rushed up the stairs.

Odessa followed her. "Not anymore."

"Did she say anything?"

"Only that her stomach hurt."

They stopped in front of Kelly's room. "Thank you. I'll let you know what time we'll be eating."

Nona walked into Kelly's room. The room was a bit dark, lit with just the early evening light that filtered through the window, but she could still see that the room was empty. She frowned.

"Kelly," she whispered. And then her frown deepened. *What is that?* she wondered. *What's that gurgling?* Nona moved slowly toward the sound. Her steps quickened as she approached Kelly's bathroom.

It took a moment for the sight before her to register inside her brain. Kelly was hunched over the commode, with half of her hand inside her mouth. She was on her knees. Heaving. Purging.

"Kelly," Nona screamed.

Kelly's body jerked as she heard her mother's voice, but

she stayed in place, the yellow bile still flowing over her hands, out of her mouth, into the toilet.

"Kelly," Nona cried. She grabbed her by her waist and lifted her away.

Kelly's gags continued, even through her cries as Nona tried to carry her. Nona stumbled a bit under Kelly's weight, but after several seconds of struggle, she finally laid Kelly on her bed.

"Kelly," Nona shouted. "What are you doing?"

"Mommy, I'm sorry."

Nona stared at her daughter for a moment. Her white shirt was soaked with the fluid that was meant to be inside her stomach. Nona pulled Kelly into her arms, and their tears flowed together.

"Odessa, Odessa," Nona yelled. Nona rocked Kelly in her arms, trying to stop her sobs. "Odessa."

"Yes, Ms. Nona." Odessa rushed into the bedroom and stopped. "Oh, Ms. Nona."

"Please bring me some towels," she shouted.

Odessa nodded and hurried away.

"Mommy, I'm sorry," Kelly said over and over.

"Kelly, why?" was Nona's mantra.

It took less than a minute for Odessa to return, and then long minutes passed as Odessa gently wiped the bodily waste from Kelly and Nona.

Still, Nona held her daughter—as she moved Kelly to the chaise while Odessa swiftly changed the bed linens and comforter, and then cleaned the bathroom.

Still, Nona held her daughter—as Odessa removed Kelly's soiled shirt and draped her bathrobe over her shoulders. Then they both helped Kelly return to her bed.

Still, Nona held her daughter—until she stopped crying. When Nona felt the calm breathing of Kelly sleeping, she motioned for Odessa to move to the other side of the room. "I'm going to stay with her."

Odessa nodded. "Let me know if you need anything else, Ms. Nona." She looked at Kelly, and then her eyes, still filled with tears, returned to Nona. "I'm so sorry."

Nona rubbed Odessa's shoulders, trying to reassure her. But once Odessa left the room and Nona was alone with Kelly, she wondered who was going to reassure her.

Nona returned to the bed and lay next to Kelly. She was sure of it now. She had to do something. She had to save her daughter's life.

The bedroom was totally dark before Nona felt Kelly stirring. Nona reached for the nightstand light, and when Kelly opened her eyes, Nona smiled.

"Hi, sweetheart. How are you feeling?"

Kelly nodded slightly. "I'm feeling better now."

Nona took a breath and held her daughter's hand. "That's good. And we have to make sure that you stay that way." She paused. "Tomorrow I'm making an appointment with the doctor."

Kelly sat up on the bed. "But I'll feel way better by tomorrow. I won't need to see Dr. Benjamin."

"I'm not talking about Dr. Benjamin. I'm talking about a psychologist. We're going to get to the bottom of this."

"What?" Kelly shrieked and jumped from her bed, as if Nona hadn't found her crouched over the toilet just hours before. "I told you, I'm not going to any shrink."

"And I told you, Kelly, that we are. I'm the parent, and I want to know what's going on with you."

"There's nothing going on, Mom. I just had a little stomachache."

"And that's why you were standing over the toilet vomiting?" It took everything within her to keep her voice calm.

"I . . . I had a stomachache. That's why I was sent home."

Nona stood from the bed. "Kelly, please. You and I both know that's a lie. You weren't feeling well because you've been forcing yourself to throw up whatever you put in your mouth. It's called purging."

Kelly's eyes widened as if she were surprised that her mother knew the truth.

"And I know about everything else too. How you don't eat around me and Odessa, but there are empty bags of cupcakes and potato chips and God only knows what else stuffed in the back of your closet."

Kelly fell back onto her bed, her eyes filled with tears. "Okay, Mom, it's true," she confessed as if she were telling Nona something new. Then Kelly looked up, her eyes filled with promise. "But I won't ever do it again. I'll get better. But please, please don't make me go to a shrink."

There were so many days when Nona had believed she and Kelly could fight this together. But the vision of what she'd seen today would not allow that hope anymore.

"Please, Mom." Kelly's pleas invaded her thoughts but didn't change her mind.

Nona looked at Kelly as if she hadn't heard a word she said. "I'll let you know when we have the appointment."

"Don't you care about what I think and what's going to happen to me?"

"That's all I care about." Nona walked toward the door. "And in thirty minutes I expect you downstairs for dinner."

Kelly slumped against her pillows and cried. Nona hesitated for a moment. She wanted to run to Kelly and hold her, comfort her, assure her that this was for her good.

Promise her that in weeks, they'd both be glad a doctor had become involved. But instead Nona walked out of the room.

Inside her bedroom, Nona crawled onto her bed and leaned against the headboard. She pulled her knees into her chest and covered herself with the down comforter. What was going on? Her daughter, her business, even her friendships . . . it was all falling apart. Was there a message in what was happening? She closed her eyes. If there was something she was supposed to hear, she had to find a way to listen before everyone and everything that she loved was completely destroyed.

## seventeen

Sarah had researched, spoken to friends, and then given Nona a list of doctors. Nona interviewed seven over the telephone and selected Dr. Rutherford, a psychologist who specialized in children with eating disorders, and more important, someone who was not affiliated with her daughter's school. She didn't want Kelly to worry about her friends there knowing that she was seeing a therapist.

Nona had wanted to visit the doctor first to explain the situation. But Dr. Rutherford insisted on seeing Nona and Kelly together.

As Ray slowed the car in front of the Park Avenue building, Nona glanced at Kelly. Her daughter hadn't uttered an unnecessary word since their confrontation two days before. And this morning Nona had almost had to drag Kelly from her bedroom. Now Kelly sat scrunched in the farthest corner of the SUV, as far away from Nona as she could get.

When the car stopped, Nona stepped out, but Kelly stayed inside.

Nona waited a moment before she said, "Kelly, get out of the car."

Kelly opened the door on her side and jumped out, but then walked a few steps behind Nona as they passed the building's doorman and entered the doctor's first-floor office.

In the next minutes, Nona felt as if she were living another woman's life—she checked in with the receptionist, filled out a mental health questionnaire for herself and Kelly, gave the receptionist her insurance information, and then sat in the ten-chair waiting room. She was relieved that only she and Kelly were there. That had been one of her concerns—being recognized by another patient and then having the story of her doctor's appointment splashed on the pages of some tabloid magazine. That would certainly push Kelly over the edge.

Nona picked up a magazine. "Do you want to look at one of these?"

Kelly barely shook her head, as if she were disgusted by any interaction with Nona.

Nona sighed and prayed that Kelly would behave differently with the doctor—act as if she had some home training and not as if she were one-half of a very dysfunctional family.

"Ms. Simms."

Nona looked up.

"Dr. Rutherford is ready," the receptionist said.

Nona glanced at the clock. Nine o'clock, exactly. She stood, took a few steps, and then looked over her shoulder.

"Kelly." Nona worked hard to keep her tone even.

"She called you, not me," Kelly said. But still, she stood and followed her mother.

"It is so nice to meet you, Ms. Simms," Dr. Rutherford said as she stood at her door. She turned to Kelly. "And how are you, Kelly?"

Kelly shrugged and grunted.

When Nona opened her mouth, the doctor shook her head slightly, stopping her. Dr. Rutherford motioned for them to take a seat in front of her desk.

Although she tried not to show it, Nona was a bit surprised by Dr. Rutherford. On the telephone, her heavy proper-Boston accent painted a picture in Nona's mind of a tall, red-haired, refined, slender woman. But the large-boned doctor couldn't be called slim at all. It made Nona wonder. Was that why she was so effective with young girls?

"Kelly, it doesn't seem like you're too happy." The doctor's voice brought Nona back into the office.

Kelly folded her arms across her chest and shrank into the chair. "I don't want to be here," she said, her eyes trained on the floor. "It's embarrassing. I don't need a shrink."

Nona shook her head and sighed. This wasn't going to work.

"I can understand how you feel," the doctor said. Her voice was soft, soothing, as if even her speech were some kind of medicine. "But since you're here, let's talk."

For the first time, Kelly looked at the doctor. "About what?"

Dr. Rutherford smiled. "I can think of a few things, but first"—she turned to Nona—"Ms. Simms, would you mind leaving us alone?"

The doctor had told Nona that she might want to speak to Kelly by herself, but Nona hadn't expected it to be this early in their meeting. Dr. Rutherford didn't know anything about them—nothing about what had been going on in their lives. Even though her brain told her feet to move, she stayed.

"It's fine, Ms. Simms," the doctor reassured her as if she

heard her thoughts. "You can wait right outside. Kelly will be fine." The doctor stood, and Nona followed.

Nona glanced at Kelly and then stepped from the room. She chose the chair closest to the doctor's office and eyed the receptionist. She was waiting—waiting for the receptionist to get up to make copies, go to the bathroom, run to the post office—anything that would give her enough time to stand and put her ear to the door.

She had to know what was going on. What family secrets was Kelly revealing? Was she telling the doctor that her mother was never there for her and cared more about her business and didn't seem to know that she existed? And that her mother was why she didn't eat? And why she binged? And why she purged?

"Stop this, Nona," she whispered to herself. "If I'm going to have a conversation, I should at least include someone else." She pulled out her cell phone and punched Leila's number.

"Hey, girl," she said when Leila answered. "How're you doing?"

"Not so good, Nona. There is so much going on."

"Tell me about it." Nona sighed. "I'm at the doctor's office with Kelly right now."

"Listen, Nona, can I call you later? There's something I have to do."

Nona stared at the cell phone once she heard the rustle of dead air. Leila had hung up. Without saying good-bye. Right after she'd told her best friend that she was at a doctor with Kelly.

She dialed Toni's number. She couldn't wait to tell Toni how Leila had treated her.

"Hi, Sam. Can I speak to Toni?"

"Hold on a sec," the cheerful assistant sang. A few seconds later, Sam returned, but the song was gone from his voice. "Nona, uh, Toni is . . . not available right now."

"Not available? What does that mean?"

"She's not available," Sam repeated as if saying it a second time would make it clearer.

"Thank you," Nona whispered before she hung up. She wanted to call Anna, but knew she was in a meeting for her Children's Literacy Outreach.

Friends . . . that's what she needed now. But none were available. She was staring into the face of one of the most important moments of her life, and she was alone.

"Ms. Simms." Nona hadn't realized that the doctor's door had opened. "Can you join us?"

Nona stepped back inside and paused when she looked at Kelly. She'd left her daughter slumped in the chair, lips poked out, arms folded. But now she was sitting up straight, and although Nona couldn't quite call the smirk on her face a smile, it was much more pleasant than what had marked her face when Nona had left the room.

"Well, I think Kelly and I have learned quite a few things, haven't we?" the doctor said.

Kelly nodded and glanced sideways at Nona.

"Now, Kelly, would you mind leaving me and your mother alone?"

Kelly stood and looked at Nona again. She still wore that smirk—a half smile filled with secrets. As if she understood things that her mother never would. Nona twisted in the chair.

When they were alone, the doctor said, "You have quite a daughter, Ms. Simms."

She'd heard that statement a few times. "I know. That's why I don't understand this problem."

The doctor nodded. "Well, there is no way for me to

make a complete diagnosis after twenty minutes, but I can safely say that Kelly's problem is classic. It's a call for attention."

Nona sighed. "She constantly says that she wants to look like me—"

"I don't think it's so much that," the doctor interrupted. "She's not really trying to look like you, although she believes that is the solution. You see, so much attention is given to you that Kelly feels . . . insignificant. So she's willing to do whatever she can to be like you. In her mind, when that happens, she'll be special and people will notice her too."

Nona frowned.

"I know this is a lot to take in right now, but the key is, Kelly really opened up to me. In just minutes, she was telling me how she was feeling."

The doctor's words didn't make her heart feel good. Nona thought of the times when she'd asked Kelly what she was feeling, what she was thinking. All she'd received were blank stares or empty words. "Well, I'm willing to do anything to help my daughter." Nona pulled a pad from her purse, ready to take notes.

"Like I told you over the phone, Ms. Simms, there is never any quick fix for eating disorders." She motioned for Nona to put the paper away. "This is not about one feel-good session. Kelly is holding much inside. I suspect some of this has to do with her father living so far away."

Nona gulped. It was another item to check off on her guilt list. She was a career-focused mother who couldn't even give her daughter that one important relationship—the one with her father.

The doctor continued, "It's going to take more time to get to the center of all that Kelly's feeling. This is really about discovery. In these sessions, Kelly will come to find out things about herself. She'll develop her own solutions, with my help. But I'm just here to listen and direct." The doctor leaned forward and made a note on a pad. "I'd like to see Kelly twice a week—alone."

Nona nodded.

"And I'm going to give her a diary to write down not only what she's eating, but what she's feeling. Any thoughts that come to mind."

"That's good," Nona replied. If Kelly wouldn't talk to her, at least she'd be able to read what her daughter was thinking.

"I'm going to explain to her that whatever she writes is private, and the only person who will ask her to share her thoughts is me."

Nona squeezed her protest back into her throat.

"In order to get to the crux of Kelly's challenges, she has to feel safe," the doctor explained, addressing Nona's hesitation.

"Did Kelly tell you she didn't feel safe with me?" Nona whispered.

The way the doctor looked at her, Nona was sure she was being analyzed. "Kelly didn't say that. I just want to provide every opportunity for her to open up—completely and honestly." She paused. "Let's try it this way for a while. Of course, I'll schedule regular updates with you."

Nona nodded.

"And one last thing, Ms. Simms. Kelly thinks you're angry with her."

"I'm not."

"I understand, but it's what she feels. I just want you to know that Kelly really can't help what she's doing. Bulimia is an illness. She is substituting a need for attention with a voracious appetite when she is alone. Then, to look like you, she makes herself vomit. It's physical and mental. She's not trained to solve this eating disorder. And unfortunately, neither are you. You can't just put a plate in front of Kelly and force her to eat and keep it down. She won't eat in front of you or others, and when she does, she feels so guilty that she punishes herself by purging. We have to find a way for her to eat normally again, and that won't happen until she feels safe."

Nona swallowed. *Bulimia is an illness.* It was as if those were the only words from Dr. Rutherford that she heard. *Oh, my God,* she thought. *I've been waiting and hoping that this would just end. Did I make Kelly worse by not bringing her in sooner?*

"You've done a good thing, Ms. Simms," the doctor said.

Nona blinked. This doctor seemed to always know what she was thinking.

"Many people wait for years before they seek medical help," the doctor continued. "People don't realize this disorder is an illness. But Kelly is here now for treatment. And part of that is making sure that she feels complete support. Not anger or condemnation."

"She's a child, my child. I would never *condemn* her."

"I know that," the doctor said in her soothing tone as if Nona was the one who now needed treatment. "I just wanted to make you aware so there won't be any obstacles as we move forward."

By the time Kelly returned to the office, Nona was slightly slumped in her chair. She barely heard the doctor's words as Dr. Rutherford spoke to Kelly about the diary and meetings the two of them would share. Nona watched her daughter. Just an hour ago, Kelly was shut off, angry, ready to step off the face of the earth if that would get her away from Nona. But after minutes with the doctor, Kelly was speaking freely, smiling even. She wasn't the daughter that Nona had brought into the doctor's office.

What did Dr. Rutherford do that she hadn't done? Countless times she'd tried to connect with Kelly—in all kinds of ways. But the doctor had done it in twenty minutes.

By the time Ray brought the car in front of the doctor's office, Nona's emotions were swirling. This session was supposed to be for Kelly, but she was the one filled with doubts. Maybe she wasn't a good mother. Maybe she wasn't cut out to be. Maybe she would never be able to help Kelly.

By the time she dropped Kelly off at school, Nona was absolutely sure. She needed her own psychologist.

Leila stared at the phone again, willing it to ring. Still, it remained silent. She wanted to pick it up and call Nona back. She hated the way she'd spoken to her friend, but she couldn't do anything about that. She'd call Nona and apologize later. Right now, there was only one person she wanted to talk to.

She tightened her bathrobe around her waist and walked to the bedroom window. She drew back the rose curtains. Outside, the sylvan peace that had drawn her to this Jersey suburban home was in fall bloom. The golden colors of the leaves urged her to remember good times, when she and Shawn had first chosen this ten-thousand-square-foot home and made plans that matched their wedding vows—till death would them part.

But the death of their marriage had come long before its legal demise. It had been ushered in through Shawn's emotional abuse and womanizing that he did little to hide. He had broken her heart, ripping feelings of love from her.

It was a miracle that those feelings had returned—a gift from her lover. There was joy in her heart now, although it was only outside the walls of this home. It was joy nonetheless—in the arms of the sweet man who made her feel special.

But now she feared the delight she'd come to know could be gone. It had been more than a week since he'd stomped out of the Ritz, and although she had called him an uncounted number of times, he hadn't returned any of her calls.

She hadn't been able to sleep, to eat—she hadn't even been to Brickhouse. When Shawn questioned her and challenged her to get herself together, she lay in bed, speechless, and left her children's care to their housekeeper. Nothing in her life mattered if she lost the best man to ever come into her life. With the other men she'd bedded since she'd been married to Shawn, it had only been about sex. But not now. With him, it was about love.

Leila reached for the phone and dialed the private number again. He'd given her this number right after their first tryst.

"Hello."

His deep voice surprised her. "Sweetheart," she breathed through her throbbing heart.

"What can I do for you, Leila?"

She blinked at his tone. As if he were talking to a business associate. "You must be in a meeting."

"No. What do you want?"

She swallowed. "I've been trying to reach you for a week."

"I know."

"I wanted to speak to you so that I could apologize." She waited through his silence and pulled her robe tighter around her. "I'm sorry for the way things ended last time we were together."

"I'm sorry too, Leila, because I thought we had a good thing going."

"We do."

"But you've become too serious, too possessive. It used to be all about fun with us, but now . . . you've taken that away."

She wondered how she had done that. Last week was the first time she'd mentioned their being together. To this point, it had all been about him, the relationship all on his terms.

But she didn't dare protest. She couldn't take the chance of his becoming angrier. "I don't know what came over me, sweetheart," she began quickly. "But I'll never ask about us being together permanently again." She paused. "Please. I need you."

She heard his sigh. "I don't know, Leila. Let's wait and see."

"But I need you now." She hated the desperation in her voice, but what she hated more was the thought of living without him. He made her life with Shawn bearable. Without him, she didn't know what she'd do.

"Let's see how things go between us at the videotaping in Marcus Garvey Park next week."

"You're going to be there?"

"Of course. I have to be. But just keep your distance. There will be too many people there, and I cannot afford a slip-up. I don't want anyone to suspect anything if they see us together."

Again, she wanted to protest. They'd attended many of the same events, and she'd never given him any cause for concern. And she wouldn't now. But she knew her words would mean little—she'd have to show him. "Baby, I promise, we'll be fine."

"We'll see." It was the first time he'd ever hung up without saying good-bye, but Leila held the phone to her ear, wanting to hold on to his last words, even if they weren't filled with the love that she was used to receiving.

Finally she returned the phone to its station. It wasn't the conversation she'd hoped for or even imagined. But at least he'd spoken to her. And he hadn't ended their relationship.

She sank back into her bed. She would be careful. From now on she would make sure that she gave him everything he wanted, all that he needed. She would become his life. And then maybe one day, he'd see what she already knew—that the two of them were put on this earth to spend their lives together.

"I don't know, Allen. It was awful."

"Well, the doctor said she'd be able to help Kelly, right?"

Nona nodded and stood looking out the window at 116th Street. Her beloved Harlem. "Dr. Rutherford said that she's able to open a dialogue with Kelly." Nona sighed. "I guess that's what's most important since my daughter won't talk to me."

"Nona, don't take this personally. Kelly is almost a teenager. In her mind, her mother doesn't know anything."

Nona grunted.

"And Dr. Rutherford is trained to use the right words and the right tone to get Kelly to open up."

Nona remembered the doctor's gentle manner. "Well, whatever works, right?" she said as she returned to her chair.

"And I'll spend more time with Kelly too. Maybe she'll open up to me."

Nona smiled. "Thanks, Allen. I can always count on you." Her smile faded when she looked at him closely. "Are you all right?"

He nodded.

"You just look a bit . . . drawn. You look tired."

He took a breath. "I guess it's all that's going on. And now, with Kelly."

"Don't worry, I know she'll be fine. Dr. Rutherford's good."

"Still, I wonder . . ." He paused and looked down at the floor. It seemed as if he had something to say, but was having difficulty finding the words.

"What are you thinking, Allen?"

When he looked up, a mist covered his eyes. "I have to wonder how much of a toll fighting Reverend Watkins will take on Kelly."

"I can't believe you're saying this." Nona slammed her fist against the desk. "What are you trying to do, make me feel guiltier?"

He held up his hands. "No, not at all. I'm just trying to be the voice of reason to get you to see the other side."

Her eyes were slits as she stared at him.

"I'm being what you've always asked me to be, Nona. A true friend. One who will tell you the truth."

The anger that had been rising in her began to descend. Allen was right; he'd always been the one to say the things she didn't want, but needed to hear. From the beginning, he'd been the reasonable voice when she operated on emotion. Was she doing that now?

"Nona, I don't want you to be mad at me, but I'm thinking about you and Kelly. Maybe what she needs is a clean break. Away from everything that's here. Everything that makes her think she's not good enough."

"And you think LA, the land of the superficial, will make her feel better?" Nona smirked.

"LA will give her a new start, with another support system. It won't all fall on you. It's time for Ronald to be a parent too."

Nona sank into her chair and allowed his words to settle. Maybe he was right. Maybe LA and Ronald would be good for all of them.

She shook her head. "You know what? I don't want to think about this right now because I'm not ready to give up."

He nodded, though she could still see the reservations in his eyes.

"I can make one last stand. The videotaping is a week from today and I think I can rally enough support against Watkins and his ideas."

"But—"

Nona held up her hand. "I promise you, if it doesn't work, then I'll truly consider what you're saying. I'll think about not fighting."

He hesitated, as if there was more he was going to say, but then just nodded. He stood and walked slowly to her side of the desk. "I hope you know how much I love you." He took her hand and lifted her from her seat. He wrapped his arms around her.

"I know, Allen. I love you too."

He held her, and she thought the embrace was to give her strength. But he held her for himself, knowing that if he didn't change Nona's mind, any day the truth would be told and then they would never again share moments like these.

# eighteen

Nona couldn't believe the transformation. Marcus Garvey Park glowed, even under the midmorning sun. Trees were filled with miniature golden lights, and gold garland was wrapped around their trunks. The Harlem park was like an elaborate movie set—which, Nona was sure, was exactly what Derrick wanted to achieve.

"Mom, look." Kelly pointed at the massive trucks that blocked traffic on 124th Street.

Nona smiled at Kelly's enthusiasm. It had been a week since their visit to Dr. Rutherford, and since then, Kelly had made every effort to return to the sweet girl that Nona remembered.

It had been Dr. Rutherford's idea for Kelly to attend the video filming.

"Of course, school is important, Ms. Simms," the doctor had explained yesterday over the telephone. "However, having Kelly participate in major projects such as this will make her feel included. That will only help. And I'll be looking forward to getting her insight on the filming. I think it will tell us a few things."

A security guard motioned for the SUV to pass through the barricades, allowing Ray to drop Nona and Kelly right behind the stage. Before they were out of the car, Derrick rushed to their side.

"How are my two favorite ladies?" He grinned.

Nona knew those words were not meant for her. It was a greeting for Kelly. In the two weeks since she'd changed the venue, her daily conversations with Derrick had been short, strained. Sometimes it sounded to Nona as if Derrick was ready to croak with pain just from speaking with her.

But this morning his greeting was filled with cheer, as if they'd never had any challenges. No one in sight would suspect they'd had so many differences.

"Hi, Mr. Carter," Kelly said. "This all looks so beautiful."

"Thank you, Kelly." He turned to Nona with a glance that made her think he was glad to see her and said, "I have a few things to finish up before the taping starts. You can look around, and then I'll go over everything with you."

Nona nodded, but before she could move away, he added, "Kelly, I could use a little extra help. Would you mind being my assistant for the day?"

Kelly looked to Nona, her face filled with a hopeful grin.

"Go ahead," she said spotting Anna on the other side of the stage.

Nona watched as Derrick handed Kelly a clipboard, then the two trotted toward a team of cameramen. When they were out of sight, Nona sauntered toward Anna, while she took in the park sights around her.

This section of the park was already packed—there had to be more than one hundred people here, and that was just the crew. But Nona knew it was nothing compared to what she expected for the afternoon taping. She prayed the community would respond to the radio ads that she had placed on WBLS, the press releases she'd sent to the *Amsterdam News*, and the announcements she made at Riverside Church, Abyssinian Baptist Church, and several of the smaller churches. This could be a very good day.

But the bit of joy she felt turned into concern as she edged toward Anna. Her friend stood close to her husband, her stance stiff and combative.

"You're my wife," Nona heard the mayor hiss through lips that barely moved.

"Suddenly that means something to you, Anthony?"

"Whatever position I take, you're supposed to be behind me."

"Not if something illegal is going on."

Nona swiveled, changing directions. She'd taken only a few steps before Anna called her name.

When she turned around, Anthony was gone. Nona paused, smiled, and said, "Anna, I didn't see you."

Anna looked at Nona knowing they both knew the truth. She kissed her friend's cheek. "This is going to be fabulous, Nona," she said with excitement and not a trace of the argument with her husband showing.

"I know. Derrick's done a terrific job."

"Doesn't he always? Listen, I have the petitions." She handed half of the pile of papers she held to Nona.

Nona glanced through the sheets. She couldn't believe Anna had designed these official papers in less than a week. This would be the community's voice to the Harlem Empowerment Office. "I can't believe you did all of this."

"I told you I'd do everything to save Brickhouse. We're going to win."

Her words were so different from the ones Allen uttered. So different from the thoughts she held in her own head. She hugged Anna. "Thank you, sweetie."

After a moment, Anna leaned away from their embrace. "Don't worry." She glanced around the park. "I've hired a few political science students from Barnard who will be gathering signatures—some are assigned here at the park and others will be walking the streets." She glanced at her clipboard. "It'll take me all weekend to verify the signatures, but then you can march right into that final public meeting on Monday with the people of Harlem behind you."

Nona breathed deeply. She'd been thinking about not attending the meeting. After all, what purpose would it serve? But Anna had just handed her a glimmer of hope.

Nona hugged Anna again and noticed Leila leaning against a tree across from the stage. She motioned for Leila to join them.

Leila took slow steps to them. "Hey, you guys," she said.

"Hey." Nona placed her hand on Leila's shoulder. "You look terrific," she said as her eyes roamed over Leila's raw silk bronze-colored pants suit that perfectly matched the color of her hair. Nona looked down at the jeans she was wearing. "But I guess I should have mentioned this was casual."

"Oh." Leila pressed her hand along her jacket, smoothing it against her hips. "This is nothing."

"I haven't seen you in the gym in I don't know how long. What's been going on?"

Leila fluttered her fingers in the air. "I've had the flu, or something."

"You should come to the gym and sweat that out."

"I have a sauna at home, Nona," Leila snapped. "Brick-house isn't the only solution."

Nona glanced at Anna, who frowned.

"I'm sorry." Leila sighed. "I haven't been feeling well."

"I understand," Nona said, although she didn't understand at all. She hadn't forgotten the way Leila had spoken to her a week ago when she was at Dr. Rutherford's office. But in the last week, with the rushed preparations for this filming, there hadn't been time to find out what was troubling her friend.

"Uh, Nona, I guess there are going to be a lot of important people here today."

Nona shrugged. "I guess."

"The commissioner, City Council members, maybe a senator," Leila rattled off a list. "We might even get a glimpse of President Clinton." She chuckled as if she'd told a joke.

"I doubt if we'll see the former president," Anna said. "I think you're going to have to settle for just the mayor, Leila."

The three laughed.

Leila said, "I'm going to take a walk around."

"I'll join you," Anna said. "You can help me get some signatures." She waved the petitions in the air.

Nona watched her friends walk away. There was a time when she, Leila, Anna, and Toni had been so close. They shared weekly dinners, monthly outings to Broadway plays—even a few long weekend jaunts to London and Paris for shopping sprees and girlfriend time. And they shared one another's secrets.

But life had stepped in the way. And time had passed, shifting their lives. Anna and Anthony were clearly at odds, and Leila and Shawn—Nona wondered just how many days were left in that marriage.

Then there was Toni. Something was definitely going on with her. Suddenly she was unavailable whenever Nona called and she'd spent her time since the premiere rushing in and out of the gym, never having even a moment to chat.

Nona looked around now; she had not yet spotted Toni. That was strange—her thespian friend never missed an opportunity to primp for flashing cameras.

It seemed all of them had troubled lives, and as soon as the taping was complete and the zoning issue was resolved, she'd get them all together. Even if she were living in LA. She shuddered at that thought.

The park began to fill, and Nona moved through the crowds, with the collar of her tailored shirt pulled high over her neck and her New York Yankees cap pulled low over her eyes. She didn't want to be recognized—she wanted to enjoy the environment as everyone else seemed to be doing. Excitement charged through the park like an electrical current.

She spotted Derrick in the middle of a six-person circle, probably his production team. And Kelly stood by his side. Nona smiled when Derrick turned to Kelly, and she jotted notes on her clipboard.

This man was a riddle wrapped in a mystery. He had disagreed vehemently with her desire to change venues, yet he'd kept the filming schedule on track. He moved through the park as if Marcus Garvey had been his idea. The consummate professional.

In the years since she'd known him, there had been times when she'd wanted to cut him open and prove that he was a man who lived without a heart. But as she watched him now, working, yet taking time with Kelly, she felt herself softening toward Derrick, and she wondered if she'd been wrong. Maybe there was something beating inside his chest.

"Okay, people," Derrick yelled to his team of assistants. "I'm going to take a short break for lunch, but let's be ready to begin taping at two sharp." He turned to Kelly. "Let's find your mom and we can have lunch together."

Instinct made her pull back and disappear into the crush of the crowd. She was close enough to hear Derrick and Kelly, but they hadn't seen her. She blended with the swelling mass, hiding, but watching.

Derrick and Kelly walked around the edges, searching, while Nona watched them. Finally Derrick glanced at his watch. "I guess it's just you and me, kid. You wanna grab a sandwich?"

Nona held her breath as Kelly nodded, and then she stepped just feet behind them as Derrick led Kelly to the catering truck.

"Do you like tuna fish?" he asked.

It was one of her favorite sandwiches, when Nona could get her to eat. She watched Kelly nod her head.

"I'd like mine on wheat, please," she heard Kelly say. "And I'll just have water, instead of a soda."

Nona's eyes remained on them as Derrick took their sandwiches, chips, and drinks to one of the park benches. She stayed in place as Derrick chatted, taking the first bites of his sandwich.

"So, what do you think of the day so far?" Derrick asked Kelly. "Do you like my job?"

"It's exciting. You work with a lot of people."

Nona held her breath as Kelly sat across from him, not moving at first.

"Hey, you don't like your sandwich?" Derrick asked. "I'll get you something else if you want."

Kelly shook her head. "No, this is fine."

It took a moment, but Nona almost jumped with joy when Kelly took the first bite. Then the second. And third. Nona cheered as Kelly chatted and ate, until she had finished the sandwich—although she didn't touch the potato chips.

"Well, young lady, it's time for us to get back to work."

When Derrick and Kelly stood, Nona turned and rushed into the crowd. She hurried through the mass of bodies to the other side of the park. As she moved, she smiled. She had been wrong—Derrick Carter definitely had a heart.

Nona closed the back door to the SUV and kissed Kelly's cheek through the window.

"Mom, can't I stay a little longer?" Kelly pleaded. "It's not like I have school tomorrow."

"You've been here all day, sweetheart. I want you to rest."

"And I promise, we'll get together soon," Derrick added. The way Kelly smiled, Nona knew that Derrick's words were like a judge's gavel. That was all her daughter needed to hear. "And, Kelly, thank you for being such a great assistant today. I couldn't have done it without you."

"You're welcome." Kelly giggled. "I had fun."

Derrick and Nona waved as Ray eased the Escalade from the curb. They stood, shoulder-to-shoulder, until the car turned left into the night.

"Are you ready to face your public?"

It took effort for her to nod her head. She wanted to jump in the car right next to Kelly and go home to her waiting bed. She'd moved and danced and lectured for six straight hours. It would have taken much longer if Derrick hadn't been in charge. Still, her legs ached from the hundreds of side kicks she'd demonstrated, her arms were in pain from the uppercuts she'd shown, her cheeks hurt from keeping that perfect smile for the cameras. And there weren't any words left inside to speak to anyone.

But the press, among others, waited. She had to work through this final act.

Nona turned back toward the park and paused, enjoying

the sight of the set now glowing in the night's darkness. It had been Derrick's idea to have the wrap party right on the set, and the caterers had accommodated. Around the perimeter, cloth-covered tables lined the area holding an international buffet of healthy fare that would rival the meals of the city's best restaurants.

As they moved toward the press circle, Nona noticed the way Derrick's hand gently rested on the small of her back, guiding her, as if he planned to never leave her side.

"Ms. Simms," they screamed when she was in their sight.

Derrick held up his hands and took control. "One at a time." He pointed to one of the raised hands.

"Ms. Simms, I'm Laverne Milner from *People* magazine. This was quite an elaborate setting for just a workout video. What gave you this idea?"

"First, this is so much more than a workout tape. The purpose is to inform and educate," Nona said. "But I'm very aware of how glitz and glamour sells." She glanced at Derrick, and he smiled as if he approved.

"Ms. Simms and I, as the executive producer, wanted a balance," he added. "We both understand the importance of the message, but we both understand the importance of marketing."

*Liar,* Nona thought. She wanted to playfully say that aloud, but she only smiled. If only the press had been privy to their battles. Nonetheless, there was no doubt she was pleased with the results. Even without viewing the final product she knew what Derrick had created.

"Ms. Simms, David Lang, with the *New York Post*. We were a bit surprised by your message before the taping began this afternoon when you asked people to sign the petitions supporting Brickhouse. So, you are concerned that Brickhouse may be closing?"

Nona made sure that the confidence she had worn throughout the day stayed with her now. No one could know that as she danced on the stage that afternoon, she was filled with doubts and fears that this would be her last event in Harlem. "Am I concerned that Brickhouse may be closing?" she repeated the journalist's question. "I know there are many who want to close Brickhouse, but I know that it will not happen. Brickhouse is here to stay."

"Then why the petitions?" the reporter persisted.

"We just wanted to make sure that as the Harlem Empowerment Office looks at the community and moves forward, they understand the importance of Brickhouse to the residents of Harlem."

"I understand that it's already been decided." The reporter refused to stop. "With the rezoning plan, your club will be closing. This is the end for Brickhouse."

Nona smiled and waved her hand in the air. "Rumors."

"More than rumors, Ms. Simms."

Derrick interjected, "Ms. Simms has more than answered your question, Mr. Lang." He looked through the crowd. "Does anyone else have any questions pertaining specifically to why we're here today?"

The questions continued, without David Lang, and Nona answered. It was so comfortable having Derrick by her side. He fielded the rest of the inquiries, allowing Nona long moments of just standing, listening, taking it all in. She watched him and finally decided that she would allow herself to change her mind—she really did like this man.

But her thoughts about Derrick were overwhelmed by her feelings for Brickhouse. As she stood in the middle of the park, surrounded by admirers, Nona thought about David Lang's words, and she prayed this wouldn't be the end.

"Nona, I'm so excited," Anna said as she approached her.

She waved the pile of petitions in front of her. "At first count, we have almost one thousand signatures. Not bad for one day."

"That's wonderful." Nona and Derrick spoke together. They glanced at each other for a long moment, then turned back to Anna.

"I still have to verify the signatures," Anna said, speaking so fast that she didn't notice the exchange between Derrick and Nona. "So I'm going to get out of here now." She hugged Nona. "I don't want you to worry," Anna whispered in Nona's ear. "You're going to walk into that meeting on Monday with Harlem right behind you." She stuffed the petitions into the bag slung over her shoulder.

"Hey, wait a minute," Derrick said. "You didn't get my signature. And I'm Nona Simms's number one fan."

While Nona raised an eyebrow and wondered why her heart fluttered, Anna smiled and handed Derrick the clipboard. "Well, sign right here." When he finished, Anna said, "Well, I'm gone. You two enjoy the rest of the evening." She waved before she disappeared into the night.

"Thank you for doing that," Nona said.

"Of course. I wish I could do more. But it looks like the mayor's wife has it under control. You really have some great friends."

"I do."

Nona glanced through the crowd that still swelled to more than two hundred even in the late hour. She searched for her other friends. She hadn't seen Leila since the taping began, and Toni . . . Nona wondered if she had ever shown up.

"I saw Leila earlier, but I haven't seen Toni," Derrick said as if he read her mind. He followed her gaze through the crowd.

She shrugged. "There are so many people here."

He nodded.

For the next hour, Nona and Derrick moved through the crowd, giving thanks to the crew and answering questions from members of the press. Nona tried to concentrate, but it was difficult with Derrick by her side. She noticed the way he stood so close, the way he touched her gently, the way he whispered in her ear.

"Are you cold?" Derrick asked softly as he guided her toward the catering tables.

She glanced up at him. "No, it's a beautiful night," she said, although she buttoned her cashmere cable sweater. She sipped a cup of Calypso punch, giving her time to watch Derrick. She'd seen him in the sexiest of outfits, but the jeans and black turtleneck he wore today was the best yet.

"I grew up right across the street." She pointed to the redbrick, six-story building. "Right there."

"Really? So you are a Harlem girl."

"All the way."

"I wish you had told me that before I tried to fight you on this venue change."

She searched his face for sarcasm, but he only smiled. "Would it have made a difference?" she asked.

He shook his head. "No."

"I didn't think so."

"Well, look at it this way. We fight so well together."

They laughed.

"Derrick, I do want to thank you, though. You didn't have a lot of time to put this together with all of the changes, and it still turned out wonderfully."

She meant for her words to be an apology of sorts—for all the dissension between them.

"You're welcome. Having the shoot here was a good idea."

There it was—his apology. It made her smile.

He returned his cup to the table. "Well, I'm going to get going," he said.

Nona was surprised that his words disappointed her.

"I have another appointment."

Nona frowned inside, but kept the smile on her face. Another appointment—at eleven o'clock? It sounded more like a Friday night booty call. She took another sip of her punch. Why should she care? She didn't know why, but she did.

"I'll see you soon, Nona." He reached for her, and she was in his arms before she could understand what had happened. It was a professional hug, or more like a spiritual one—the kind that men and women gave each other at church. Only he held her longer than he had to. And she stayed in his embrace because she wanted to. She closed her eyes and inhaled his scent again. When he finally pulled away, Nona wondered what she saw in his eyes. Was it desire? Was it yearning? She was sure he was going to kiss her. She braced herself and almost closed her eyes.

"Good night," he said and turned away.

She was startled and could barely nod her good-bye. She watched him inch through the crowd, stopping for moments to say good-bye, or congratulate someone on a job well done. She watched until he disappeared into the mass of people who remained.

Nona sighed. She was certainly ready to go now.

"Hey, you."

She grinned at Allen as he lifted a water bottle from a steel bucket in front of them. "I haven't seen you in a while," she said, forcing herself to keep her eyes from searching for Derrick.

"I've been moving around. Whew," he said, "this has been some day."

"Yeah, but I'm ready to go home."

"Okay." Allen took Nona's arm and tried to rush her through the people, but they had to pause every few steps, just as Derrick had minutes before, until they reached the curb where Ray had returned.

"Do you want a lift?" Nona asked as she climbed into the SUV.

"Sure."

She told Ray they'd be dropping Allen home first, then leaned back into the seat and closed her eyes.

Allen took her hand. "This was a good day." He paused. "You know, Nona, you've accomplished so much in this city."

She knew his next words before he spoke, so she kept her eyes closed.

"You can be proud of today . . . you can be proud of every moment you've spent in Harlem."

"But it's time to leave," she said for him.

"I think so." He let his affirmation rest in the air. "You and I have always been that one-two knockout punch. Imagine how much bigger and better we could be in LA."

*Bigger and better is not what I want,* Nona thought, though she kept that reflection to herself.

"It's always best to move when you're on top," he said.

*Who made that up?* she wondered.

"The event today was something that Harlem hasn't seen in years," he continued. "This could be your last hurrah."

She was glad when the car slowed in front of Allen's Ninety-sixth Street walk-up, stealing his opportunity to toss more daggers into her heart. She hugged him, without saying a word, but then directed Ray to take off the moment Allen stepped from the car.

"Ray, before I head home, can you take me up 125th Street?"

"Sure thing, Ms. Simms."

Alone, she kept her eyes open as the Escalade rolled through the spirit of Harlem. The clock was inching toward midnight, but it wasn't apparent by these streets. People still walked, shops were still open, the streets pulsed with life. It was Friday night. Nona stared at every sight, photographing it in her memory.

She tried to imagine riding down the streets of Los Angeles and feeling this way. Feeling as if every avenue, every boulevard was part of her DNA. But there was no room in her mind for that. No place else would ever be called home. There was no place like Harlem.

Still, what Allen said made sense. There was too much going on here. Brickhouse, Kelly, this was even taking a toll on Allen. Every time she saw him, he was thinner, paler. This was too much for him too.

It was time to give LA serious consideration. She could force a better deal from Reverend Watkins and his goons. She could make them pay big for what they were doing to her.

Nona leaned back in the seat and closed her eyes again. She couldn't look at Harlem anymore. She had to prepare herself. As she tried to envision the streets of Los Angeles, a single tear slipped from the corner of her eye.

It was almost midnight when Leila glanced out the living room window. The black sky was the canvas for the twinkling of the stars that filled the night. A beautiful sight. At least that had been her thought in the first years of her life in this house. But there was nothing that resembled beautiful now.

She was miserable—as she'd been all day. This morning, she'd fought the thought that she shouldn't go to Nona's filming. She didn't want to see Nona, or Anna, or Toni. But she needed to see her lover.

Too much time had passed since she'd been with him last, and she found that she could barely breathe. For months, her life had been all about him. He kept her beyond happy, and her plan was to feel that way straight to forever.

But just a simple slip of the tongue, just speaking a wonderful thought aloud had pushed him away.

She'd been sure it would be fixed today. She'd purchased just the right suit to remind him of her assets. To force him to remember the pleasure her body gave him. But even when she spotted him from afar, and then stood shoulder-to-shoulder with him in front of the stage, he'd treated her as if they'd never met.

She'd left before the taping began, not wanting anyone to see her tears. What was she going to do if she lost him? That had been her only thought all day as she called his private line and left message after message.

The creak of the garage door opening and rap music thumping from inside the Hummer surprised her, and she glanced at the grandfather clock in the corner of the foyer. It was just after midnight, a bit early for her husband on a Friday night after a game. She almost wished that he would have kept his normal hours, creeping in just before the first sign of morning light.

Shawn opened the door and stopped when he saw her. "What are you doing up?"

She stared at him for a moment. "What are you doing home?"

He chuckled. "If you don't want me here, I can leave easily."

She held up her hand as she passed him. In that instance, she took in the smell of him saturated with another woman's fragrance. "Whatever." She rushed up the stairs. A fight with Shawn Lomax was not what she needed. There was only one place where she wanted to put her effort. And that was finding a way to be with the only man she'd ever really loved.

# *nineteen*

Reverend Watkins barely acknowledged her when she walked into the Harlem Empowerment Office conference room with Allen. Nona walked to the back as the reverend opened the meeting. She leaned against the wall. This time, there were no chairs for the public—no need for other input. It was as if the future had already been decided.

"This won't be a long meeting," Reverend Watkins said and glanced at Nona. "This is to review the schedule now that all permits have been attained and many of the leases have been signed. At this point, we have a seventy-two percent occupancy rate for Harlem East."

The reverend paused, and the committee members gave their nods of approval.

"Mall construction should be complete in sixteen months."

"Reverend Watkins," Nona interrupted. "I have something for the committee."

He didn't hide his sigh. "What is it, Ms. Simms?"

She handed him the pages of the petition. "The people of Harlem would like to be heard," she said as he glanced through the papers. "I have over seven hundred signatures from people who believe in the mall, but also believe that Brickhouse should remain a part of this community."

The reverend shuffled through the papers, took off his reading glasses, and leaned back in his chair. "It appears you have a lot of support, but where are all of these people?" he asked, waving his hands toward the empty space in the conference room. "People are concerned, but why aren't they here to let us hear their voices in person?"

"That's what petitions are for, Reverend," Nona said as if she were explaining the concept to a two-year-old. "People have to work, take care of their children. They don't have time to run behind you and your bandits of—"

Allen touched her arm, stopping her.

She took a breath. "You have to give consideration to the people who will be affected by this."

Reverend Watkins pushed the papers aside. "We will . . . consider your petitions." He looked at the men in front of him and continued, "Now, as I was saying, the contractors have assured me that we will be in business . . ."

Nona tried, but couldn't listen to the reverend's scratchy tone as he droned on. She glanced at the pages of the petition, tossed to the side—which was exactly where Nona suspected they would stay.

*Why am I fighting?* she thought. She stared at the reverend as he spoke, his mouth moving, sounds that made no sense bombarding the air. She felt as if she were jabbing a brick wall. She couldn't win against this man who had probably purchased his doctor of divinity from the *National Enquirer.*

As the reverend continued his "blah, blah, blah" soliloquy, Nona glanced around the table. The committee was attentive, all eyes watching him—all except the mayor. Nona stared at Anthony Leone as he scribbled on the pad in front of him. It was his frown and lack of attention that made Nona wonder if Anna had spoken to her husband. After the argument she'd overheard at the taping on Friday, Nona had decided not to ask Anna about going to her husband anymore. Besides, Anna had done more than any of her friends to help her with this issue.

But clearly, something was troubling the mayor of New York. Maybe Reverend Watkins didn't have all the support he needed.

For fifteen more minutes, Nona stood until she couldn't stand it anymore. She tapped Allen on his arm and motioned toward the door. Before she stepped outside the room, she glanced back at the reverend. He paused and looked at her, then smiled. It was a smirk of victory.

Nona and Allen rode the elevator in silence, and the quiet continued between them until they climbed into the SUV and Ray pulled away from the building where her future was being decided.

"It's over, isn't it?" Nona asked, keeping her eyes focused outside the window.

For the first time since they'd begun these discussions, Allen stayed silent.

"LA is a good market to start over," she said, making the arguments herself now.

Still, Allen was quiet.

"It'll be good for me, the business, and most importantly, Kelly."

Without a word, he took her hand.

She turned to him. "Will you go with us?"

"If you want me to." He squeezed her fingers.

"I couldn't do it without you," she said with tears in her voice.

She leaned back. This was the end. She knew it now. It

didn't make sense to keep fighting. She had to move forward, plan her life for the way it was going to be.

She would be strong. For herself, for Kelly, for Allen. But even with that resolution, she couldn't hold back, and the tears that were in her heart moved to her eyes. She cried.

Allen glared at the phone number on the paper in front of him as if it were a poisonous snake. He had taken his pills a few hours ago, but just looking at the digits made his nausea return.

He reached for the telephone, then pulled his hand away. He stood and walked to his office door, locking it. Then he dialed the number.

"Reverend Watkins," Allen said when the call was answered.

"I've been waiting to hear from you. What the hell was that about petitions? I'm warning you, Allen—"

"You can keep your threats, Reverend. Nona is leaving. She's not going to fight you anymore."

He paused. "Are you sure? It didn't look that way when you two left the meeting."

Allen closed his eyes, remembering every word of Nona's conversation in the car. Even now, what she'd said tore his heart. "Yes, she's ready to leave."

"Brickhouse and Harlem?"

Memories of the years he'd spent with Nona building Brickhouse flashed through his mind. "Yes." It was a struggle for him to say that single syllable.

"Well, Mr. Wade." The reverend paused and laughed. "I guess your reputation is more important than your friendships."

Allen felt bile rising from his stomach.

Reverend Watkins said, "Just make sure that Nona

doesn't change her mind. I don't need any more interference from her. Some members of the committee are already a bit concerned."

"Yes."

"And, Allen, you'd better truly come through or else the entire world will find out that you're more than a traitor. You're a murderer."

Again the reverend laughed, and Allen hung up. He waited a few seconds before he reached for the trash can at the side of his desk. Then he heaved, releasing all that had been building inside him since Reverend Watkins answered the phone.

Nona had been able to stop the tears in her eyes, but cries continued to fill her. She sat behind her desk, staring at the walls of her office, and years passed through her mind. She remembered the days at the beginning when it had been a struggle to pay the bills. She recalled the month when her accountant called to say that she was in the black for the first time. She was reminded of the time when she'd made a ten-thousand-dollar donation to the Boys and Girls Club of Harlem—her first charitable contribution of any size. All because of the success that came with Brickhouse.

She blinked, not wanting to cry again. It was true, she was leaving, but the reverend could never take away what she'd accomplished.

She picked up the phone, needing to hear the reassurances of a friend.

"Hey, Sam, it's Nona. May I speak to Toni?"

There were seconds of silence. "Toni's not available."

Nona frowned. There it was again. The same words. "Sam, what's going on?"

"Nothing. She's just not available."

"Is Toni all right?"

"She's fine. She's just not available."

Nona hung up without saying good-bye. She couldn't take the chance of hearing him say that Toni wasn't available again. She didn't want Sam to be on the bad end of all that she'd been saving for Reverend Watkins.

*What is going on?* she wondered. But before she had time to contemplate that thought, her phone rang.

"Nona, how did the meeting go?" Anna asked.

She shook her head. "I think it's time to let it go, Anna," she said, her voice filled with fatigue. "I've accomplished a lot here and maybe—"

"Don't talk like that."

"I have to face reality."

"I have to see you, Nona."

"No, that's okay. I'm fine really."

"I have to see you," Anna repeated. "Stay in your office. I'll be there in ten minutes."

Anna was gone before Nona could protest, and she hung up the phone. Nona didn't know what her friend wanted, but from the firmness of her tone, she knew she'd better stay still.

Nona was sure now. Kelly had been praying, because God had personally stepped right into the middle of her life.

"I've been gathering this for weeks, Nona. I didn't want to say anything until I had spoken to Anthony. It took me a while to come to terms with things. I was hoping to find something that would prove that what's inside this folder isn't true."

Nona couldn't say a word as she turned the pages in the folder that Anna had given her. It was all here, the back-room deals, the payoffs, the promises of future bonuses—

everything that Reverend Watkins had used to push his project through. Everything that Nona needed to bring him down.

"I can't believe this," she whispered.

"It's all true. Anthony confirmed it."

Nona looked up for the first time since she'd been given these sheets of gold. "Anthony was involved in all of this?"

Anna shook her head. "I don't think so. I believe most of it was done by the time he found out. But still, he didn't do anything about it." Anna sighed and sat in front of Nona's desk. "Anthony feels some strange allegiance to that jerk Watkins because they went to college together and because the reverend helped him get elected."

"I still have a hard time believing Reverend Watkins went to any college."

They laughed, although the sound was not filled with cheer.

Anna said, "The key is that Anthony did nothing, and now he's vulnerable."

Nona caressed the folder as if it were a child. "But Anna, if I go public with this, it could ruin Anthony. I don't want to do that."

"I don't think you'll have to go public, Nona. Once the reverend finds out what you know, he'll have to back off."

Nona shook her head as if she were unsure.

"Look, you're only asking to keep Brickhouse. You're not trying to stop the building of the mall. Hell, I think Harlem East is still a good idea—even if it's going to make Reverend Watkins a multimillionaire."

Nona sat still, staring at the papers. When she looked up, her eyes were filled with tears, but they were different from the ones she'd shed just an hour before. She stood and walked to her friend.

"Anna, you have saved my life."

"It's nothing more than you've done for me. I'll never forget how you were there for me after Todd's death."

Nona nodded. "But . . . I'm afraid. I'm thinking about what this is going to do to you and Anthony."

Anna's eyes were sad. "This didn't destroy me and Anthony. A wall has been building between us brick by brick, day by day. The only thing I can hope for now is that we don't destroy each other."

"Oh, Anna."

Anna held up her hand. "Don't feel sorry for me. Surprisingly, I feel better now than I have in years. I have the Children's Literacy Outreach program that makes me very happy." She smiled and took Nona's hand. "And now I know that I will have you. Still here at Brickhouse, taking care of me and my body. And being my friend."

Nona hugged her. "I don't know what to say. I'm so grateful. I won't ever be able to pay you back."

Anna leaned away. "Just go kick that reverend's butt. That's all the payback I need."

"I think I can do that."

Anna smiled. "And once you get the reverend to see things the right way, please keep this information just between us." She looked away, and her smile was gone. "I'm not trying to ruin Anthony. My husband is doing a good job of that all by himself." When she glanced up at Nona, she was smiling again. "I think you have an appointment to make, girlfriend."

When they hugged again, Nona could feel her friend's strength in her embrace. And with all that she'd been through, this was the first time that Nona was absolutely sure. Anna would be all right.

# twenty

On the one hand, Nona couldn't wait to be in front of Reverend Watkins and hand him the grenade that would blow his world apart. On the other hand, the thought of being alone with him made her want to throw up. It was the side of her filled with fight that pushed her to make the call.

"Well, Ms. Simms," the reverend said when she was put through to his line by his secretary. "It is a pleasure to hear from you."

She wanted to laugh—he wouldn't be saying that in an hour. "Reverend, I would like to meet with you this afternoon, if possible."

"Sure." She heard the smirk in his tone. "We can get together." He paused. "I'm sure you want to finalize some things."

"That's exactly what I want to do."

"Great. You know, Nona, I wanted to tell you this morning, but you left so quickly. This is going to be good for you too. You've worked hard all of these years. Now you will only have your restaurant to be concerned with. This is really for the best, you'll see."

His words made her almost gag, but she'd let him have his moment. She glanced at her watch. "I can be there in an hour."

"Five o' clock. That's good," he said. "By then everyone will be gone and I'll be able to concentrate on you."

"Thank you," she said, keeping as much civility in her voice as she could manage.

When she hung up, she imagined that he was leaning back in his chair, his fingers entwined behind his head, wearing a smile of victory. She couldn't wait to slap that smirk off his face.

She made copies of the file and made a note to herself to put the originals in the safe, located in the building's security room, on her way out. Then, she called Ray to take her to what she prayed would be the final meeting with Reverend Watkins.

In the car, she couldn't keep her thoughts away from the one paper in her arsenal that still shocked her. The one designed to destroy her and her business. She pulled that letter from the folder in her lap and reread the words that she'd just about memorized. She'd always known the reverend was a crook. But what amazed her now were the people willing to lie in bed with him. Make any kind of deal—for the sake of making money.

She shook her head. Not only was she going to bring the reverend down, but she'd be going against old adversaries. And she was about to knock every one of them out—with a single Brickhouse side kick.

It was just after five when she stepped into the receptionist area of the Harlem Empowerment Office, but there was no one behind the desk.

"Hello," she yelled out.

A moment later, the reverend walked into the hallway. "Ms. Simms, it's good to see you."

She wondered if he had purchased all the powder-blue polyester in the country and then had some tailor make him a dozen leisure suits.

"Let's go to my office." He motioned with his hand, letting her walk ahead of him.

Nona could feel his eyes, watching her from behind, and for a moment she wondered if it had been a good idea to come alone. Maybe she should have told Allen.

No, she thought. Reverend Watkins might be a snake, but he was a coward. And she was sure he was a smart coward. He knew that she could kick his butt anytime she wanted.

"Nona," he began when they were finally in his office. "Like I was saying on the phone, I don't want you to feel bad about this."

"I don't feel bad at all, Reverend."

He motioned for her to sit on the couch, but she chose a chair in front of his desk. He chuckled. "I'm glad because I don't want us to be enemies. I've always liked you, and I promise we'll work out a deal that will be incredible for you."

"I know we'll be able to work something out." She crossed her legs, and when she saw the tip of the reverend's tongue slide against his lips, she tugged at the edge of her skirt.

The reverend coughed. "Well, let's begin. Why don't you tell me what you expect in this deal?"

For a second, she wanted to draw out the moment. Savor the knowledge that the reverend was about to drown in his own dirty pool. But she didn't want to stay with this man a minute longer than she needed to, so she pulled out the paper that was most damaging. She slid it across his desk, and before he could put on his glasses to examine the page, she said, "I know about the deal you have with the New

York Fitness Club, Reverend." She paused and watched his eyes widen. "You know, you got them to do what I was never able to. I tried to convince Marilyn Gagney years ago to bring one of those clubs to Harlem, and you were able to do it."

"What is this?"

"This," Nona began, holding up the folder, "is what I need to stop you from destroying me."

She couldn't remember a time when the reverend had been silent.

"I can't say that I blame you, Reverend. I mean, you are going to make a fortune by getting me out of Harlem, bringing the New York Fitness Club here and giving them a ready-made clientele—all of the members of Brickhouse. This really was brilliant."

"I don't know where you got this—"

"Well, if this isn't enough for you, why don't you take a look at these?" She handed him paper after paper of the deals he'd made—the kickbacks from the contracts he'd awarded, the percentage from the leases he'd negotiated. She let him soak in the damaging papers. "I'm sure you realize that I can bring you and everyone on that committee down with what I have here. Although I'm sure you're the only benefactor. Isn't it a shame that men may go to jail who had nothing to do with this?"

When he looked at her, she almost thought he was going to cry. "What do you want?"

She smiled. "I want Brickhouse. That's it. I don't really care about your other dealings. You're a criminal, but the people of Harlem will find that out sooner or later. I have no doubt you'll live your last days shriveled up in some top-security penal institution."

His wide eyes became as wet as his drippy hair.

"But that's not my concern, right now," Nona said. "I keep Brickhouse and none of this has to come to light."

He shook his head. "I don't know how I can do that."

"You'll figure something out, because I have it on good authority that if any of this ever comes out, not even the mayor will be able to save your sorry ass."

"I don't know how to change things."

"Oh, Reverend, you don't have any imagination." Nona leaned back in her chair and smiled. "All you have to do is say that you've had a change of heart. Not that anyone believes that you have a heart. But you can lie, like you always do, and say that when you reviewed the petitions, you were so moved that you had to listen to the people of Harlem."

He leaned back in his chair, taking the stance that he always did, but there was little arrogance in him now. "Well, Ms. Simms, you've certainly given me something to think about."

She raised her eyebrows. "You're smarter than that, Reverend Watkins."

"I need some time."

"I understand." She looked at her watch. "I'll give you sixty seconds," she said without looking up.

"Ms. Simms, I can't possibly—"

"Fifty seconds."

"There are other people involved."

"Forty seconds."

"You can't expect me to just change everything—"

She looked at him. "In thirty seconds, this news hits the papers, and the only thing you'll have to think about then is how you're going to keep your cellmate, Bubba, off your greasy behind."

"You're being unreasonable."

She glanced at her watch again. "Ten seconds." They were silent until Nona stood. "What's your decision?"

"Ms. Simms, I don't believe—"

She walked to the door.

"Fine," he yelled out.

She took her time turning back to him. "Brickhouse stays." Her question really was a statement.

He glared at her and nodded.

She smiled. "You've made the right decision." She glanced at the folder on his desk. "And you can keep those papers. I have *plenty* of copies." She returned his stare. "Have a good evening."

Nona almost ran from his office, and instead of waiting for the elevator, she trotted down the stairs, needing to release the adrenaline that was raging inside her. She was out of breath when she got to the car.

"Do you want to go home, or back to Brickhouse?" Ray asked before he started the SUV.

Nona looked at her watch. "You know what? We still have thirty minutes. Let's pick up Kelly from the doctor. I'll call Odessa."

She called her housekeeper, then leaned back in the car as Ray turned south onto Park Avenue. New York City. This was her home, and now she knew for sure . . . it always would be.

"Mom, what are you doing here?" Kelly asked.

"I wanted to spend some time with my daughter, is that okay?"

Kelly smiled. "Yeah, that's great."

Nona looked over Kelly's shoulder to Dr. Rutherford's closed door.

"Mom, let's go," Kelly said.

Nona nodded and took her hand. "So how was your day?"

"School was okay, but it was good with Dr. Rutherford."

There was a pang in Nona's heart as she and Kelly climbed into the Escalade. Although she was so pleased that Kelly agreed Dr. Rutherford had been a good idea, she still wished that Kelly would open up to her. But the doctor had assured Nona that would come with time.

"Anything you want to tell me about?" Nona asked as Ray pulled the car into traffic.

"Not yet." Kelly paused. "I hope that's okay, Mom."

"Of course. As long as you're feeling better."

"I am."

Nona squeezed her hand. "Good. Well, I want you to know that everything is fine with Brickhouse. The zoning committee has decided to let everything stand the way it is."

"Mom, that's terrific. But I knew it was going to work out. I've been praying for you."

Nona squeezed her hand. "I know you have. Thank you, sweetie." She looked out the window. "I think I want to celebrate."

"That sounds like a good idea."

"Let's stop at Baskin-Robbins."

Kelly hesitated. "Before dinner?"

"Now who's the kid and who's the parent?"

Kelly laughed. "I just didn't think we should have dessert first."

"Since today was such a good day for both of us, let's do something different."

A few seconds passed before Kelly said, "Okay."

"Ray, there's a Baskin-Robbins on Seventy-sixth Street. Can we stop there?" Nona aked.

In the store, Nona ordered a double scoop of Strawberry Crunch.

"I'll just have a small vanilla yogurt," Kelly said.

The clerk nodded.

"Is that nonfat?" Kelly asked.

The clerk nodded again.

Outside the store, Nona said, "Let's take a walk around the block."

While Kelly chatted about her day at school, Nona watched her dip the tip of the spoon into her cup, taking the smallest nibbles. Within minutes, Kelly tossed the still half-filled cup into one of the street trash cans.

Nona finished her ice cream, then put her arm around Kelly's shoulders as they continued to walk and chat. She wanted to go back and get that cup of yogurt. Tell Kelly that she was beautiful, and wonderful, and smart, and the perfect daughter. And with all of that, it was certainly safe to eat.

But she said nothing, following the advice of Dr. Rutherford. *You cannot force Kelly to eat.* Nona remembered the doctor's words. *Kelly's been opening up. I know she's getting better.*

It was clear to Nona that Kelly was trying. After her third session, Kelly had agreed that Dr. Rutherford had been a good idea. And Nona could tell just from conversations that Kelly was feeling better about herself. Surely normal eating couldn't be far away.

Kelly was doing better. Brickhouse was going to stay in Harlem. Nona squeezed Kelly in a hug. With just a little patience and a lot of tenacity, life had certainly turned out better than good.

Allen groaned when his toes hit the edge of the shower stall. He grabbed a towel, wrapped it around his waist, and hurried to the telephone. He shivered in the cool room as water dripped from his chest onto the carpet. His forehead creased with concern when he glanced at the caller ID.

"Nona, what's wrong?" he asked as soon as he put the phone to his ear.

"Nothing. I'm sorry to call you so late."

Allen glanced at the clock. It was five after eleven. Nona never called him once she left Brickhouse. Years ago she'd established that home time was for Kelly.

"Don't worry about it being late. What's going on?"

"I have incredible news." She took a breath. "Our fight with Reverend Watkins is over."

He slumped onto the bed, reminded that she was losing her business because of him. "I know this is tough, Nona. But it's for the best."

"Oh, no, Allen. The fight's over, but not that way. Reverend Watkins has backed down. He's agreed to let Brickhouse stay."

Allen stood, moving as if he'd heard her words in slow motion. "He's agreed?" he asked, knowing her words hadn't reached his brain correctly. "How? Why?"

Nona chuckled. "Let's just say he wants to stay out of jail."

The chill that Allen felt when he first jumped from the shower was replaced by a heat that made him feel faint. "What did you do?"

She hesitated. "Nothing. Reverend Watkins just realized that he messed with the wrong woman. But the key is we won't have to deal with that counterfeit preacher ever again."

Now it felt as if ice were pumping through his veins. He knew for sure that Nona's words weren't true. They would never be rid of that man. "I don't understand. What happened, Nona?"

"Nothing happened that you need to be concerned about. The most important thing is that it's over. I had planned to tell you in the morning, but I couldn't wait. And I wanted you to sleep better tonight too, knowing that the fight is over."

With this news, Allen was sure that he wouldn't sleep at all.

"Thank you, Allen."

"For what?"

"For being there for me and telling me the truth. Even when I didn't want to hear it. You were right, but God gave us a last-minute reprieve."

Allen swallowed the lump in his throat.

"Good night," she said before she hung up.

He returned the phone to his nightstand and slowly fell onto the bed. How did Nona get the reverend to back away? A million scenarios flashed through his mind, but he couldn't find one that made sense.

Reverend Watkins was not the kind of man who walked away from anything. There was more to this story, and Allen knew it wouldn't have a happy ending. Would the reverend call Nona in the middle of the night and tell her about the drugs? Would there be a front page article in the *New York Post* tomorrow about drugs being supplied through Brickhouse?

He took the towel from around his waist and wiped the perspiration that once again covered his body. When his cell phone began to ring, he stared at his jacket folded against the chair next to his bed. Another lump, larger this time, choked him. He tossed the towel onto the floor, grabbed his cell phone, and looked at the incoming call number. He didn't want to answer.

"What do you want, Watkins?"

"Don't use that tone with me, Allen. You have some big problems right now."

The reverend's speech sounded slurred, as if he'd been drinking. "I told you I was not playing games. But I guess you didn't believe me."

He stood, in the middle of his bedroom, naked, listening and waiting for the reverend to pull the trigger that would destroy him.

"Why didn't you tell me what your boss planned to do?"

"I don't know what you're talking about. Last time I talked to Nona, she agreed to move to LA."

"That's not what that bitch said tonight. She threatened me."

He wished he could smile. He wished he could cheer. He wished he'd been a part of that meeting—when Nona brought this man to his knees.

But he could find no joy, knowing that Nona's victory was fleeting.

"Have you forgotten we have a deal, Allen?"

"Of course not. But I don't know what I can do now. If Nona—"

"If Nona doesn't get out of Harlem, I'm going to reveal everything about the drugs and Todd's death. Brickhouse will be closed anyway."

He was a grown man, built like a contestant for Mr. Olympia. But right now all Allen wanted to do was sit in the middle of his floor and cry. Or die. It really didn't matter which to him.

"Reverend Watkins, I don't know what I can do. I used everything I had—"

"Well, it wasn't enough." His speech was suddenly clearer. "I should have known not to send a boy to do a man's job." He paused. "Be at my office at eight in the morning. I have a plan."

Allen wanted to protest. He wanted to tell the reverend to drop dead. But as he opened his mouth to utter those words, the images returned in his mind: The police rushing Brickhouse. Nona in handcuffs. Kelly screaming.

"Allen, did you hear me?"

"I'll be there."

"I know you will."

Allen stared at his phone for a few minutes before he clicked "end." Still naked, he fell onto his bed and lay on his back. He closed his eyes, folded his hands across his stomach, and imagined himself dead. But not even that would help Nona.

He sat up, opened his nightstand drawer, and slipped three pills into his palm. He'd never taken that many at once, and he couldn't wait for the peace to fill him. He swallowed the drugs and returned to his position. As the steroids streamed into his blood, new visions filled him. Of the days before his pain started, before he had returned to the drugs. Before he had ruined his best friend.

Soon, unconsciousness relieved him, and on the night that he was sure he'd never close his eyes, he slept.

# twenty-one

Nona wiped the perspiration that still rolled down her neck and took a deep breath. That had been a great work-out. She'd returned to her classes and her own training with a new vigor. She couldn't remember a better time in her life. After five sessions, Dr. Rutherford said that Kelly was making superior progress. And Brickhouse was here to stay.

The only issue facing her now was her friends. She'd called all of them, wanting to see if they wanted to chip in and put together a Thanksgiving gala. But Leila was still distant, Toni was still missing in action—Nona couldn't even find her in the gym—and Anna said she wasn't in the mood for any holiday festivities. Even Allen had passed on her idea to spend Thanksgiving together. He was the biggest surprise of all. She didn't understand it. She was sure her news last week about Reverend Watkins would have made Allen relax, return to normal. But he seemed even more listless and distracted. She'd even had to cover two of his personal training sessions over the weekend, and that had never happened before.

Well, now that Brickhouse's zoning was resolved, she could put more of her attention to her friends.

As she passed her assistant's desk, Sarah said, "Nona, you have a call. It's Derrick Carter."

Nona smiled, surprised at how good it made her feel to hear his name. "I'll take it in my office."

A few seconds later, she lifted her phone. "Derrick, good to hear from you."

"Good speaking to you as well. How's Kelly?"

She smiled. "She's well. Thanks for asking."

"Great." His tone turned somber. "Nona, do you have time to meet with me this evening?"

"Sure, is something wrong?"

"There is something we need to discuss."

"Sounds serious. What's wrong?"

"I'd rather do this face-to-face."

"Okay, why don't we have dinner?" The words came out before she had a chance to think about it.

She cringed at his long silence. *What was I thinking?* she asked herself.

"Dinner?" he repeated as if it were a foreign word.

She wanted to slap herself.

He said, "I was just thinking about having you come to my office."

She wanted to slap him.

"But dinner would be great," he finally agreed.

She could hear his smile, and she exhaled. "We can eat here at my restaurant."

"Let me take a raincheck on that, because tonight we need to meet far away from Brickhouse."

She frowned. "This is beginning to sound quite serious, Derrick."

"It is, Nona."

"Now I'm really concerned. What's going on?"

"I'll tell you everything tonight."

By the time she hung up, she knew where they were meeting and what time, but nothing else. She tried to imagine what news he could have, but then she shook her head. She wasn't going to sit and imagine the worst. Everything bad was behind her. Whatever news Derrick had, she'd handle. She'd beaten Reverend Watkins, and that was close to winning a match with the devil. If she could do that, she could do anything.

She smiled. "Bring it on, Mr. Carter. I'm ready for whatever you have." She stood and headed toward the locker room for a shower.

Nona was pleased that Derrick had chosen the Sugar Hill Bistro. Not only was this one of her favorite restaurants, but she was pleased that Derrick Carter was a man who recognized that some of the city's best eateries were in Harlem.

Derrick held her velvet-covered chair out for her as she sat. "I think you'll like the food here," he said. "This is one of my favorite places."

She smiled. "I've been here a few times." She placed her napkin on her lap as the tuxedoed waiter filled their crystal water glasses.

When the waiter stepped away, Derrick said, "Thank you for meeting me on such short notice."

"Of course, business is top priority."

He smiled. "Yes, business is number one."

Beyond the Armani suit, beyond the Versace Man cologne, she saw something new today. His brown eyes seemed to dance when he smiled. Through the light of the candle that rested in the middle of their table, his eyes glowed, and it made her wonder why he wasn't married.

"I do have some good news," she said. "I'm out of danger with the Harlem Empowerment Office. Brickhouse is going to remain in place."

His smile widened, and he lifted his water. "Congratulations." He tapped his glass against hers. "You've had quite a few successes over the last few weeks, haven't you?"

*If you only knew,* she thought. Kelly, Brickhouse—life was going well. "The past few months have been challenging, but I've come out on top. I'm certainly blessed."

"That you are."

When he paused, Nona wondered what he saw when he looked at her.

"I enjoyed the wrap party," he said, leaving her wondering.

"The entire day was good. You did a great job. I still can't believe all the people you got to attend."

"I'm still surprised Toni Lee wasn't there since the two of you are such good friends."

Everything that had made her happy in the minutes before was gone. The compartments where she'd hidden the memories of that awful Derrick Carter opened and poured out all that she'd forgotten. And she remembered. This was a man she almost hated. How could she forget that? And how could he even form his lips to say Toni's name to her?

"Maybe she didn't attend because she knew you'd be there," she said. "Especially after the way you treated her."

He looked at her for a long moment. "Nona, my relationship with Toni is really none of your business."

She took a sip of water, drowning the words she wanted to say.

He continued, "But since I was the one who brought up her name, I want you to know something."

She put her glass down. "Let's get back to business, Mr. Carter. We're not here to discuss you and Toni."

He bristled when she addressed him formally. "I know why we're here."

The waiter interrupted them. "Are you ready to order?"

They scanned the menus, but the appetite that Nona had brought with her was gone. Still, they had business to finish, and she ordered the catfish salad, while Derrick asked for filet mignon—medium rare—and Caribbean potatoes.

The waiter had taken only a few steps away when Derrick said, "I'm sure you believe you know everything about me and Toni. But you only know it from the way she tells it." He paused. "Did you know that Toni and I broke up before I knew she was pregnant?"

Nona shifted in her seat. This was private ground, and she didn't want to discuss her friend, not with this man. But it was Derrick who kept her silent. As he spoke, his eyes, which had flickered with delight just minutes before, were filled with sadness. And misery slumped his shoulders.

"But once I found out about the child, I made it clear to Toni that I would be there for her and the baby, always."

Nona tried to keep her surprise inside. All she'd known was that her friend was pregnant and Derrick Carter was nowhere to be found. Toni had never told her anything more.

He continued, "But even though I made that commitment to Toni, she had an abortion. Without my knowledge." He paused, letting his words set with Nona.

She stayed still.

"I called Toni for weeks," he continued. "When she finally called me back and told me that she'd gotten rid of the baby—" He stopped, and his voice became softer. "I was shocked and I was devastated because the one thing I've always wanted to be is a father."

The candle on their table flickered wildly, then slowly went out.

Nona wanted to reach across the table and take his hand. She had never heard such sadness in a man.

"I don't know, Nona. Maybe Toni and I would have married, maybe not. With what I've learned about her, whatever we had never would have lasted anyway. But the one thing I would have been was a good father."

Nona swallowed.

"I'm almost forty, extremely successful by most standards. But I'd give it all up to be . . ."

In that moment, she remembered his times with Kelly. His patience, his concern, the ease with which he spoke to her and encouraged her.

"Derrick, I'm sorry. I didn't know."

He looked at her for a moment, then lifted his shoulders, sat up straight, and took a deep breath. "There's no need to feel sorry for me. I have a life that I'm grateful for. And who knows—maybe there's still a plan for me to have a family."

She nodded.

"Anyway . . ." He paused and cleared his throat. "Like you said, we're not here to discuss this." He stopped when the waiter returned, and as Nona looked at Derrick's plate, she wished she had a mound of the spicy mashed potatoes in front of her. Her appetite had returned.

After he said grace, they chatted about Kelly, but a few minutes later, Derrick put his fork down.

"I hate to be the one to bring this to you, but this time at least I caught it early," he said.

She stabbed at a catfish slice. "What's going on?"

"You know we worked frantically last weekend to get the video edited and ready for production to get last-minute distribution for the holidays."

"I know. I received my copy last Tuesday. I have my master locked in my safe."

"Really? Well, someone is already making unauthorized copies of your video."

She dropped her fork. "What?"

"Because of the problems we had with the last video, I had my tech guys put a plan in place. This time, I only made two formatted discs of the video—you have one and I have the other."

"Okay."

"I programmed both of the discs so that if either were being copied, my computer would be alerted."

"How did you do that?"

He waved his hand in the air. "It's a complicated process, if you don't understand programs. Suffice it to say, I know copies are being made."

She picked up her fork again. "Well, Derrick, it has to be your disc or some problem with the program you installed. My disc is locked up."

"Not only am I sure it's yours because the computer knows which disc is being copied, but I can even tell you the date and time when it was done."

Her fork slipped from her hand and onto the floor with Derrick's words. This wasn't possible. There were only two people who had access to the main safe where she kept the disc—she and Allen.

The waiter rushed over and handed Nona a new fork, but she put it down, knowing she wouldn't eat any more tonight.

"I don't understand," she said, more to herself than to him.

Without a word, Derrick lifted a page from his briefcase and handed it to her. He looked as if he felt sorry for her. "I wanted to let you know as soon as possible because these bootleg videos could really affect our holiday sales."

On the page he gave her was the time and date that the

disc had been copied. It was three nights ago—Friday. She'd been home, having dinner with Kelly, helping her daughter practice her lines as Lady Macbeth. She remembered how she had basked in that time, knowing that her life had turned around, knowing that it would all be easy from this point.

She tucked the paper into her purse and stared at her salad.

"Nona, I'm sorry. Maybe I should have told you this after we finished eating."

"No, I had to know." She paused. "Derrick, would you mind if I left now? I really want to get to the bottom of this."

"But it's after eight. I don't know what you can do tonight, except check to see if the disc is still missing."

She shivered—imagining her disc being passed from one bootlegger to the next—possibly traveling across the country already. She slipped her purse strap onto her shoulder. "I'll check on the disc in the morning, but I know I won't be good company anymore tonight."

He nodded and motioned for the waiter.

"No, please stay," Nona said. "I don't want to ruin your dinner."

He shook his head. "I need to get home too. And my dinner is already ruined if my dinner partner is not here with me."

Nona tried to smile, but her head was filled with confusion. Someone was making copies of her video. Someone she knew. Someone she trusted.

As Derrick paid the bill, she tried to imagine all the reasons Allen would make copies of her video. Without her knowing.

By the time Derrick stood and she followed, she was sure—there was no way Allen was involved.

Still, there was someone out there—who knew her, who had access to her safe, who had betrayed her.

Outside, she wrapped her cape tighter around her shoulders. But it wasn't the night air that filled her with chills.

"Will you call me and let me know what you find out?" Derrick asked.

She nodded. "I don't know whether to be sad or angry."

"Don't decide until you find out what's going on. No need to waste hours wallowing in the wrong emotion."

She couldn't help but smile at his words. "That's good advice."

"And I promise I'll be sufficiently outraged along with you when we figure out what's going on."

"Thank you." She almost chuckled.

Ray eased Nona's Escalade to the curb, and Derrick walked her to the SUV.

"I'll call you tomorrow," he said, helping her inside. Before he closed the door, he added, "I had a good time tonight, Nona. Even if we wasted a couple of minutes because you tried to get on my case."

"That's not what I meant to do."

He smiled. "Yes, it was. For a few minutes there, when I was talking about Toni, you couldn't decide if I should live or if I should die."

As they laughed, neither noticed the limousine that pulled up behind the Escalade.

Derrick said, "But I'm glad you've decided that I should live."

"It was an easy decision, Mr. Carter."

He paused. "I think you're a very special lady." He leaned forward and kissed her cheek, letting his lips linger against her skin.

No one saw the woman when she stepped from the car, then paused and stared at them.

It took Toni a moment to recognize Derrick and Nona. She watched as Derrick kissed Nona, then she rushed back to her car.

"I've changed my mind," she said to her driver. "Take me home."

When her Town Car eased around the SUV, Toni strained to catch a glimpse of her friend. And at the same time, she fought to keep the tears from her eyes.

Leila paced the length of the hotel room. The robe that accompanied the satin teddy she wore fluttered at the top of her thighs. She looked at the clock. It was almost nine. Her lover was two hours late. She picked up her cell phone again, but before she could punch in his number, the lock on the hotel room door clicked.

He had stepped inside but hadn't closed the door when she yelled, "Where have you been?"

He let the door close and stared at her. "If you don't lower your voice, I'm out of here."

She glared at him.

"I mean it, Leila. I've had it."

She exhaled. "It's just that we were supposed to get together two hours ago."

His expression said, *So what.*

"I was worried," she said, softening her quivering voice. She sucked in her stomach and sauntered toward him, allowing the robe to flow behind her. She wrapped her arms around his neck. "I don't want to fight. It's been weeks since we've been together. I've missed you." She pressed her lips against his.

He leaned back. "I don't know why you're dressed like that. I told you we were only going to talk."

She pouted, poking out her lips the way he had told her

he liked. "But I want you so badly." She kissed his neck. "And I know you want me." She pressed against him. "I can feel you," she panted.

He grabbed her wrists and pushed her away, making her stumble backward onto the bed. "I told you, Leila, it's over between us."

"But I don't understand. We have such a wonderful relationship."

"We used to have a good thing, but you ruined that by talking about marriage."

"I said I was sorry."

"And now you're stalking me. Like some damn obsessed fanatic."

She closed her robe, covering her breasts. "I'm not doing that."

"You call me fifteen, twenty times a day. You interrupt me in meetings; you harass me when I'm home. You're worse than the paparazzi." He paused and turned his back. "I'm sorry, Leila. I told you. It's over."

"I promise, sweetheart. I'll be better." She lifted herself from the bed and let the robe slide from her shoulders. She posed, the way she'd seen Toni Lee do in so many movies, and she could tell from the way his Adam's apple jumped that the see-through teddy was working. "I'll do whatever you want me to do," she purred.

His eyes moved from her crotch to her eyes, and he twisted his mouth in disgust. "Put your clothes back on, Leila. Begging doesn't become you." He looked at his watch and sighed. "Look, it's more than what's been going on between us. There's a lot happening, and I can't put my life and career at risk anymore."

"But I love you."

He shook his head.

"No, please . . ." She grabbed his wrist as he turned to the door.

"I've said all I came to say."

"But, sweetheart, how can you just leave me like this? Don't you know how much I love you?"

He yanked his hand from her grasp. "Don't make me sorry that I ever got involved with you, Leila."

"Please, I said I'd do anything."

He moved toward the door and reached for the doorknob. When he looked back, his eyes were blank, as if he no longer even knew her name.

"Anthony, please. Don't go."

"Good-bye, Leila."

And she cried as she watched the mayor walk through the door and out of her life forever.

## twenty-two

It had taken almost everything Nona had inside her to stay in bed until the first morning light. Still, she'd dressed and walked into Brickhouse before the clock ticked to seven.

She entered the building, nodded at the first-shift employees, and then rushed to the security room. There were three keys—only she, Allen, and Charles, the chief of security, had access. But only she and Allen knew the combination to the master safe.

She stepped inside the darkened room that was the size of a small walk-in closet. In here, she kept her most important business papers, membership files, anything that she wanted to make sure would never become available to the public.

She walked slowly to the safe in the back and trembled as she punched in the digital code. She paused a moment when it beeped three times. After taking a breath, she pulled the door.

It took seconds for the sight to register. The disc was in the safe—lying on top of a pile of folders. She was surprised, and relieved. At least the vision that had filled her dreams all night of her disc traveling across the country from one counterfeiter to another wouldn't come true. Unless multiple copies had already been made.

Nona sorted through the rest of the files, making sure nothing else was missing, especially the file that Anna had given her. Everything was where she'd left it—although she didn't know what else had been taken and returned. She closed the safe, then shuddered as she looked around the room. Who had been here?

There was little comfort in finding the disc. If it had disappeared once, it could happen again.

In her office, she glanced at her watch. It was just ten after seven. Charles, the chief of security, would be in at nine, and Nona wondered how she'd survive that long. She shifted through the mail Sarah had left on her desk, but the words blurred together on every page. She shoved the pile of letters aside. From the moment Derrick told her this news till now, it had consumed her, but she hadn't been able to make sense of it. Who would make copies of her video? And, how did they get into her safe? She was more convinced now than she'd been last night that it wasn't Allen, but that left her with a blank mental canvas of suspects.

By eight o'clock Nona was staring out the window watching Harlem come alive. Residents moved through the streets, tending to their lives—on their way to work, to school, to taking care of whatever business needed to be done. It was a normal day. Normal for everyone except her.

By quarter to nine, she was speed-walking across her office, checking her watch every thirty seconds. At nine, she was waiting at Charles's door.

"Nona, good morning," Charles said, taken aback by her standing guard in front of his office. "Did we have a meeting?"

She shook her head. "I just need to speak with you." She

folded her arms as he unlocked his office, and then she followed him inside.

"What can I do for you?"

She waited until he hung his jacket behind the door and sat at his desk. "I want to review the security check-in log."

He frowned a bit. "Sure." He unlocked his bottom desk drawer, pulled out the ledger, and rested it on his desk.

After her first two years in business, Nona realized that not many members used the club after nine. Since then, she'd made nine o'clock the closing hour, but Brickhouse was open until midnight during the week for members to have access to retrieve any personal effects from lockers. It was Charles who suggested, when he joined the Brickhouse team, that after nine, everyone should sign in.

It hadn't made much sense to her then.

"Just extra precautions," he said at that time.

She was grateful for it now.

Nona flipped back the pages. "You were on duty on Friday night."

Charles looked at the page Nona turned to. "Yup. That's my late night. It was pretty quiet. Fridays always are."

Nona looked down at the page and at first sighed with relief. Allen's name was not on the list. But then lines of anxiety creased her forehead. There were only two names: Tracie, a young trainer she'd hired two months before and . . . Toni Lee.

Nona inhaled when she saw Toni's name, but she harnessed the runaway thoughts that were ready to take her to places she didn't want to go. "Do you remember these two women?"

Charles squinted at the names. "Oh, yeah. I remember both of them." He leaned back in his chair. "They came in about ten minutes apart and both stayed about fifteen minutes."

Nona glanced down at the log that kept check-in and

check-out times. He had it almost down to the minute. "You have a good memory."

He grinned. "Part of security." He turned serious. "But I remember both because, well . . . who doesn't know Toni Lee. But that night she was acting weird. And so was that other woman, Tracie. She's one of the trainers, right?"

Nona nodded.

"Well, I teased them both about acting like they were running from the cops. They were acting all nervous, like they were doing something wrong. I remember laughing, but neither one of them thought that my little joke was funny."

Nona closed the book and stood. "Thank you, Charles."

"You're welcome. Is there something wrong?"

"No, I just needed to check out something."

He looked as if he didn't believe her. "Okay, but let me know if you need my help."

She felt faint as she stepped outside his office and closed the door. Toni Lee. Could she be the one? There was also Tracie, but she'd been with Brickhouse for only a few months. What could she possibly gain? Nona shook her head—neither one of them had any motive to harm her.

"Nona?"

She looked up, into Allen's concerned face.

"Are you all right?"

She nodded.

"You look like you're not feeling well."

"I'm fine," she whispered.

"What were you doing in Charles's office?"

She looked into Allen's eyes and remembered his warning about Toni at the premiere. Had he been right?

She shook her head slightly. She didn't have any information. She couldn't say anything until she was sure. "I . . . I'm thinking about expanding the security team."

"Really? I didn't know that."

"It's only because of a few articles I've read recently." She waved her hand in the air as if it wasn't important. "Anyway, I have a class." She rushed to her office.

She couldn't wait to be alone. Toni Lee. It just wasn't possible. It seemed as if they had been friends forever. Toni was the one who helped her get financing for Brickhouse. She wouldn't have this business without Toni.

*She doesn't seem to like the idea of you working with Derrick. I think she might be jealous.* Nona remembered what Allen had said to her at the premiere.

"It can't be," Nona whispered as she sank into her chair.

The telephone rang, taking her away from the disturbing thoughts.

"Nona, how are you this morning?"

She almost smiled at the sound of his voice. "Not good, Derrick."

"Have you found out anything?"

There was no way she was going to tell him what she suspected. No one would know anything until she had all the facts. "I haven't found out much, but I'll call you as soon as I know something."

"Just know that I'm here for whatever you need, Nona."

His words made her pause and remember the way he'd kissed her last night. "Thank you, Derrick."

"I'll be waiting for your call," he said, then hung up.

She rested the phone on her desk, but a moment later, she picked it up and dialed.

"Hello, Sam. This is Nona. May I speak to Toni, please?"

She knew what was coming before he even said the words. "I'm sorry, Nona. But Toni is not—"

Nona had hung up before Sam could utter the last word.

\* \* \*

Tracie or Toni. Nona didn't know what to think. She wanted to get into her car and track Toni down, but she had a class to teach in two hours.

She'd have to start with Tracie, although Nona didn't expect to find out anything from the young woman. She was a graduate student at Columbia, studying physiology, and had come to Brickhouse with a few clients whom she'd been personally training at school. During her first month, Tracie had worked with her clients under Allen's guidance, but since then, she'd been working on her own. According to the monthly performance reviews that Allen and Isaac provided to Nona, she was doing very well.

"I think Tracie is one of the best new trainers we've hired in a while." Allen had told Nona about three weeks ago. "She's ambitious, she's hungry. We can use that to our advantage . . . and hers."

Nona shook her head. Tracie wasn't the one. It was Toni whom she wanted to speak to. And she wouldn't be able to search for her for a few hours.

It felt as if the air was being sucked from her office, and she stepped outside. "Sarah, call me on the walkie-talkie if you need me. I'm going to walk around and check on things."

As she wandered to the front of the gym, she wondered if she should tell Allen what she'd found out. He'd have ideas about Toni. He'd probably suspected something all along—after all, he was the one who warned her.

She didn't have any information, but she needed her friend. As she knocked on Allen's office door, Isaac came out of his.

"Hey, Nona. Allen's not here."

"I just saw him a little while ago."

"Yeah, but he had to run out. He asked if I would cover his first client. Said he'd be back about noon."

She sighed. "Thanks."

"Is there something I can help you with?"

"No, thanks." She forced herself to smile and turned toward the workout room.

She glanced through the glass windows. There were three trainers inside; two were working with clients. One was working alone—it was Tracie.

Nona edged closer to the glass doors and watched the petite woman with shoulder-length twists as she lifted a dumbbell. Tracie's back was to Nona, but Nona could see her face through the mirror. There was nothing unusual—she was working out, before meeting her clients.

As Tracie raised one of the weights to do a biceps curl, she looked in the mirror, and her glance met Nona's. She froze. Tracie dropped both dumbbells and turned toward the door where Nona stood.

Nona's heart pounded as she walked into the room, taking slow steps across the carpet to Tracie.

Even from several feet away, Nona could see the young woman's fear, the trembling of her hands, the widening of her eyes.

"Nona, I'm so sorry."

Nona wanted to ask Tracie what she was sorry for. She wanted to ask why. She wanted to ask what she had done to her. But shock kept her silent, and she stared at the woman she'd just hired.

"I knew it was wrong because you told me that room was off-limits to employees when you hired me, but I was only returning the disc."

Nona couldn't breathe.

"I didn't want to do it, but Allen has been so good to me. And it was only opening the safe and putting the disc back."

Allen? It felt as if her heart had stopped beating.

"And I really needed the money. And it didn't seem like it was too big a deal. I swear I didn't mean to do anything wrong."

Nona inhaled to get oxygen to her lungs and to get her heart pumping again so that her lips would move.

"I asked Allen what was going on, but all he would tell me was that you couldn't know—"

Nona held up her hand, stopping the girl. It was too much, coming too fast. Tracie's words were jumbled in her mind, like jigsaw puzzle pieces. She couldn't put them together—not yet. Even though the final picture was very clear.

"Tracie, you have fifteen minutes to get your personal belongings and leave Brickhouse." Nona was surprised at the calmness of her tone, so different from the emotions that raged inside, fighting to burst out.

The girl took a step toward Nona, but Nona backed away.

"I'm so sorry, Nona. I wanted this chance. I was only trying to help Allen."

"Get out of my gym." Nona turned, not noticing the stares from the others in the workout room. She rushed to her office.

"Nona, what's wrong?" Sarah asked just before Nona slammed her door.

With hands that were still unsteady, she called Charles.

"I just fired Tracie Santos. Please escort her out of Brickhouse in ten minutes."

"Yes, ma'am."

"And she is not to return for any purposes."

Nona slammed down her phone.

Allen. Allen. Allen. He had taken the disc, given an employee the key to the security room and the combination to the main safe.

Her eyes watered as the full understanding of the betrayal sank in. She felt heavy, and sank into her chair.

She and Allen had been a team—from the beginning. But it was obvious she was the only one who still felt that way.

She thought about the conversations they'd had in the past weeks. How he'd tried to get her to leave Brickhouse and Harlem. How he'd tried to convince her that one of her best friends was jealous of her. He was trying to destroy her at every level of her life.

She closed her eyes and lowered her head onto her desk. Her mind was blank for a moment, but then the image of the night when she discovered Ron was cheating on her filled her thoughts. Even now she recalled how that news hit her, the pain of her husband tossing aside his marriage vows—and his wife at the same time. He had kicked her, right in the center of her heart. Breaking her into tiny, irrelevant pieces. She had never known a greater pain. Until now.

Allen paused the moment he stepped inside his office. "Nona, what are you doing here? Did I forget about a meeting?"

Her back was to him, and she used a tissue to blot at the tears that still rolled down her cheeks.

He stepped in front of her. "Nona," he called her name gently. "What's wrong?"

She had it all planned—how she was going to show her indignation and then demand that he leave the premises and never enter her life again. She wasn't even going to ask him why—she wasn't going to give him the satisfaction of providing her with an explanation.

But the moment she heard his voice, her tears started

again. This man could have come from her mother's womb. He had been more than a brother to her. And she thought he'd felt the same way. From the moment they met and she found out that he had no family, he'd become part of hers. But something had changed, and she didn't know why he had betrayed her.

When he noticed her tears, he knelt at the side of the chair where she sat. He took a breath. "Did something happen with the rezoning committee?"

She sobbed and shook her head. She kept her eyes down, knowing the moment she looked at him, their friendship would be over forever.

"Nona, please tell me what's going on. You know I'm always here for you."

*Always here for you?* His words made the water that flowed from her heart through her eyes stop. She looked straight at him.

She tried to decipher what she saw in his eyes. Worry? Love? His fake concern pulled her emotional trigger.

She raised herself from the chair slowly. Her eyes blazed with anger. "You mother—"

"Nona."

"You betrayed me. I trusted you," she screamed.

"Nona, what are you talking about?"

"About the disc, Allen. And how you made copies," she yelled, pointing her finger at him. "And how you're selling them on the street. Were you the one selling bootleg copies last time? How long have you hated me, Allen?" she cried.

He backed away, her words striking him like bullets. "Nona, I don't hate you, I love you."

Her laughter was filled with pain. "Keep your love, Allen. I don't want to have anything to do with you and your love and your concern and your—"

Before Nona could utter another word, Allen stumbled backward, then collapsed onto the floor, his body limp, as if there was not a bone inside.

It took a moment for Nona to comprehend the sight. The anger that filled her twisted to fear.

"Allen?" she whispered. When he didn't respond, she rushed to him. His eyes were wide open, but Nona knew that he did not see her staring down at him. "Allen," she called, louder this time. A second later, she jumped up and opened the door to his office. "Help," she screamed.

Then she rushed to his desk and dialed nine-one-one. "Help, please . . . my friend collapsed."

"Nona, what's wrong?" Isaac asked as he ran into the office.

"I don't know," she said to Isaac, even though she could hear the operator asking her questions. "We were . . . talking and he just fell down." She handed the phone to Isaac and returned to Allen's side.

His eyes were now closed, but there was a slight dampness under both lids, as if tears were trying to seep through. With her thumb she wiped the water away and felt the heat of him.

"Isaac," she screamed. "He's burning up."

Isaac pulled the phone off the desk and knelt beside her. "The paramedics are on their way, Nona. Don't worry."

"How can you say that?" Nona cried. "Look at him."

Isaac looked up as Sarah rushed into the office.

"Nona, what happened?"

"I don't know." She was sobbing now. "We were talking and he just dropped to the floor."

Isaac hung up the phone. "The paramedics are right outside. I'm going to show them in." He stood. "Sarah, stay here." He pushed through the crowd that had formed at the door. "Stand back," he yelled. "We've got to let the EMTs through."

"He's going to be all right, Nona," Sarah tried to assure her. "He's healthy, he's strong."

Her words meant nothing to Nona as she held her unconscious friend.

What happened? She was speaking to him, screaming, declaring that she wanted him out of her life.

She remembered the horror in his eyes. The way he had backed away from her. And then he dropped to the floor.

She closed her eyes. "Please, God. Make him well."

The office door slammed against the wall as the paramedics pulled a stretcher through.

"Step back," the male emergency worker said.

Sarah stood, but Isaac had to help Nona move away.

The female paramedic asked, "What happened here?"

The words were stuck in Nona's throat.

Isaac looked at Nona, but when she remained quiet, he said, "Ah, he collapsed."

"What was he doing?"

Nona closed her eyes. "He was just talking. Then he fainted. There were no signs. Nothing."

When her tears started, Isaac hugged her.

"He's going to be fine, Nona," he said.

Nona knew Isaac was just trying to say the right thing. It was what everyone told anyone who had illness in the family. "It's going to be fine."

But all she had to do was look at Allen and know that those words weren't true.

She paced behind the emergency workers as the man took Allen's blood pressure, pulse, and temperature and announced the results to the woman, who jotted numbers onto a chart.

"Can't we do all of that at the hospital?" Nona asked. "We have to get him to a doctor."

"We can't move until we take his vitals."

Only minutes passed, although it seemed like days to Nona before they rolled Allen onto the stretcher. "Okay, we're on our way."

Nona grabbed her purse and rushed behind the paramedics. "I'm going with you," she said as she pushed through the crowd that gathered in the hall.

The whispers bombarded her ears, and she wanted to scream at all of them—telling them to go away. They didn't care about Allen. No one cared for him the way she did.

*I don't want to have anything to do with you.*

Her last words to him came to her mind. She closed her eyes, willing those thoughts to go away.

Outside, another crowd had formed. The paramedics lifted the stretcher into the back of the ambulance, and Nona tried to climb in.

"You'll have to ride up front, Ms. Simms," the paramedic said, recognizing Nona. "We've got to do everything by the book these days."

She wanted to argue, tell him that Allen needed to hold her hand, hear her voice. But there was no time. She jumped into the front passenger seat. The emergency vehicle sped uptown to Harlem Hospital. She twisted, but there was no way to see what was happening in the back. All she heard was the radio transmitter, and numbers being uttered back and forth. She closed her eyes and pleaded with God.

In the emergency room parking lot, Nona ran behind the paramedics. She was oblivious to the gradual crescendo of shouts and stares as people rushed through the parked cars trying to get a better glimpse of Nona. She tried to see Allen's face, but the oxygen mask hid even his eyes. She followed as a doctor met them inside, but she was stopped as

Allen was taken through the large double doors into the emergency room.

"I'm sorry, you'll have to stay here," an emergency room nurse said.

Her eyes protested.

The nurse put her hand on Nona's shoulder. "We're going to need some information. Can you help us with that?"

Nona nodded, and the nurse motioned toward a private waiting area. "You can sit in there, and I'll bring the papers to you."

Nona sat in a chair at the edge of the room. Through the door, she could hear that life was continuing. Cast members of *The Young and the Restless* yelled at one another on the television bolted to the table in the corner. A toddler cried as she fought to wiggle from her mother's lap. A woman spoke loudly, angrily, trying to explain to the admitting personnel that she had no insurance but she felt sick enough to die.

Nona stuffed her hands into her sweat suit pockets and closed her eyes, but she opened them a moment later. She couldn't stay inside her head—where the images reminded her.

*I don't want to have anything to do with you.*

What if Allen died? she thought. What if those were the last words he'd ever hear from her? She shook her head. Allen was sick, but it wasn't that serious. It couldn't be.

Nona sat, waiting. Minutes later, she jumped up. She couldn't sit still another second. She walked into the hallway. Around her, token signs of the holidays hung from the ceiling—cutouts of sorry-looking, two-color turkeys and silly-looking men dressed as Pilgrims. Nona guessed that the dangling shapes were supposed to bring a bit of holiday comfort and joy to people overcome with worry about the health of their loved ones.

But she felt no joy; and she had to hold back the rising fear inside her that screamed to be released. She looked at the television. Now it was *The Bold and the Beautiful,* where people screamed from the corner of the room. As she waited, the soap operas changed, although the tribulations were all the same.

Here in the emergency room, Nona Simms was just a regular person. Every few minutes, Nona walked in front of the admitting window, hoping that someone would remember that she was there. For the first time since she'd become a household name, she craved the attention she had grown to despise. Every so often she would ask if a doctor was going to take the time and speak with her about Allen Wade.

"We'll call you as soon as we know anything," was all she was told in that tone hospital personnel used when they wanted to convey that you had crossed the line and were now an annoyance.

The sitting and waiting was driving her beyond crazy. She couldn't use her cell phone and she didn't see any public phones.

But there was no way she could leave. If it meant waiting another one hundred hours, she would be here for Allen.

"Nona."

She wanted to collapse as Leila ran toward her. They held each other for several moments.

"I was at the gym. I've been there for hours and then in the locker room, I heard someone say Allen fainted. I couldn't believe it. What happened?"

They sat and held each other's hands.

"I don't know anything yet. We were in his office . . ."

Nona paused. She couldn't tell anyone what happened—what she'd said to Allen just before he'd fallen to his knees. "We were talking."

"It can't be too serious," Leila said as if she wouldn't accept any other conclusion. "He's so healthy."

The image of her friend lying on the floor—ashen, taking shallow breaths, with skin so hot that it almost burned when she touched him—flickered through her mind.

"He's so healthy," Leila repeated, needing to hear those words aloud again.

"Ms. Simms."

Both Nona and Leila stood at the voice. Nona recognized the six-foot-seven, bald, clean-shaven doctor whom she was sure was often mistaken for Kareem Abdul-Jabbar. The doctor had treated Allen years before for his steroid use and had even advised Nona on how she could be an asset in Allen's healing.

"Dr. Sawyer?"

He nodded, but there was no smile in his greeting.

"How's Allen?" Nona and Leila asked together.

The doctor motioned for the two to follow him. They walked through the double doors where Nona had been stopped hours before. Inside, the oversized room was divided into rows of cubicles by sheets of cloth that hung from the ceiling. The sounds and smells of a hospital filled the space. As they passed the compartments, Nona searched for Allen, but there was no sign of him. That made her heart pound.

The doctor stopped in front of a small room and led Nona and Leila inside. Dr. Sawyer sat behind the desk.

"How's Allen?" Nona asked again as she sat in front of him.

"It's best to be honest," the doctor began.

Her heart was already beating fast, but now she was sure it would burst through her chest.

"It appears Allen is having an adverse reaction to steroids."

Nona's mouth opened wide. "Steroids? Doctor, you know he stopped using years ago." It was something that Allen had fought hard to overcome. He'd been using steroids for years—from the moment he decided he wanted to be a fitness trainer. At that time, the industry was so competitive that being fit wasn't good enough—you had to look fit. The major gyms didn't hire anyone who didn't have the body of a Greek god. And although he had fought hard not to even start, it wasn't until Allen began using steroids and the muscles began to bulge in his arms and legs that the gyms began to look at him. The offers poured in. Allen looked the part.

But then the news came that steroids killed. And Allen tried to stop. But willpower alone was not enough. He was addicted and needed a doctor's help. So with all that Allen had gone through, Nona was sure there was no way he'd start using what he called "death drugs" again.

"Allen came to me two weeks ago," the doctor continued, interrupting Nona's thoughts. "He's been using drugs again." The doctor paused when Nona and Leila gasped. "It's not what you think. He was abusing again, but to Allen, it was medicinal."

Nona frowned.

Leila asked, "What do you mean?"

The doctor sighed. "I wish he had come to me sooner. But you know how long he was using steroids before. Well, over time, steroids will take its toll on the body, and Allen was suffering from major pain to his joints and muscles. That's why he started using the drugs again."

"I don't understand," Nona said. "If the steroids caused the pain, why would he be using them again?"

"It's strange, but to make it simple, the pain he's been suffering was caused by his long-term abuse. But the only relief he could find came from using those same drugs. Steroids alleviated the pain that came from steroids."

Nona glanced at Leila, and they both shook their heads.

"It's complicated. Just know that the new drugs he put into his system may have alleviated some of his pain, but worsened his condition."

"Okay," Nona said slowly. "So he has to fight this, just like he did years ago. We can help him."

Leila nodded. "We did it before."

The doctor said, "Allen's been moved into intensive care." He stopped, knowing those six words said much more. "His prognosis isn't good. All of his major internal organs have been adversely affected."

Leila gasped.

"What's wrong with him specifically?" Nona asked.

"We're not sure yet. We've done a lot of tests, and we're going to be looking at a number of things."

Nona could tell that the doctor knew more, but she didn't want to know. Not now. Not yet. "Can we see him?" The question squeaked through her throat.

The doctor looked at his watch. "It will be a couple of hours. We're trying to stabilize him. You probably won't be able to see him until very late tonight, and I would really recommend waiting until the morning. Even then, I don't know if he'll be conscious."

Nona felt as if she were barely conscious herself as the doctor stood and led them back to the waiting area. He handed Nona a card. "Call me if you have any questions. You can have me paged if I'm not here."

She could feel the tears beginning to rise inside her, so she only nodded and watched the doctor turn back to the emergency room.

"Nona, what are we going to do?"

She'd forgotten that Leila was with her, and she thanked God she wasn't alone. They held each other for long minutes, saying nothing aloud, but screaming their prayers to God inside.

They held hands as they walked to the parking lot. Inside Leila's car, they stayed silent as Leila drove Nona back to Brickhouse.

In front of the club, Leila whispered, "Nona, do you think Allen could die?"

She shook her head. "No," she said because that was the only thing she could accept. She remembered what everyone had said to her today and then she uttered those same words. "He's strong. He's healthy. He's going to be fine."

Leila nodded, needing to believe her friend.

Nona put her hand on the car door, but then let go. "Leila, could you do me a favor and take me home?"

Leila looked at her for a moment, and her eyes filled with tears. She nodded.

The silence returned between them, and when Leila stopped her Mercedes in front of Nona's brownstone, they hugged, holding each other for several minutes.

"I'll call you," was all Nona could say before she got out of the car.

Nona stood on her steps and watched Leila speed up the street, heading back to New Jersey, and getting as far away from all this pain as she could.

Nona sighed and turned to her front door. It was time to break the news to Kelly.

\* \* \*

"Mom." Kelly ran to Nona the moment she stepped through the door. "Allen's sick," she cried.

Nona dropped her purse to the floor and held Kelly in her arms. "Honey, how did you find out?"

"I asked Odessa to stop at Brickhouse on the way home from Dr. Rutherford's office to surprise you, and Isaac told us. I wanted to go to the hospital," Kelly continued through her sobs, "but Odessa wouldn't let me."

"I didn't think you'd want her at the hospital," Odessa said as she joined them in the anteroom. "It's so sad, Ms. Nona. I'm so sorry."

"Thank you, Odessa."

"I'm going to make dinner."

Nona nodded as Odessa walked away. She took Kelly's hand and led her into the living room. They sat on the couch, and Nona wiped away Kelly's tears with her fingers.

Kelly said, "I wanted to call you but I knew you couldn't use your cell phone in the hospital. I didn't want to do anything that could make Allen sicker."

"Oh, honey, you could never do that." She hugged her daughter again.

"Mom, what happened?"

There it was—the question that brought the image back again. Her screaming. Allen's shock. His fall to the floor.

*It wasn't you, Nona. It was the steroids,* she said to herself. To Kelly, she said, "We're not sure what happened yet, but the doctors are taking very good care of him."

Her assurances did not end Kelly's tears.

"I'm scared, Mom."

Nona squeezed her hand. "There's no need to be because Allen's going to get well, and when he gets out of the hospital, we're going to be here to take care of him."

"Will he stay with us for a little while?"

"I don't know yet. But whatever we have to do, we'll do, okay?"

Kelly nodded. "I know one thing I could do." She paused. "I'm going to pray . . . a lot."

Nona leaned back against the couch cushions and held Kelly in her arms the way she used to when her daughter woke in the middle of the night screaming from a bad dream. This had to be as frightening as any nightmare Kelly ever had. Nona wiped the constant tears from Kelly's face, and wished she could wipe away the ones that were in her heart. But she knew that would be difficult. Kelly and Allen had been close since Kelly was a toddler. He was much more than her mother's friend and had been more of a father to her than Nona's ex-husband had ever been. But most importantly, he was Kelly's buddy. Nona was sure Kelly and Allen discussed things that she was not privy to. And that was fine with her. She trusted Allen, knowing he was there for both of them.

The image of Tracie and her words rushed into Nona's head and she shook her head to keep all those thoughts away. All that mattered now was that Allen recovered.

The doorbell chimes rang through the apartment, and Nona frowned. But then her heart hammered in her chest as she imagined Dr. Sawyer standing on her doorstep with news of Allen's demise.

"Stay here, sweetie," she said to Kelly. "Let me get the door."

Nona took a deep breath, peeked through the peephole, and then exhaled.

"Derrick," she said. "What are you doing here?"

"May I come in?"

She stepped aside. "Of course." She closed the door behind him and led him into the living room.

"Mr. Carter." Kelly ran to him, her eyes still filled with tears.

He knelt down and held her. "I'm so sorry to hear about Allen," he said, still holding Kelly, but looking at Nona. "I heard he collapsed at the gym."

Nona nodded.

Kelly leaned away from him. "But Mom says he's going to be okay," she said, still sobbing.

"I'm sure he will be."

This time it was Derrick who led Kelly to the couch. "Does anyone know what happened?"

That question . . . haunting her.

Nona shook her head. "Not really." She glanced at Kelly.

Derrick looked at Kelly, and then back at Nona. "Well, I know he'll be fine. I just wanted to stop by to make sure that my two favorite ladies were doing okay."

"Can you stay for dinner?" Kelly asked.

Just yesterday, she'd asked Derrick to dinner. Nona couldn't believe it was only twenty-four hours ago. "Kelly, I'm sure Mr. Carter has other plans."

He unbuttoned his suit jacket. "Actually, I don't and would love to stay." He paused and looked at Nona. "If that's all right with you."

It was the first time Kelly smiled. "I'll go tell Odessa." She ran from the room.

Derrick smiled as he watched Kelly, but his smile faded the moment she was gone. "I hope it's not a problem with me staying."

"No, I'm so glad to have you here." She paused and added, "You're so good with Kelly, and I want her to feel better."

"Is that all I do?"

She felt her face heat, and she lowered her eyes.

"Anyway," he whispered, "I can tell there's more to the story. What happened with Allen?"

"I'll tell you later," Nona said as Kelly returned to the room.

It was amazing to Nona, the transformation that came every time Kelly was around Derrick. Even though she could tell her daughter still carried the weight of worry about Allen, she chatted freely with Derrick.

As they ate dinner, Kelly talked about school, her assignments, her friends, her upcoming role as Lady Macbeth. Although times had been much better since Kelly began meeting with Dr. Rutherford, Nona couldn't remember an occasion when her daughter had been so animated. She talked straight through the dinner of grilled trout and a tomato and cucumber salad, and even had a bite of the triple chocolate bundt cake Odessa had baked.

After dinner, Nona called the hospital, but there was no new news about Allen.

"You can see him in the morning," Dr. Sawyer advised.

Nona tried to decipher what she heard in the doctor's voice, but then decided it was nothing. Allen was going to be fine. She'd see him first thing tomorrow.

When Nona joined Derrick and Kelly in the living room, her daughter had already coerced Derrick into watching one of her favorite DVDs.

"Are you sure you want to stay?" she asked him.

He smiled. "Yes. Come on and join us."

Nona sat on one end of the couch, while Derrick was on the other end. Kelly sat between them. As they watched Halle Berry slink across the screen in *Catwoman*, Nona reflected on her day—first, the news of betrayal and then the fear of sickness. But in the hours that Derrick had spent with them, she felt lighter with the hope that the future could be challenging, but in the end it would be all right.

When the movie ended, Nona clicked the remote, blackening the large plasma screen. "Okay, young lady," she said as she turned on the table light next to her. "It's after nine. I think it's time for bed."

"Do I have to go upstairs right now?"

"Yes, you have school tomorrow."

"But what about Allen? I thought I'd be going to the hospital with you."

"Allen wouldn't want you to miss school."

"But it's the day before Thanksgiving. It's not like we're going to be doing a lot of work."

"Kelly, you have to go to school. But I'll be at the hospital, and I'll let Allen know that you're thinking about him."

Kelly folded her arms across her chest. "Well, how am I going to find out how he's doing, Mom?"

"Why don't I meet you after school tomorrow?" Derrick said.

Kelly's smile returned. "You can do that?"

"Sure. I'll meet you here after Odessa picks you up and I'll make sure that you know everything that's going on with Allen."

"Thank you." She hugged him. "Good night." Then, she turned to her mother. "Good night, Mommy." She kissed Nona's cheek.

"I'll be upstairs in a little while."

Nona waited until she heard Kelly's bedroom door close before she rested her arm against the back of the couch and twisted her body to face Derrick. "I'm sure this is not how you planned to spend your evening, but thank you."

"No, I was happy to be here. I really had a good time with Kelly . . . and with you."

Nona sighed. "This has been the longest day."

"It's been a lot to handle. First you find out about the disc, and then this happened to Allen."

"That's the thing, Derrick," she whispered and looked toward the stairs, making sure there was no sign of Kelly. "I'm trying to figure out if this is all connected."

He frowned. "What do you mean?"

"It was Allen making copies of the disc."

"What?"

Nona told him what she knew—from the security log to her suspicions about Toni, and finally the one-sided conversation she had with Tracie. "It was when I confronted Allen that he collapsed."

"You told him what you knew?"

She nodded. "But he didn't have a chance to confirm or deny. He didn't say anything." She shook her head, fighting to keep that image from her mind. "He just fell to the floor." She wished she could take back her words.

He reached for her hand.

"He just fell," she repeated as the scene played over in her mind.

"Nona, it wasn't your fault. What you said couldn't have made him collapse."

She nodded, wanting to believe him. "Actually, the doctor said that Allen has been abusing steroids."

"Oh, my God."

"It's a long story, but he was using steroids as medicine."

"Oh." He squeezed her hand.

"Derrick, I don't understand how Allen could do what he did with the disc, but I'm convinced now that it's not what it seems. Allen's like my brother, has been like a father to Kelly. He's taken care of us for years."

"Sounds like he's a good man."

She looked at him. "He is. He's wonderful." And then it began. Nona told Derrick how she had met Allen when they both worked at the New York Fitness Club, how he helped when she decided to bring a health facility to Harlem, how he had never believed in the concept, but had faith in her. How he spent weekends and school holidays taking Kelly to movies and amusement parks. How she had lived her life with him and couldn't imagine a moment without him.

Nona talked as if speaking about Allen's history would keep him alive, make him well. And Derrick listened, knowing that was all Nona needed.

She had no idea how long she talked without taking a breath, without Derrick saying a word. But finally her mouth felt as if cotton had been stuffed inside. And she became silent.

Derrick was quiet too, letting the stillness rest comfortably between them. When she looked down, she noticed for the first time that Derrick was holding her hand, and she wondered when that had happened. It felt strange—to have a man holding her like that, gently caressing her fingers.

"I can't believe you just let me go on like that," she said.

He squeezed her hand. "You said what you needed to say."

"Thank you."

He reached for her other hand and held her. Long seconds seemed to pass as Nona stared into his eyes. When she felt her heart begin to pound, she pulled her hands and her eyes away from him.

The silence continued until he said, "I think it's time for me to go." His voice was husky. He stood and slipped on his jacket.

Nona walked him to the door. "Thank you again, for

spending the time with me and Kelly. You made what could have been a tough night a little bit better."

"I'm glad. Let me know if you need anything." He leaned forward. She held her breath. Her first thought was that she loved the way his lips felt against hers—as if they were meant to be there. His lips were soft—he was gentle. He pulled away and looked at her, but only for a moment. "Good night," he said before he opened the door and walked outside.

As she watched him trot down the steps, Nona's hand touched where his lips had been. She smiled. She didn't know what was happening between the two of them, but things were changing. She allowed her hand to linger on her lips for a moment longer before she closed the door. When she turned around, she glanced at the grandfather clock. It was midnight. Derrick had helped her make it through the day. Now it was time to pray that Allen would make it through the night.

## twenty-three

The morning sounds of Brickhouse coming to life floated through Nona's door. She looked at her watch and cringed. She hadn't planned to be in the office past eight o'clock. She had wanted to run in, scan her mail, answer a few e-mails, gather phone messages, and be on her way to the hospital before too many people could see her, stop her, and question her.

But it was already quarter to nine. Well, it didn't matter. No one would stop her. She had to get to the hospital.

She stuffed her mail into her backpack, glanced at her messages once again, and walked toward her door. As she touched the doorknob, the door swung open, startling her. She stood toe-to-toe with Toni Lee.

They stared at each for a moment, and then Nona reached for her friend. She closed her eyes as they hugged, and thought about how she'd been sure Toni was the culprit who had taken the disc. She remembered her anger, and that memory made her hold Toni tighter.

They stepped into her office, and Nona closed the door.

"Toni, where have you been? I've been trying to reach you."

Toni nodded and lowered her eyes.

Nona couldn't hide her surprise. Her normally flamboyant friend was missing her zest, her energy. Even her bright green eyes, which always shone with the promise of a wonderful life, seemed dull. And then she knew; Toni had heard about Allen.

"You know?" Nona asked as she dropped her bag to the floor and they sat on the couch.

She nodded. "Late last night. Sam heard from someone here at the club. I couldn't believe it. I called the hospital, but the only thing they would tell me was that he was a patient. And it was after midnight, so I didn't want to call and wake you." When Toni looked up, her eyes were filled with tears. "What happened?"

"The doctors aren't sure. But I'm on my way to the hospital." She took Toni's hand. "Come with me," Nona asked, standing and returning her purse strap to her shoulder.

Toni nodded. "But first there's something I have to talk to you about."

"Sure." Nona sat down again. "Sounds serious."

Toni looked at Nona and then turned her gaze away. "I have to apologize. I know you've been trying to reach me."

Nona remembered Sam's words. Yeah, she thought. For weeks.

Toni continued, "I've been avoiding you."

"Why? What did I do?"

"Absolutely nothing, except be your wonderful, charming, beautiful, smart self." Toni took a deep breath and tossed her blond hair over one shoulder. "And with that, you took Derrick Carter away from me."

"What?"

"The funny thing about this is I never had Derrick for you to take away. But in my mind I did, or at least I was hoping to have another chance with him. And then all of a sudden, there was you." She looked at Nona. "And my best friend became the enemy."

Nona shot up from the couch. "Toni, that is ridiculous. Nothing is going on with me and Derrick." She paused and remembered their kiss last night. "If you still want that man, you can have him."

It was Toni's turn to show her surprise. "Nona, I'm telling you it's okay with me now. I've been acting like a jealous schoolgirl. I had to stop myself. With what's happened to Allen, I realize that our friendship is what's most important. So I wish you well."

"That's all good, but there's nothing going on with me and Derrick."

Toni raised her eyebrows.

"Well, yes, we've had a few meetings." Nona waved one hand in the air as if that wasn't important. And she tried her best to ignore the way her heart seemed to take an extra beat every time she said Derrick's name. "But that's all," Nona continued objecting. "It's just about business."

"I think you protest too much."

"I don't even like the man, Toni. Do you remember that?"

Toni folded her arms, and a smirk filled her face.

"Okay," Nona continued. "Well, maybe I do like him now. He's not as bad as I thought. But it's only business."

Toni's smirk turned to a smile.

"Look, I don't care what you say. The fact is, there is nothing going on with me and Derrick. I'm not interested in him, and I know he's definitely not interested in me."

Toni chuckled. "Whatever you say."

"I'm not going to talk about this anymore. I need to get to the hospital." Nona was surprised that her tone was filled with frustration, and she lowered her voice when she asked, "You're coming with me, right?"

Toni nodded, stood, and hugged Nona again. "Of course. I just wanted to make sure that you weren't mad at me."

"I'm not mad," Nona said.

Toni leaned back from the embrace and looked at her friend.

"Okay," Nona agreed, remembering that it wasn't just her friend's lack of access that had made her angry. She still wanted to talk to Toni about her relationship with Derrick and why their stories about what happened with Toni's pregnancy were so different. But the more she thought about it, the more Nona realized that Toni had not lied. She had just given Nona her version of the truth—her truth that made the entire situation easier for Toni to handle. "Maybe I was a little . . . annoyed. But I could never be angry with you for long. It's a good thing I didn't know what was really on your mind. I'd have been pissed."

Toni smiled. "I'm glad we had this talk. I feel so much better connecting with my friend again."

"Good, because with all that's going on with Allen, I know there's nothing more important than friendship. Certainly not any damn man drama."

Toni chuckled and followed Nona to the door.

"Before we go, I do want to say one thing." Toni paused as Nona opened the door. "Don't be fooled, Miss Thang. You think Derrick is not interested in you? Please. You are exactly the kind of woman that Derrick Carter has always wanted." Toni tossed her gold-colored shawl over her shoulders, letting the fringes of her wrap gently flutter against Nona's face. She strutted into the hallway with her leopard leggings hugging her legs.

Nona looked down at the black velour Juicy sweat suit she wore. She shook her head, but then she couldn't hold back her smile. At least she had solved her challenges with one friend. Now it was time to see what they could do for Allen.

The small piece of cheer she'd found in seeing Toni that morning dissipated as Ray drove the two to Harlem Hospital. They rode in silence, each wondering what news this day would bring.

Inside the hospital their silence continued, interrupted for moments only when Nona asked for directions to the intensive care unit.

Outside room 205, Nona took a deep breath and turned to Toni. Without an exchange of words, Toni nodded and held Nona's hand. They stepped inside the room, and Nona tried not to gasp.

Against the starkness of the white—white walls, white curtains, white chairs, white linen—lay a man Nona didn't recognize. This certainly wasn't the strong, muscular man who for years had protected her.

In front of them lay a stiff body, connected to life by machines and tubes and other apparatus that Nona couldn't define. It didn't seem possible, but Nona was sure that Allen had lost weight—even though he'd been in the hospital for less than twenty-four hours.

Nona knew the same tears that were in her eyes were forming in Toni's.

"He looks so weak," Toni said.

Nona only nodded. She didn't want to say anything, not sure of what Allen could hear. She pulled one of the chairs closer to the bed and sat.

She knew there was still life in him because of the rhythmic beep of the monitor and the green lines that peaked every few seconds. But through the sheet that covered him, she could barely see his chest move.

"Allen," she whispered.

Toni stood next to her. "Do you think he can hear us?"

Nona shook her head. "I don't know. But just in case . . ." She left the sentence unfinished, hoping that Toni would understand.

"He looks awful," Toni said.

Nona shook her head. Toni would always be Toni. She just didn't get it.

They both looked up when the doctor stepped into the room.

"Good morning," Dr. Sawyer said.

They nodded.

"Would you mind waiting outside for a moment."

When they walked into the hallway, Nona leaned against the wall and closed her eyes, her mind a ball of confused emotions. This wasn't just a fainting spell or a collapse brought on by exhaustion. She didn't need the doctor to tell her that Allen's condition was beyond serious.

She hadn't allowed that thought to enter her mind yesterday. She couldn't handle the ramifications of what that would mean to her life.

"I'm going to the bathroom," Toni said.

Nona watched her friend walk away, the pep once again gone from her.

"Ms. Simms?" the doctor called, breaking her attention from Toni. "I'd like to talk to you. Let's step over here." She followed the doctor through the hallway, past machines and stretchers and carts filled with supplies. She sidestepped nurses and visitors for other patients until they were finally at the end where three chairs were lined up under the small window.

"How's Allen?" she asked as they sat.

"Ms. Simms. It's much more serious than I originally thought," the doctor began. "Allen had a stroke."

"Oh, my God." She covered her mouth with her hand, but she couldn't stop the tears that instantly flowed from her eyes. "A stroke? How can that be? He's only thirty-five."

Dr. Sawyer nodded slowly. "It's the steroids, Ms. Simms. One of the effects is the restriction of blood flow to the brain. That's what happened to Allen."

"How serious is it?"

"He's in a coma."

Nona wanted to just close her ears and run away. Could the news get any worse?

"We won't know the extent of the damage until he's conscious," the doctor continued. "But I have to tell you, Ms. Simms, Allen's condition is grave."

Nona wanted to scream and tell him not to use that word. It meant death. Instead she nodded and took a deep breath, trying to find strength. "Okay, so what can I do? How can we make sure he gets better?"

"It's a waiting game right now. We have him stabilized." The doctor stood. "If anything new develops, I will let you know."

The doctor nodded at Toni as she walked toward them and then sat by Nona.

"What did the doctor say?" Toni asked when Dr. Sawyer was far enough away not to hear her question. "Is Allen going to be all right?"

Nona looked at Toni. How was she supposed to say the words to her or any of their friends? But Toni was the worst, with her theatrics. Nona took a breath. "He's had a stroke."

Toni was still, as if she didn't comprehend Nona's words.

"That's impossible," she breathed, holding her hand over her heart. "He's not old enough to have a stroke."

Nona didn't have the strength to explain what Dr. Sawyer had said. She just leaned back in the chair and waited for Toni's hysteria to set in.

"Okay, well, all this means is that it will take a little longer for Allen to get well. But that's okay. We'll all be here for him."

Nona looked at Toni as if she didn't recognize her.

"We'll have to set up a schedule so that he has round-the-clock care," Toni continued. "Do Leila and Anna know what happened?"

Nona was still waiting—for the tears, the fainting—she was waiting for the Toni that she was used to.

"Leila knows," Nona started slowly, still waiting. "I expect her here at any moment. But Anna . . ." She shook her head. "I wasn't sure if I should call her."

"I'm looking for Allen Wade's room."

Both Nona and Toni looked up at the sound of the voice. Their mouths were still open when Anna spotted them, waved, and then walked to where they sat.

"Oh . . . my . . . God . . ." Toni said as if she were going to faint. "We were just talking about you."

"I hope you were saying good things," Anna said. She hugged them both.

"What are you doing here? I thought you didn't like Allen," Toni said. When Nona elbowed her, Toni added, "I mean, we didn't expect you . . . we didn't know . . ."

Anna held up her hand. "That's okay, Toni. I know what you mean. I had to come to talk to Nona. Toni, would you mind if we had a few minutes alone?"

"Sure. I'll go back in with Allen." Toni hugged Anna again before she stepped away.

Nona took Anna's hand as she sat. "I'm glad to see you here."

Anna lowered her eyes. "It's not what you think, Nona." She looked up. "I mean, I hope Allen gets well, but . . ." She took a breath. "There's something I have to talk to you about."

"What?"

"I found out something that you should know. From that sorry husband of mine. It was divorce or talk." She paused. "I don't know if this has anything to do with Allen being . . . in here, but Reverend Watkins has been blackmailing him."

"Blackmailing Allen?"

Anna nodded. "Apparently the reverend found out that Allen was using drugs again, and he used that. Allen was supposed to get you out of Brickhouse and out of Harlem."

"I don't believe this."

"Well, things turned worse when I gave you those papers." She twisted her body to face Nona directly. "I don't know if you know this, but the reverend has a master copy of your new videotape. After I gave you those papers—"

"He blackmailed Allen into giving him the disc," Nona finished for her.

"You knew?"

"Not all of this." She shook her head. "Yesterday I found out Allen had taken the master disc, but I didn't know why. I never had a chance to ask him." She paused, trying to digest this news.

"I think you should know, Nona, that according to Anthony, Allen's primary motivation was to protect you. Even though he didn't want you to find out he was using steroids again, the main reason he went along with Reverend Watkins was because the reverend was threatening to bring you into it. He was going to accuse you of supplying drugs through Brickhouse."

"You've got to be kidding me."

"I wish I were. The way the reverend was playing, it was going to get ugly. And that was Allen's fear. The reverend planned on sabotaging you anyway he could. Figured he'd bootleg your videos on the streets so that your sales would flop and you would have less resources to fall back on for your fight for Brickhouse."

This was too much to take. First, the news that Allen was in a coma. Then, that he was being blackmailed. And then, that Anna was the one bringing her this news. Bringing it all to light. Vindicating Allen.

"How . . . how is Allen?"

"Not good. It's very serious, Anna."

She nodded. "He was using steroids. Just like he was doing when . . . Todd died. Todd was in such awe of Allen. They trained together for years and I always knew that Todd only would have taken the steroids himself if Allen approved it. I'm not surprised they were doing the drugs together."

Nona stayed quiet. There were no words to defend him. She hadn't been able to do it in five years. Allen had told her that he had stopped using the drugs, but he had been taking them along.

Anna stood. "Well, I only came by because I wanted you to know that the reverend had your tape. But I don't think he's going to do anything with it right now. Both Anthony and that slimy reverend are scared shitless that the reverend's blackmailing schemes are going to come to light with what's happened to Allen. I think Reverend Watkins will be laying low for a while."

"Did Anthony know about all of this? There was nothing in the file about the tape or Allen using steroids."

Anna nodded. "Most of it. Apparently, quite a few from

the Harlem Empowerment Office were in on this—not all the way. The reverend was clearly the leader, but the rest of them had enough information to stop that disaster to the ministry. Including Anthony." She shook her head. "I don't even know my husband anymore, Nona."

"I'm sorry."

"Don't be. I don't know what's going to happen with us, but one thing I can tell you. He won't be running for re-election. I'll stand on top of the Apollo and shout to the world what I know. I won't let the people of New York go through that."

"I wish there was something I could do."

Nona hugged Anna, and they walked down the hall. In front of Allen's room, Nona stopped and asked, "Do you want to see Allen for a moment?" There was hope in Nona's question.

Anna hesitated. "No, I can't, Nona. I'm still not ready . . . with Todd . . . with everything. But I will be praying for him."

Nona hugged Anna again. "Thank you, sweetie. For being the best friend I could ever have."

"We're supposed to be here for each other." Anna kissed Nona's cheek. "Keep me posted."

Nona waited until she saw Anna step into the elevator, and then she went into Allen's room.

Inside, Toni sat at the edge of Allen's bed, holding his hand, stroking it lightly. "You're going to be fine," she said. "We're going to make sure of it."

Nona stood at the door and watched Toni utter those words over and over. She stared at Allen in the bed, lifeless to her, making her grateful for the monitors that assured her he was alive.

She wondered if he could hear, if he could think. She

wondered what thoughts were in his mind. How he must have suffered—knowing her love for Brickhouse, knowing it was his mistakes that had given Reverend Watkins what he needed.

Tears came to her eyes as she tried to imagine his pain—both physical and mental. Knowing him, the mental anguish was worse. She needed him to get well. So that she could tell him that it was fine. That she understood. That she knew of his mistake. But also that she knew *him*. And that she knew he was bigger and better than any of this.

Nona walked to the bed, and Toni smiled at her. While Toni held one of Allen's hands, she held the other. And together, they told Allen that he would be all right.

"King me! King me! King me!"

Nona frowned when she stepped into her brownstone. Whom was Kelly yelling at?

The moment she walked into the living room, Kelly ran to her. "Hi, Mom." She hugged her. "I beat Mr. Carter at least ten times." She held up her arms and jumped around in a boxer's stance. "I'm the checkers champion."

Derrick and Nona laughed.

"I don't think you beat me that many times, Kelly."

"Yes, I did. Mom, you can ask Odessa. She came in here and watched one game. And she left because Mr. Carter was so pitiful." Kelly fell back onto the couch, laughing.

Nona tossed her bag onto the chair. "Sounds like you guys are having a good time."

"We are." Kelly laughed, but then she became serious, as if there was something that just came to her mind. "Mom, how's Allen?"

How was she supposed to tell her child all that she had

learned today? "He's . . . the same, honey. The doctors are really working with him."

"Do you think I can see him?"

Nona hesitated and shook her head slightly.

"I really want to."

"I'll check with the doctors."

Kelly nodded. "I hope he's going to be all right. But I decided today that since tomorrow's Thanksgiving, I'm only going to think good thoughts. And I'm just going to thank God for making Allen well."

Nona rubbed her hand over Kelly's head. "That's what you should do, sweetheart. Hey, would you take my bag upstairs for me, please?"

"Sure."

When they were alone, Derrick said, "I promised Kelly yesterday that I would come by this afternoon."

"I remember, but you didn't have to stay this late. I'm sure you have plans . . . to get ready . . . for tomorrow."

He nodded. "But I wanted to wait for you."

She smiled and remembered Toni's words from this morning. And she remembered how she had professed the truth. How she declared there was absolutely nothing going on between the two of them. "I'm glad," was all she said.

"How's Allen?"

She shook her head and joined him on the couch. "Not good. He had a stroke," she whispered. "And now he's in a coma."

He let out a soft whistle. "Wow. This is really deep." He shook his head as if he were trying to understand what she had told him. "I don't know a lot about steroids, but I didn't know it could do all of that."

"Apparently using those drugs for years can kill you." She sighed.

"You know what? As soon as Allen comes out of this, we need to do a video on steroids and abuse. Get the word out."

"Derrick, that is a wonderful idea."

"Mom," Kelly interrupted them. "Odessa wants to know what you want for dinner."

"I have an idea," Derrick said. "Why don't we go out?"

"Derrick, thank you, but I don't think so . . ."

"Oh, Mom, could we? Please."

"But it's the night before Thanksgiving. Nothing's open."

"I'm sure we can find something," Derrick said.

"Please," Kelly begged. "We can go get pizza. They're always open."

Nona had been on an emotional roller coaster all day, but there was no way she was going to deny Kelly's request. She couldn't remember the last time Kelly had asked to go anywhere to eat. "Derrick, I think we're about to have a pre-Thanksgiving feast of pizza."

He stood and put on his jacket. "Pizza. Yum. My favorite."

Nona laughed as she moved toward the stairs. "Let me tell Odessa and then change into some jeans."

"Sounds good to me."

As she started up the stairs, she heard Kelly ask Derrick if he wanted to play one more game of checkers. She paused as Derrick laughed and said, "Sure. But just be ready this time because you're going down.

Kelly giggled.

In the hospital, she'd been surrounded by the bustling of the nurses, the beeping of machines, the coughs and calls of the patients—the sounds of sickness. But now all she heard was laughter and cheer. And she thanked God that there was this place called home.

## twenty-four

Nona tapped her fingers across her desk. She grabbed the phone from the speaker station when she heard the voice on the other end.

"Dr. Sawyer?"

"Yes, Ms. Simms."

"I was just calling to check on Allen's progress."

She heard the doctor sigh. "There's been no change since yesterday. There's been no positive change in a week. Frankly, Ms. Simms, it's like I told you. The tests have shown that there is decreasing brain activity."

"But each day that he holds on . . . isn't that good?"

"I know what you want to hear, but I want to prepare you. I'm not sure how much longer Mr. Wade will last."

She'd been asking the same questions for a week. But each time she heard the doctor's answers, new tears squeezed through her eyes.

"I'm sorry, Ms. Simms."

"Thank you, Doctor. I'll be there this afternoon."

She hung up the phone and held her head in her hands.

What was she going to do? How was she supposed to live without one of the best friends she'd ever had?

"No, Nona," she scolded herself. "I am not going there. Allen is going to make it."

Those were the same words she said to herself every time she spoke to the doctor. But the conviction that was in her voice faded a bit with each passing day.

She blinked, fighting to keep back her emotions. She had work to do before she returned to the hospital to sit with Allen. Every day she sat with him, and talked with him, and tried to convince him that he had to get well.

Maybe it was time to let Kelly see Allen. Kelly asked every day if she could visit. And the doctors said they didn't know what a person in Allen's state heard. Maybe Kelly's voice would help bring him closer to consciousness.

But she had to consider what seeing Allen so sick could do to her daughter. She couldn't take the chance. Especially since Dr. Rutherford said that Kelly was making remarkable progress. She didn't need the doctor to tell her that. She could see it herself. And most of it was because of Derrick Carter.

She couldn't believe that just a month ago, she had hated being in the same room with that man. Now she looked forward to seeing him. Every night he was there when she got home. Staying with Kelly and Odessa. Eating dinner with them. It eased the pang of her being at the hospital so much. Nona knew Kelly understood, but now Nona knew that Kelly was in good hands too. And at the end of the day, Derrick was there for her. Ready to listen. Ready to talk. Whichever she needed.

She pushed those thoughts aside. She'd decide about Kelly and Allen later. Right now, she had to get this preliminary press release written for the publicist. She looked down at the page in front of her.

This was Derrick's idea—to have a publicist get out this information about Allen, since reports had been circulating for the past week.

"It's time to get our truth out there," Derrick told her last night.

She agreed. But she had been here since nine, and it was almost twelve. In the past, she'd been able to write something like this in thirty, forty minutes.

But she couldn't get the doctor's words from her mind.

*I'm not sure how much longer Mr. Wade will last.*

"No," she exclaimed to the words in her head.

The knock on the door made her sit up straight.

"Nona, may I come in?"

She smiled. "Sure, Leila."

Her friend was dressed in leggings and an oversized T-shirt. Nona couldn't remember the last time she hadn't seen Leila in some shape-showing outfit.

She walked to the other side of her desk, and the friends hugged.

"How's Allen?" Leila asked as they sat in the chairs in front of Nona's desk.

Nona shook her head.

Leila said, "I saw him yesterday."

"I know. The nurse told me I just missed you."

Leila nodded. "I didn't get to see him over the weekend. I took the kids to my parents in Ohio for the Thanksgiving weekend."

"That's great. Did you have a good time?"

She shrugged. "It was kind of good to see the folks."

"Kelly and I stayed home. I didn't want to be too far away from Allen."

"You've been spending a lot of time at the hospital."

"I'm all Allen has." She looked up at Leila. "Well, not all . . ."

"I know what you mean. The two of you were . . . are so close."

Nona nodded and remembered the doctor's words. "Leila, I am really scared. I don't think Allen's going to make it."

Leila laid her hand on top of Nona's. "Let's not think that way. Not yet."

Nona nodded.

"But whatever we have to go through," Leila continued, "we'll go through together."

"I can't imagine life without Allen. I don't want to."

"Then let's keep our prayers going that Allen will come out of the coma and make a full recovery. Let's think good thoughts."

Nona tried to smile. "You sound like Kelly."

"That's probably a good thing. I wish this had been my life's philosophy over the past months rather than—" She stopped.

Nona looked at her friend and remembered how distant she'd been. "With all that's been going on, we haven't had a chance to talk in a while. What's been going on with you?"

Leila clasped her hands together in her lap. "There's something I have to talk to you about."

Nona cocked her head. It was odd. Both Anna and Toni had uttered the same words to her in the last week.

Leila continued, "I wanted you to hear this news from me." She paused. "Shawn and I have split up. We're separated for now, but I'm pretty sure we're headed toward a divorce."

"Oh, no. Leila, I'm so sorry."

"Don't be. It's been coming for a long time."

Nona thought about how similar Leila's words were to

Anna's, and she knew that soon Anna could very well be sitting next to her in this same place speaking similar words about her and Anthony. What was going on with her friends?

"Separations are always difficult, I know," Leila continued. "And it hasn't been easy on the kids. But it really is for the best."

Nona nodded.

"This last year has been hard on me. First, trying to live up to something that I thought Shawn wanted, when in actuality, he didn't want me in any way, shape, or form."

"Leila, I'm sure that's not true."

"No, it is," she said. "There's no need for polite words. I need to focus on what's true. If I had been doing that all along, I wouldn't have gotten caught up . . ." She paused and shuddered. "I lost myself. I did so many things . . ." She took a breath. "Anyway, I'm past all of that. And I'm ready to move forward as the new and improved Leila Lomax."

"If this makes you happy, then I'm happy for you." Nona hugged her. "You know, if there is anything that I can do—"

"I know. Listen, are you going to the hospital? I'm on my way over there."

"Great. We can ride together. Let me just get these papers together for Sarah."

They both looked up when they heard the knock on the door.

"I hope that's not some well-meaning member wanting to talk about Allen," Nona whispered. "I've been trying to avoid the masses."

"Do you want me to get rid of whoever it is?" Leila asked.

Nona nodded. "Sarah must not be at her desk."

Leila stood, opened the door, and smiled. "Well, if it isn't the impeccable Mr. Carter."

"Oh, is that who I am?" He chuckled as he stepped inside. "I hope I'm not interrupting anything."

"No, we were just having a little girl talk," Leila said, but his attention was already on Nona.

"How are you?" he asked her.

"Okay. I did the press release. I was going to call the publicist this afternoon."

"I can do that for you."

"You don't have to."

"I want to."

Leila stood at the door with her arms folded and watched the exchange. It was all business, but there was something more inside the words they spoke. "Ah, Nona, I'm going to go now . . ."

"Okay, Leila," Nona said, barely looking away from Derrick. "I'll catch up with you later."

Leila waited for a moment before she turned to the door.

Before she closed the door behind her, Leila heard Nona say, "I feel like I'm your new full-time job, Derrick."

"Well, it's a position I'll gladly accept."

Leila smiled. With all the negativity that seemed to be around them, maybe this was Nona's harvest. And she couldn't think of anyone who deserved it more.

As Leila hurried to her car, she couldn't help smiling. She had walked into Nona's office filled with the sadness of Allen and her crumbling marriage. But Nona had brought a little joy to her day.

She had spoken to Toni last night and had been surprised when Toni mentioned Nona and Derrick.

"There is something going on between those two, Leila. Mark this date on your calendar and remember."

She had been skeptical, chalking Toni's words up to her actor's imagination. Leila didn't know anyone who disliked Derrick Carter more than Nona Simms. But from what she'd just seen in that office, obviously those feelings were in Nona's faraway past.

Leila was happy. They could all use a little cheer. Toni sounded as if she was having her own challenges, and Anna . . .

Every time Leila thought of her other best friend, she shuddered. How could she have done that to her? How could she have slept with her best friend's husband?

Leila opened the door to her car and slipped inside. She leaned back, closed her eyes, and said a long prayer. There was so much regret that she harbored in her heart. It sickened her that she could ever do what she'd done to a friend. Where was her loyalty? She knew the pain of adultery and the hours of hurt she'd had to endure thinking about Shawn's infidelity. How could she do this to Anna?

And what was worse was that even though she knew what kind of man Anna was married to, there was nothing that she could do. She could never tell her. She could only pray that one day, Anna would find out—in another way—who Anthony Leone really was.

But on the other side of regret, Leila was grateful for two things—that she had accepted that her affair with Anthony was over and that no one had found out about that one-sided romance.

Leila shook her head, ridding herself of the thoughts, and started her car. She didn't want to think about her sins anymore. There was someone more important who needed her and her prayers right now. She turned from the Brickhouse parking lot and headed toward Harlem Hospital.

Nona pulled the sheet up to Allen's chin. His chest barely moved. But at least the green lines on the monitors continued to indicate that her friend was alive.

She stared at his face and again wondered what the last weeks had been like for him. "If only I'd known, Allen," she whispered. "We could have gotten through this together."

She continued to stare, wanting to see him blink or to see a muscle in his face twitch. But there was nothing.

Nona sighed and sank into the chair at the side of the bed. She was so tired, but refused to give in to the exhaustion. Allen needed her, Kelly needed her, Brickhouse needed her. She would find a way to balance them all.

She glanced at Allen again, before she closed her eyes, but she would rest only for a moment. She would go home in just a little while.

She felt peaceful, she felt calm; the space she was in was serene.

"Nona, Nona."

She tried to force her eyelids apart, but they stayed closed.

And then she saw him.

"Allen." She smiled. "You're better."

He returned her smile and sat up in the bed. "I am now."

"I am so glad. I was worried."

"There's nothing for you to worry about." He took her hand. "I have to tell you something. I'm so sorry, Nona."

"For what?"

"For hurting you. For giving Reverend Watkins room to try to destroy you." He paused. "And for using drugs again."

"It's all right, Allen." She squeezed his hand. "Dr. Sawyer explained it all to me. I know you weren't abusing again, not really."

"Still . . ."

She put her fingers to his lips, stopping him. "I understand what happened. You were trying to protect me from

Watkins and you were trying to stop your pain. None of it matters, because I forgive you."

"Thank you. That's all I needed to hear." He looked away, but when he turned back to her, his eyes were sad. "I've always loved you, Nona. You and Kelly. You were the only family I had, and I wanted to take care of you and protect you for the rest of your life."

"You can still do that, Allen, now that you're well."

"I'm well, Nona, but not in the way you think."

She frowned. "What do you mean?"

"Just know that I will always love you."

And then he was gone.

"Allen, Allen," she called.

"Ms. Simms, Ms. Simms." Someone was shouting her name.

Nona opened her eyes. It took a moment for her to focus. The small hospital room was packed with doctors, barking orders to the nurses.

"Ms. Simms, you have to wait outside," a woman who was standing over her said.

"What . . . what's going on?"

"We're losing him," she heard one of the doctors yell.

"Allen?" she whispered before the nurse escorted her out of the room.

"What's going on?" Nona asked again, straining her neck to look around the nurse.

"I'm sorry, Ms. Simms," the nurse started, "but you'll have to wait out here," she said before she turned away and returned to Allen's room.

Nona stood, close to the door, wanting to rush back inside, but knowing it was best for Allen if she just waited.

*What happened? I was just talking to him. It was wonderful. He was well; we were both at peace.* Her thoughts paused. Had she really been talking to him? Nona closed her eyes and tried to remember the conversation. It was so real. She opened her eyes and looked at her right hand; he had held her as he spoke.

*Was I dreaming?*

*Just know that I will always love you.*

She remembered his last words before more doctors rushed inside the room. "Please, Allen," she whispered. "Fight. You've got to stay alive."

Then another thought filled her, and as tears burned her eyes, she said, "I will always love you too, Allen. May God bless you and keep you."

## *epilogue*

*Six months later*

Nona held Kelly's hand as they walked down the steps of Brickhouse. Derrick trotted in front of his Jaguar and opened the passenger door.

"How're my two favorite ladies?"

"Fine," they said together.

As Nona slipped into the front seat, Derrick opened the back door for Kelly.

"Seat belts on," he said as he started the car and veered from the Brickhouse parking lot. He turned east, toward the Triborough Bridge. "How was church?" he asked.

"Fine," Kelly said. "I really like the new pastor. I can understand almost everything Pastor Jerome preaches about."

"That's a good thing," Derrick said. He glanced at Nona. "I'm sorry I missed services. When I got that emergency call last night, I insisted that the production manager meet with me this morning because I knew I wanted to be with you and Kelly this afternoon."

She smiled. "I understand. I'm just glad you're with us now."

For thirty minutes, they chatted about church, school, Kelly's appointments with Dr. Rutherford, and her upcoming part in a new play—*Othello.*

"I think I'm going to like playing the part of Desdemona better than even Lady Macbeth," Kelly said. "Although I don't know how I always end up playing the wife." She sighed.

Nona and Derrick exchanged glances and smiled.

Kelly continued, "But Desdemona is strong. And the notes said that she was very beautiful. I think I can play that part." She laughed.

Nona wanted to turn around and hug Kelly. Just another sign that her daughter was getting better.

As the city sights metamorphosed into suburban serenity, their chatter lessened, until silence filled the car. Nona stared at the passing images of homes that were farther apart and trees that grew much larger and fuller than any in the city. Westchester County was so different from where she lived. Here there were few signs that they were still in New York. There were no people walking or car horns honking or fire engine sirens blaring. Here there was just quiet. Nona shuddered. It was too peaceful for her.

"Look, there's a flower stand." Kelly pointed.

Derrick slowed the Jaguar and stopped in front of the roadside stand. Nona stayed in the car while Kelly and Derrick got out. She watched as the two examined the rows of flowers, and Kelly finally chose a bouquet. Nona smiled. Derrick was so good with Kelly. And Kelly was so good with him. They made each other happy.

Kelly handed the bouquet to Nona, and its fragrance flowed through the car. She closed her eyes and inhaled.

Lilies were one of her favorite flowers, but their reason for purchasing them today filled her with sadness.

An hour and fifteen minutes after they had left the city, Derrick turned the car around the curve into the King of Kings Cemetery. He followed the driveway, remembering the way from the funeral six months before.

Nona put on her sunglasses when Derrick stopped the car. She stayed in place as he got out, then walked to the passenger side and opened the door for her. She took his hand and stepped outside. Then he did the same for Kelly.

In silence, Nona led the trio past perfectly lined rows of gravesites until they came to the headstone they were seeking: ALLEN WADE 1970–2005. Most beloved friend and our angel forever.

Nona stood for a moment, then swayed slightly, but Derrick was right behind her. He wrapped his arms around her, easing her back against him. As he held her, she felt the first tear seep from under her glasses.

The cemetery administrator had called this week to tell her that Allen's headstone was ready. She'd been pleased, but was not prepared for the impact of seeing her best friend's name on the stone. At that moment, it all came rushing back. The pain of the doctor's final words, "I'm sorry, Nona." How she had stayed in Allen's hospital room and cried until she had no more tears. And then how she had gone home and held Kelly as she sobbed for hours until sleep finally rescued her from her grief.

Nona had felt barely conscious as she made Allen's final arrangements, and then maintained her zombie state through the services. She'd held her tear-filled daughter and just stared at the black and silver coffin, willing Allen to rise and convince them this was all a bad dream. She'd heard none of the minister's words, nor understood any of the condolences as friends passed by shaking her hand and whispering their words of sorrow. She didn't hear the wailing from Toni Lee or Leila's eloquent reading of Allen's eulogy—although Nona had noticed Anna as she walked past the open casket and paused, saying her own teary farewell to the man she had considered an enemy during the last years of his life.

When it was Nona's turn to say good-bye, she had stood looking down at Allen, grieving for the man who had protected her, saved her, loved her. But in the end, her love hadn't been enough to save him.

Now, as she stood at Allen's grave site, it didn't feel as if six months had passed. The pain was as fresh as the flowers she held in her hand.

Kelly took the lilies from Nona and knelt beside the gravestone. "Hi, Allen," she said as she positioned the flowers right under his name. She paused. "I miss you so much. I—" She stood up, sobbing, and leaned against Derrick.

While he held Kelly, Nona knelt in front of Allen's resting place. "We do miss you, Allen, but we're doing well. Brickhouse is fine. Better than ever. Reverend Watkins didn't try to put up a fight when Derrick went to him and demanded any copies of the disc back." She paused and smiled at Derrick. "I have a feeling Derrick did a little more than just ask for the disc," she continued. "But whatever he did or said, it worked. Brickhouse is still here. And it will be, for a long time."

"And I'm doing good too, Allen." Kelly sniffed. "I got all A's on my report card, and Dr. Rutherford said I'm her best patient ever. I'm eating all the time, but it's just the right stuff. Like you always told me."

Nona stood, and the three stayed in silence, staring at the headstone. As the minutes passed, memories rolled through their minds. And it was time that gave them more smiles than tears.

Finally Nona said, "I'll always love you, Allen."

Derrick held Nona's and Kelly's hands as they walked to the car. He helped them inside and then said, "I'll be right back."

Nona frowned as she watched Derrick return to the spot where they had just stood. He knelt, for no longer than a few seconds, then walked slowly back to them.

When he got inside the car, Nona turned to him, her expression asking the question.

"I just wanted to thank him for taking care of my two favorite ladies." He took Nona's hand. "And to say that from now on, that's my job." He leaned over and let his lips meet hers. They kissed, almost forgetting that Kelly was with them until she clapped her hands.

"I love it when you guys do that." Kelly giggled.

Nona and Derrick turned to her and smiled.

"I just want to know one thing," Kelly said.

"What?" Derrick started the car.

"When are you going to get married?"

"Kelly!" Nona exclaimed.

"What? I thought it was a good question," Kelly said.

Derrick agreed, "It's a very good question." He lifted Nona's hand and looked at the five-carat, emerald-cut diamond that he'd given her three months ago. "So, when are we getting married?"

The three of them laughed, and Nona squeezed Derrick's hand before she leaned over and kissed his cheek.

She sat back just as Derrick drove through the burial ground exit. In her side view mirror, she could see the sign with the gold letters—"King of Kings Cemetery." She stared as it got smaller and smaller until it was completely out of sight.

She turned away from the mirror and took off her sunglasses. It was wonderful the way life worked. Sometimes what seemed to be the end was really a new beginning. She looked at Derrick, who was staring straight ahead, maneuvering the car along the curves of the expressway. Moving with caution. Taking care—for his two favorite ladies.

Nona's eyes moved from Derrick to the ring that glittered on her finger. She smiled and thanked God for her new beginning.

Want More?

Turn the page to enter
Avon's Little Black Book —

the dish, the scoop and the
cherry on top from
RITA EWING

Read on to see Leila, the New York Knicks wife in *Brick-house,* make contact with her two friends, Rita Ewing and Crystal McCrary Anthony, the co-authors of *Homecourt Advantage* (Rita's first novel) and two women who were once New York Knicks wives and lived to tell about it!

Get a peep at the never-before-printed epilogue to the original manuscript of *Homecourt Advantage,* which reveals a very different ending from the one published in the finished book—an ending where Casey leaves her husband, Brent!

"Damn, damn, damn!" Leila winced.

She remembered the character Florida from the ghetto sitcom *Good Times.* Damn if she didn't feel as miserable as that woman always appeared on that damn show every damn day.

Even as a small child, Leila knew the popular character from her parents' favorite TV show was one unhappy woman. Leila counted the blessings that came from her own charmed existence on a regular basis. Unfortunately, a lot of bullshit came hand-in-hand with the fairy-tale life. Particularly a husband who couldn't seem to keep his dick in his pants!

Leila knew her game was just as bad. She was pissed off at the hand she had been dealt, yet deeply ashamed at the foul hand she herself played. It had come down to one affair after another. She had to talk to someone!

She rummaged through her nightstand and grabbed her

BlackBerry two-way pager. Using her thumbs to key in information, Leila sighed with relief when the names scrolled across the unit's small screen.

She plopped on the side of her bed and let herself fall backward into the soft pillows. A slow smile spread across Leila's face, stretching from one three-carat diamond stud to the other. She was so glad she had kept the numbers. They had all been so close back in the day when their men were all members of the Knicks.

Basketball fans at the games had jokingly referred to the trio as the Knicks Chicks, the real Dream Team. Rita Ewing and Crystal Anthony were her girls! Leila missed her friends dearly.

"That's it," she thought, swiping at a fat tear as if a fly had just landed on her face. She would call both of them today.

Leila remembered the day when Rita and Crystal had invited her out to dinner. They had something private they wanted to share with her. Leila had been shocked when Rita pulled the neatly typed manuscript of *Homecourt Advantage* out of her bag and pushed it across the table with a flourish.

"Bam!" Rita had declared, giggling in her silly way.

"We want you to read this for us, Leila," Crystal explained. "We want your opinion before we submit it to our editor."

Leila had been terribly flattered that Crystal and Rita valued not only her opinion, but her editing skills as well.

Damn if those two hadn't been like prophets telling their story! *Homecourt Advantage* was the Nostradamus of the National Basketball Association!

It had been their secret until her friends turned authors came clean, and all of New York started talking about the now infamous roman à clef about the New York Knicks basketball team. Yup, even Leila knew who the gay Knicks player was. There was no lying going on in that book, that was for sure.

Leila remembered the *Homecourt Advantage* storyline only too well. Hell, she might as well have been one of the main characters in the book. She was still living the part.

Leila just wished, as she had many times since the book

had been published, that her friends had not decided at the last minute to change the ending of the book. She knew the real deal, the true story, what happens in real life.

That was why she desperately needed to talk to Rita and Crystal. They would understand what she was going through with Shawn. They would know why she felt it was time to leave her husband. Leila knew her baller girlfriends would understand. They could relate to things that even her best friend Nona would never comprehend.

For the very same reasons that Crystal and Rita had Casey leave her husband Brent's tired ass in *Homecourt Advantage's* original storyline, Leila was about to leave her own husband. She remembered the original story like it was yesterday . . .

# Epilogue

## From the original manuscript of
### *Homecourt Advantage*

Casey stared at the beautiful Kosta Boda vase sitting in the middle of her living room coffee table. Sunlight poured through the double French doors that opened onto a small private bluestone courtyard. The light created the effect of a dazzling myriad of colors swirling through the interior of the vase. Casey sank down onto a large brown suede floor pillow and read Alexis's letter for the second time.

It was difficult for Casey to believe that Coach's wife, Alexis, had written the letter. Obviously, there was a side to Alexis O'Neil that she had never revealed to anyone affiliated with the New York Flyers. Casey looked up at the vase and gazed at it for what seemed like an eternity. She had always considered herself to be a good judge of character, but she realized now that not even she had been able to see through Alexis's tough exterior.

As the sun began to set, Casey walked around the room lighting one scented candle after another. She then tuned in her stereo to her favorite jazz station and let the music course through her. The bare walls in her newly refurbished SoHo loft were already covered with her favorite pieces of art. It was ironic, Casey thought, that she had found her new place through the relocation program offered to the NBA players and their families.

She walked into the kitchen to arrange the Thai food she had had a local restaurant cater for her housewarming party that evening. Her friends would be arriving shortly, and Casey was anxious for them to see her new place. She loved her two-story loft with its soaring ceilings and its brick walls. Most importantly, Casey enjoyed her newfound independence and relished the freedom that came with living by herself.

"I don't believe it . . . Trina!" Dawn exclaimed. "Is that M.A.C. lipstick you're wearing?"

"Yeah, girl." Trina said, laughing. "I figured I could use a new look. It's not too dark on me, is it?"

"No! It's perfect," Dawn answered. "It's hard to go wrong with any M.A.C. product."

Casey thought that the changes Trina had made to herself on the outside as well as the inside were amazing. Not only had she started eating healthier, she had gotten a stylish short cropped haircut that showed off her glowing ebony skin and deep-set brown eyes. Casey happily realized that the biggest difference in Trina was reflected in her self-esteem.

Casey had welcomed all her friends: Trina, Lorraine, Remy, and Dawn, one by one, to her housewarming party. Casey laughed with her friends, enjoying the camaraderie of the group. They were all sitting on the floor on huge pillows thrown around a low mosaic tile table Casey had recently purchased at an estate auction. Several authentic Thai dishes were spread on the table in hand-painted clay dishes. Though Casey had gotten together with all of them at various times over the past summer, the five women had not all been in the same room since the season.

Casey had filed for divorce back in July, only two weeks after the season had ended. Although Brent had tearfully sworn that he had changed and even wanted to renew their marriage vows, for Casey, it was simply a case of too much, too little, too late. When she explained her feelings to Brent, she had never before felt such clarity of mind about a decision.

All Casey wanted was a place of her own that had no haunting memories of her life as Brent Rogers's wife. Her new Village retreat was just what the doctor ordered, especially for those cozy evenings she spent with Jason Ennis, the new man in her life.

"Come on, Casey, we want the truth," Trina demanded, smiling at Casey.

"Why bother with your own place? How come you just didn't move in with Jason when he asked you to?" Trina wanted answers.

"Trina!" Lorraine said, appearing shocked by what she had just heard.

"Casey can't just up and move in with a man, they're not even married, for goodness' sake." Lorraine's hand had slowly moved up to caress the small platinum cross she wore on a chain.

The women all started to laugh, but Casey was quick to explain.

"You all know how crazy I am about Jason, and even though I've never felt this way about a guy before, I'm not ready to jump into another serious relationship right away. I plan to take my time, enjoy life, and live one day at a time to the fullest." Casey had never been more sure of herself.

Dawn nodded her head in agreement with Casey. "That sounds similar to what Michael and I are doing."

"What do you mean? Aren't you supposed to be tying the knot soon?" Trina asked.

"As long as you keep the Lord in your lives, He will show you both the way. There's no need to rush it yourselves." Lorraine smiled at Dawn.

"You're right, there's no rush here." Dawn said, shaking her head and taking a sip of her wine. "I think Michael and I will get married one day, but for now we're taking our time. Right now we're just having fun learning about ourselves and growing together.

Casey stood up to get another bottle of wine, and as she walked toward the kitchen amid their constant chatter, she was thankful for her friends.

"Dawn, I never thought I would say this, but you're young, girl, enjoy yourself while you can." From within the kitchen, Casey was surprised at what Trina was saying. Her friend had changed so much since last season. As far as she was concerned, what she was hearing from her girlfriends today was all good.

"Don't give up your independence until you are good and ready," Trina continued.

"Not that I would do anything differently where my children are concerned." Trina shook her head back and forth and wagged one pointed finger in the air as she spoke.

"But maybe with Rick, I wouldn't have given every ounce of myself on a silver tray." Trina paused, looking straight at Dawn.

"I was lucky in a lot of ways to get the second chance that I got, but maybe it was a fluke that I was able to do what I've done," Trina continued.

Casey returned to the room, catching the tail end of Trina's comment. "Trina, it was no fluke. You have talent, and it paid off, big time. Don't be ashamed of it, Ms. Businesswoman," Casey said, referring to the recent lucrative multiyear contract Trina had entered into with Sutton Bakeries to supply various recipes for cakes, pies, and cookies.

"That's right, Trina, don't make excuses for your success." Remy was intent and crossed her slender legs as she spoke.

"You earned it, fair and square. I used to do that to myself constantly, and it was counterproductive. Save your energy for your family and some new cake recipes for me," Remy told her.

"Speaking of sweets," Remy continued, "did you bring my sweet potato pie? I want to make a good impression on this guy I've been dating for a few months. I want him to think I can at least bake desserts."

"Girl, I'm so sorry." Trina looked at Remy sheepishly. "I walked right out of the house and left it on the kitchen counter. I'll call Rick and tell him to bring it," Trina said.

"Don't have him come all the way from Connecticut just to bring me some pie," Remy said.

"Oh, it's no problem, he has to pick me up when I'm ready to leave anyway. I'll just have him bring it then," Trina said.

"That's so considerate of him to pick you up," Lorraine said.

"That is nice," Dawn playfully chimed in. "Michael would probably just send a car service to fetch me."

Trina splayed her hands out in front of her.

"You all would not believe Rick, he's like my shadow these days. He hasn't been like this since we were in college. You know, it seems like the instant I stopped pressing him about coming back home, he couldn't stay away." Trina sounded surprised at her own words.

"Now you would think he's Mr. Mom, especially with little William, and he sticks to me like white on rice. Of course, making some money of my own didn't hurt. But I can't complain 'cause he's still my baby and we're a family." Trina was grinning from ear to ear.

"So, Remy, fill us in on this guy you're trying to impress," Dawn pressed, smiling mischievously.

"Is it serious?" Lorraine asked.

Casey watched Remy look around the room uncertainly, and she knew that it was a big step for Remy to open herself to people, even this group of women whom she considered her friends. She always kept her guard up. But Casey also realized that Remy had begun to make a concerted effort to allow people into her life more.

Remy swallowed before she elaborated on her new friend. "Well, his name is Phil and he's always cooking exotic dishes for me, so I bragged to him about my nonexistent culinary skills, and he's been patiently waiting to taste something ever since then."

Casey gave Remy an encouraging smile.

"My mother won my father's heart through his stomach," Lorraine interjected. "And if Trina's doing the baking for you, then his heart is as good as won. Ever since I took some cakes that Trina made to my church, none of my parishioners will eat the usual coffee hour desserts anymore. They're waiting for the real deal," Lorraine said.

"Well, I'm not really aiming to capture his heart as of yet . . ." Remy hedged and shifted on her pillow.

Casey gave Remy a knowing look. "Come on, out with it, girl."

"Okay, well, maybe I am trying to capture his heart," Remy said slowly.

"He's an incredible man and I have so much respect for him. And, let's see . . . it doesn't hurt that he's fine as I don't know what and . . . that's about it other than . . . he could be the one." Remy clasped her hands in her lap. She had nothing more to say . . . as far as she was concerned, her new man was as good as it gets.

"The one?" Casey repeated.

"Funny, but for the first time in my life, the idea of settling down with someone is quite appealing." Remy smiled as she blushed.

All of the women started ooohing and aaahing at Remy.

"It's a wonderful thang," Remy sang.

"Well, as only you can say it, Remy, 'Happiness is divine.' It sounds like you got some of your own medicine," Trina said.

Casey noticed Lorraine looking at her watch and yawning.

"Are we boring you or do you have someplace to go, Raino?" Casey asked, calling her by her childhood nickname. Casey knew that Lorraine had embraced her past and was moving forward with her life.

"You all are not boring anybody, but I really do have to go," Lorraine apologized. "I'm so sorry to have to break up our soiree but tomorrow is the groundbreaking ceremony for the community center that Paul and I are opening. Between planning that and my double shifts, I'm about to run out of gas." Lorraine was visibly exhausted.

"That's tomorrow?" Casey asked. "I thought it was next Thursday. I would have planned this for another night."

"Casey, I wouldn't have missed this for anything in the world," Lorraine said, hugging her friend tightly with tears in her eyes.

"I'm so happy for you girl." Lorraine was sincere as she pulled back and looked into her friend's eyes.

"What type of a center is it, Lorraine?" Remy asked.

"It's going to be a place where our youth can go and participate in productive activities instead of only having the streets and gangs as extracurricular activities," Lorraine explained.

"This center will be an outlet for them and a haven from the streets. I'm praying to God that will help our children. It's going to be called the Christine Jackson Community Center."

"Well, I wish you the best of luck," Remy said. "Let me know if there's anything I can ever do to help."

"Me too, Lorraine," Dawn chimed in eagerly. "What a wonderful idea."

Casey jumped up, thinking of Alexis's letter, and ran into her kitchen to retrieve it. As she returned to the living room, she stopped Lorraine from leaving. She knew she did not have to worry about the other three leaving. They were enjoying the wine and ambience far too much to budge.

Casey was anxious to let her friends in on the latest twist with Alexis.

"Wait one minute before you go, Lorraine." Casey said. "Ladies, listen up. Dawn, would you turn down the music please? I want to read you all this letter Alexis sent me along with a housewarming gift."

"What is it?" Dawn teased. "A chastity belt for your use while you're away from Brent?"

"Be nice," Casey said as she glanced at the ivory linen paper.

"I think it may surprise everyone. She starts out with the usual Alexis kiss-kiss greeting but she continues by writing how she knows what a difficult step I made by leaving Brent but that she was proud of me for taking a stand in my life and doing what I wanted to do, for once," Casey said, scanning the letter.

"Is this the Alexis I know?" Remy asked incredulously.

"Wait," Casey said. "There's more."

"She continues by saying that despite all that transpired last season between herself and us that we were the group of women she admired the most in all of her husband's years of coaching.

"And get this," Casey continued. "She says that she especially appreciated us for our intelligence, inner beauty, honesty, and most importantly, our forthrightness in our decision making. She even ends it by saying perhaps there's hope for her beyond her husband's coaching career."

"You know," Dawn said, "I'm about to surprise myself here, but let's give a toast to Alexis." Dawn raised her glass of wine high above her head.

"To Alexis, I suppose," Remy added. "She had to suck up a lot of pride to write that letter, and I respect her for doing it. I just hope she meant it." Remy was the last to hoist her glass into the air.

"I hope she meant it too." Casey toasted, "Here's to friendship. The kind that transcends time, place, or circumstances."

"Here. Here. Here. Here." Everyone chimed in.

Cheryl Spencer

**RITA EWING,** A.K.A. Rita Williams prior to her marriage to NBA All-Star Patrick Ewing, did not start out as a writer. After graduating from La Reine Senior High School in Suitland, Maryland, Rita accepted a four-year National Merit Scholarship to attend Howard University in Washington, D.C. Starting out with a major in chemical engineering, Rita quickly decided by the end of her freshman year that she had no burning desire to pursue a career in engineering and switched over to the College of Nursing, with the intent to prepare for a future in medicine.

It was during her tenure at Howard that Rita met her future husband, Patrick Ewing, who at that time was a student at

Georgetown University. While working as a summer mail clerk and receptionist for Senator Bill Bradley, Rita had to accept packages from the likes of Ewing, who worked as a summer intern for the Senate Finance Committee. What began as lunch breaks blossomed into seven years of dating until the pair decided to tie the knot.

Upon completion of the four-year nursing program and with a bachelor of science degree in hand, Rita began a career in critical care nursing at Howard University Hospital. After two years of working on various medical, surgical, and cardiac intensive care unit wards, while at the same time trying to assist her fiancé with his newfound fame and responsibilities, Rita decided to put her nursing career on hold and go back to school. Georgetown University Law Center welcomed her into the JD/MBA program with open arms. But after one year, it was the law portion that Rita felt most suited her aspirations. In December 1992 Rita proudly tossed her tassel to the side and walked across the podium with a Juris Doctorum in law.

Admitted to the Pennsylvania Bar Assocation in June 1993, Rita turned her entrepreneurial dreams into a reality. Through her first start-up venture, One on One Management, Inc., Rita was able to provide home office management techniques and consulting services to professional athletes. Working with the athletes, including her own husband at the time, Rita was privy to the nuances of the world of professional basketball and the relationships that play a major role both on and off the court. She decided to put pen to paper.

Rita created the children's book series Patrick's Pals,

which was based on Patrick Ewing, Alonzo Mourning, and Dikembe Mutombo's real-life friendships portrayed by childhood friends growing up in the 'hood. Her next penned venture and first published novel was *Homecourt Advantage,* which Rita coauthored with Crystal McCrary Anthony, coauthor of *Gotham Diaries.* Rita and Crystal sold the film rights to *Homecourt Advantage* and still have hopes of bringing their story to the silver screen.

Two years ago, Rita helped bring the nation's largest African American–owned bookstore to Harlem, New York. She is coowner of the Hue-Man Bookstore and is proud to be able to bring renowned authors to the Harlem community. It was in Harlem where Rita conceived her most recent baby, *Brickhouse. Brickhouse* is Rita's current novel and certainly won't be the last. She wrote *Brickhouse* while living in New Jersey with her three daughters, Randi, Corey, and Kyla. Rita credits her ex-husband, Patrick, for her juicy NBA experiences; her parents for their unconditional love; and her friends for all of their support.